DAME MURDER

When Flora Coombe, best-selling author of murder mysteries, disappears she hits the headlines. Flora surprised everyone when she took a second husband, years younger than herself, whom she has saved from the gallows. Her pride and vanity shattered by her husband's betrayal, she stages her own disappearance and apparent murder at the hands of her young husband. How does a famous writer lay low when half the country are looking for her? By taking on the persona of a Victorian-style nanny on a mysterious Cornish estate – where guilty secrets make her venture into childcare as dangerous as anything she has written.

DAME MURDER

DAME MURDER

by

Terence Kingsley-Smith

Dales Large Print Books
Long Preston, North Yorkshire,
BD23 4ND, England.

British Library Cataloguing in Publication Data.

Kingsley-Smith, Terence
  Dame murder.

A catalogue record of this book is
available from the British Library

ISBN   978-1-84262-722-8 pbk

First published in Great Britain in 2007 by The Book Guild Ltd.

Copyright © Terence Kingsley-Smith 2007

Cover illustration by arrangement with
The Book Guild Publishing

The right of Terence Kingsley-Smith to be identified as the
author of this work has been asserted by him in accordance with
the Copyright, Designs and Patents Act, 1988

Published in Large Print 2009 by arrangement with
The Book Guild Publishing

Dales Large Print is an imprint of Library Magna Books Ltd.

Printed and bound in Great Britain by
T.J. (International) Ltd., Cornwall, PL28 8RW

DEDICATION

To my younger sisters, Susan Durney
Mickelson and Christine Durney
Armanasco, the second half of the
Dorothy Kingsley dynasty, in appreciation
for all the kind and generous things.

FOREWORD

To my faithful readers upon publication of this book after the year 2000, which, if my estimation of my mortality is correct, will be several years after my death.

When this book is published, I will have travelled to that 'undiscovered country from whose bourn no traveller returns'. Mr Shakespeare always said it best, didn't he? If he had written mysteries instead of plays, I never would have had the courage to take up my pen. There would have been no Flora Coombe if he had. It took great fortitude, as it is, to follow in the wake of such distinguished mystery writers as Mr Wilkie Collins and the celebrated Sir Arthur Conan Doyle.

I know that many of you were disappointed in my autobiography. Some reviewers actually called it a Pollyanna view of my life; however, I did have a happy childhood and my days spent writing were always filled with the joy of constant discovery. I never lacked for ideas or for the enthusiasm to transcribe them onto paper. If there is really such a thing as writer's block, this peculiar malady never visited at my door.

If I did not dwell on the unhappiness of my first marriage and my painful sojourn in India as a military wife, it was to spare the feelings of the remaining members of my husband's family. I suppose when this book is finally published they will all be gone. Perhaps I shall meet them in some sort of paradise. If there is truly such an 'undiscovered country' I certainly hope there are no heavenly plans to rejoin me with my late husband. One time around with him was more than enough.

If I did not mention a second husband in my reminiscences, these pages will make evidently clear why; for he will play a major part in what you are about to read. I still find it painful – these many years later – to dwell on such an upsetting period of my life.

There was also great consternation when I neglected to mention my celebrated 'disappearance' in my memoirs. Even now, so long afterwards, it is still difficult to reveal the facts of that singular period of my life. Long after I am gone, you shall judge these facts for yourself and ascertain how great was my guilt in what transpired.

I go to my grave a storyteller at heart. I could never allow a good one to pass me by or prevent myself from inventing one. What happened those many years ago is a very good story indeed.

I shall tell it all now exactly as it happened. If it reads like fiction rather than the truth, that is because I cannot help myself from writing in that manner.

No doubt my readers will think less of me after they learn the truth of those long ago days. After I'm gone, it will no longer matter what anybody thinks.

Your faithful storyteller,
Dame Flora Coombe
Dovecote Cottage
Winter, 1972

ACKNOWLEDGEMENTS

To my typist, Bonnie Petros, the first to see and encourage; to Jan Harris, the first to edit this in the British way; to Joanna Bentley and Janet Wrench of The Book Guild, who completed the job so magnificently; and to the late Agatha Christie, who gave me the idea.

And to Faye Whitlock for a final and thorough proofing.

ONE

How I shall miss Dovecote Cottage, near Oxford, when one day in the distant future, I plan to die peacefully in my Chippendale four-poster bed. There is already talk of turning my home into some sort of museum after I am gone. I detest the very idea of it, but if this means the small estate can be kept intact, as lovely as it is now, I suppose I shall set some money aside for this very abhorrence.

The dovecote, the small stone tower that still houses my beloved pigeons, is all that remains of a medieval castle that once dominated these grounds. It stands at a short distance from the two-storey structure that I call my cottage, although I suppose it is larger than a cottage – yet not quite a manor house – somewhere in between, the perfect size for a contented widow such as I. How happy I was to sell my late husband's estate at Tunbridge Wells upon his welcome death (yes, *welcome*, I can say it now) and move here close enough to Oxford University for intellectual stimulation, yet far enough away in the beloved country for contemplation.

I look in the dictionary for the official

definition of my first name – Flora. 'Flora' is defined as the plants of a particular region or period, listed by species and considered as a whole. True to my moniker, the myriad flowers of a typical English garden grow here beyond my cottage in great profusion. It is a delicious private park, the paths of which I have walked contemplating the solution of my latest murder mystery. These gardens have always been the highlight of the yearly Oxford Garden Tour; I suppose, after my death, they shall be visited by the curious six days a week instead of only once a year.

Perhaps I shall haunt these precious acres myself, and tourists will glimpse my shadowy form waltzing around the sundial that is surrounded by yellow roses or dancing through the small maze of tall hedges, or by chance reading on my favourite marble bench beneath the willow trees, or sipping tea and munching crumpets at the green wrought iron table on the lawn.

Rather than a further description of these precious acres of flowers, I refer my readers to my novel *The Chrysanthemum Murders*. Although fiction, the story provides as apt a description of my garden as I shall ever give, for it was the inspiration for my mystery. Those who have read me know that I like to get on with things and not dwell over lengthy descriptions. Vita Sackville West wrote a lovely book describing her Sissinghurst Castle and gardens. I could never do so unless a story was attached.

Suffice it to say that the interior of Dovecote Cottage is warm and comfortable, with a fire burning through winter – now for instance – and with French doors thrown open to welcome spring and savour summer. I furnished for comfort, and, if I may say so myself, for taste: good sturdy pieces from celebrated periods of history that have stood the test of time. I shall not take the time to describe them now.

I remember so clearly the day it began. Naturally I didn't realise then that I was opening a December window to something that would alter my life in a way that I did not believe possible. It is only in retrospect that we are able to pinpoint the precise day of change.

I was relatively new to Dovecote Cottage then. The remodelling and painting were finished. I had settled in, but the gardens were not yet extensive. Since it was winter, I was devoting myself to writing my latest mystery and putting off the gardening until spring. My beloved Persian kitty, Lucretia, named after the conniving Borgia poisoner, was asleep upon her special cushioned basket beside my desk.

The day before I inadvertently set something in motion is one that few of us in England will ever forget. On December 11, 1936, our new King, Edward VIII, abdicated his throne for the 'woman he loved', that (I don't blush to say it and still feel it is true) American tart, Wallis Simpson. With hindsight now, I realise that Edward did my country a great favour. He would have been a rotten king, as his abandonment of duty initially showed. We were blessed, instead, to have his younger brother, King George VI, as our steadfast leader in the difficult war years that were to follow. I can't imagine how Edward would have managed. Greatness can be thrust upon you, but I doubt that Edward would have worn the mantle well.

Few of us slept well the night following Edward's terse announcement. In the morning, sitting at my Sheraton desk in my comfortable office next to my downstairs master bedroom, I fretted over the dénouement of my latest Inspector Hecate mystery, *The Mysterious Disappearance*. It certainly was not writing itself, so I laboured over the *Times* crossword puzzle instead. Besides, I was waiting for my assistant, Miss Hewitt, to complete typing what I had written the previous evening in bed, my most creative place in winter, beneath a comforter, beside a fire with Lucretia purring beside me. I have always written in longhand in the same blue school notebooks I loved as a little girl growing up in Brighton.

Mary Beth Hewitt will figure prominently in the story I am about to tell. Certainly neither of us realised the day after the abdication that she would prove to be an unexpected, unwelcome catalyst.

I find it more difficult to describe a beautiful girl than a plain one such as myself. I know that I have sometimes been described as 'attractive' and 'aristocratic', but interviewers were just being kind. All the adjectives for 'beautiful' have been so over-used. I suppose what made Mary Beth Hewitt's prettiness so unusual was her attempt to disguise it. Neither horn-rimmed glasses, nor the severest of hair-dos nor the total lack of make-up could conceal that this was still Venus Rising upon her own Botticelli Shell. Here was hair blonder than gold, eyes as blue as turquoise, colouring as radiant as the skin of a summer peach; a luscious mouth as pink as a damask rose and a nose perfectly formed to complement the pleasing symmetry of her face; in addition, a sumptuous figure that a matching tweed skirt and jacket could not conceal.

Mary Beth Hewitt was an American girl from New Orleans, Louisiana. I marvel to this day how she came to be in my employment. If I had spurned her when she showed up unannounced at my doorstep those many years ago, I suppose there would be no story to relate now.

I wonder if it was just a coincidence that I had so recently lost my faithful secretary to a marriage that came late in her life. Her new husband was an Oxford don who had accepted a teaching position in Australia. I was happy that the prim and proper Rosemary could finally find happiness, but I hated to let her go. We had become as accustomed to each other as a pair of old socks. Sometimes I wondered if the elderly professor wasn't just looking for someone to darn his own, but I couldn't deny that Rosemary was happier than I had ever seen her. Was I perhaps just a little jealous? I had assumed that Rosemary would see me through many decades of widowhood; instead I had to content myself with her letters from Melbourne.

I hadn't even begun to interview for a replacement when the luscious American creature appeared on the doorstep.

'It's one of them fan ladies,' Bertie, my young parlour maid from the wrong part of London, announced. 'She says she's come all the way from America.'

I seldom refused them. I signed their copies of my books and sent them on their way, but this one, this Mary Beth Hewitt, was somehow different: so determined. If she hadn't announced that she had just graduated from secretarial school, I would have sent her on her way as well.

'I told Daddy I was going to be a famous mystery writer just like you, but he said, "I don't care what you're going to be, you are going to learn to type and take shorthand so you can earn a decent living if the need ever arises, like the Crash we had in '29." Of course, I was just a little girl then, and times were hard, but in the South we had more to eat than apples.' Her voice dripped with honey and molasses and laboured slowly over each and every vowel. How different from the clipped British speech of those of us who just want to 'get on with it'. I must say it was refreshing and I am easily flattered, especially by someone who has read all of my books and remembers the plots better than I do.

'I just feel like Inspector Hecate is alive somewhere here in England and you are going to lead me straight to him.'

'What else brings you to Europe, Miss Hewitt? Surely not just to see me?'

'It's the only reason, Miss Coombe. Daddy treated me to a tour of the continent for a graduation present. I beat a path straight to your doorstep. I'm just hoping that some of that wonderful fiendish imagination of yours will rub off on me.'

'Certainly there are more interesting things to see in Europe than a widow at her pad and pencil.'

'I can't think of one thing. They told me at

this hotel in Oxford about you losing your secretary. The lady at the hotel is as big a fan of yours as I am. I'm just wondering if I can't help out a little, typing and such while I worship at your feet, so to speak, until you find somebody else.'

What made me put her to the immediate test? I suppose it was because I had a deadline to meet and had just worn myself out scribbling the final chapters of my latest Inspector Hecate into my blue notebooks.

Amazingly, Mary Beth Hewitt was a faster typer than Rosemary and she made few errors. Although she was not a perfect speller, fortunately I seldom made a mistake. Before I thought things through clearly, she had moved her belongings into Rosemary's old room at the end of the upstairs hall, and made herself indispensable.

I now had a new secretary in addition to a cook and a parlourmaid who both slept in quarters off the kitchen, and a housemaid who came to us but slept out. There was one gardener then and he lived off the premises. I suppose we were too many women in one house. That was about to change.

I shall now begin a chapter of my life about which there has been much speculation and entirely too much written. It began innocently with an American newspaper. It became the most painful period of my life.

TWO

I was at my crossword puzzle. Mary Beth was pounding at the dependable Remington typewriter. Bertie, tears running down her hollow cheeks, pushed inside my study.

'It's me, ma'am,' she half sobbed, 'with the post.' She smelled of lavender water, as she did every morning after her ablutions. I preferred the trace of gardenia worn by my secretary, or my own *L'Heure Bleue*.

'Bertie, dear,' I said, forced to look up from my puzzle by the tear in her voice, 'whatever is the matter? Some bad news from home? Is it your mother?' Bertie's mother had a fondness for drink. She worried that the portion of her salary she sent home was spent on too many pints.

'No, ma'am. It's him ... what he said on the wireless last night, and what was printed in the paper this morning.'

'Oh that,' Mary Beth pooh-poohed. Being an inveterate American, she had little respect for the traditions of royalty or our family Windsor.

Bertie, although she had the appetite of a wart hog, was as thin as a sparrow. She flapped her arms about as if they were wings, her big brown eyes overpowering her small beak of a nose, her black and white uniform giving her the aspect of a penguin. 'It's enough to break your heart,' she sniffled, now quoting our monarch herself. "I have found it impossible to carry on the burden, and do my duties as King, without the help and support of the woman I love."

Mary Beth was having none of it. 'If an American president like Roosevelt wanted to marry a divorced woman...'

'President Roosevelt isn't descended from kings!' Bertie interrupted.

'You had better not tell him that,' Mary Beth retorted. 'It's because this Wallis Simpson is an American. That's what all the fuss is about.'

'She's a *divorced* American,' I interjected.

'I bet your people would have let him marry Barbara Hutton, divorced or not. This country could use her kind of money.'

Bertie, the little chauvinist that she was, protested. 'We British can get along very well, thank you, without any dirty money from America.'

It was obvious from the day that Miss Hewitt arrived that Bertie was suspicious of her intentions. She had scant understanding that a woman that young and beautiful could possess such a burning desire to write. Bertie had little use for literature herself.

Before the two of them were clawing at

each other like cats, I thought perhaps that I should change the subject. 'Mary Beth, what's a six-letter word meaning to kill?'

'Why "murder", Miss Coombe. You, of all people should–'

'But it starts with a "q".' And then it dawned on me. 'Of course, it's "quarter", to cut someone up in equal sections. And it's seven letters. I miscounted.' I shook my head ruefully. 'Do you remember Inspector Hecate when he was confronted by the victims that were drawn and quartered?'

'I wouldn't know, ma'am,' Bertie responded for Miss Hewitt. 'You wouldn't catch me reading that frightful stuff. I don't even like coming in here with all these hideous creatures staring down at me like I was going to be their next victim.' She was referring to my collection of photographs of some of the most famous murderesses in recent history. I just happened to mention in an interview that I had a picture or two of the likes of Lucretia Borgia and Mrs Lovet and Lizzie Borden. Photographs began arriving in the mail. A recent addition was the American trunk murderess, Winnie Ruth Judd. They glared down at us from their burgundy-coloured frames about the walls and were often an inspiration for future books. I always conjure up the murder first. Everything else follows.

Bertie picked up the front page of the

Times and presented it to me. 'Did you read it, ma'am? Every word His Majesty said?'

'Yes, Bertie,' I replied impatiently. 'It was exactly as he said over the wireless. But he's not His Majesty anymore.'

'So romantic. Like out of a storybook.'

I had heard enough of our former king. I attempted to change the subject again. 'You can give me the mail, Bertie.'

'I'll go through it first, Miss Coombe,' Mary Beth volunteered.

'No, you keep at your typing. I get a much better idea of what I've written after I see it all typed out.'

'Such mail you get, ma'am,' Bertie commented, handing me a large bundle. 'It never stops. It just seems to pile up and up.'

'The curse of being a successful novelist.'

'Will there be anything else, ma'am?' Bertie was awaiting her instructions.

'Isn't it about time for the silver again?' I knew how Bertie hated to polish the silver. 'As soon as I finish the new book, I shall begin entertaining again.'

'Rosalie isn't coming in today. I can't do the silver without Rosalie to help.'

'We mustn't depend on Rosalie to do everything, must we?'

'No, ma'am,' Bertie replied, attempting not to make a face. She started out but turned back, determined to have the last word on the subject. 'I suppose it's just as well he abdicated. I wouldn't have wanted to see that American bit of rubbish on the throne.' This was directed at Mary Beth, who shared a look with me as Bertie closed the door.

Have I spent too much time setting the scene and introducing two of the prominent players in this drama that was my life? To the day of my death, I am still a novelist at heart. My readers must permit me an occasional recidivism to the kind of book I used to write when there was no such thing as television and civilised readers curled up in an armchair and took time to peruse a book.

I suppose I did make a comment about the Duke of Windsor after Bertie left the room and I began to leaf through the mail. 'I met him on more than one occasion, you know, although I wasn't pretty enough for the Prince. He looked right through me to some film star.'

'Well, I certainly don't think Wallis Simpson is anything to write home about.'

'I suspect she has hidden gifts we don't know about.' If I was shunned by Edward Windsor, his younger brothers had paid more attention to me when I was invited to tea by their lovely mother, Queen Mary, who was a devoted fan of mine.

'It certainly is the ultimate sacrifice a man can make for a woman. Giving up everything for the woman he loves. Doubtless he will gradually regret it, finally blaming and detesting that woman so much that he wants to do away with her. I must remember that. What a plot it would make. Of course I wouldn't make him King. That would be too obvious, but somebody who must give up something very important in his life – perhaps his peerage and his fortune. Now how would he do away with her in such a way that only Inspector Hecate could suspect?'

'I'm sure you'll think of something, Miss Coombe. Here I am still struggling over my first novel and you've got your next five all planned.'

'The ideas are the easy part, Mary Beth. It's plotting them that requires great concentration.'

'I'm finding that out.'

'How is your own work coming, dear?'

Mary Beth flushed as if I had caught her at some infraction. 'I can't turn them out the way you do.'

'The first novel is always the hardest, dear. I agonised over mine.'

'Yes, I know,' she said with a trace of bitterness in her voice. *Murder at the Crossroads*, an instant best-seller.'

'That didn't make it any easier to write.'

She was becoming defensive. 'I want my book to be more than just a mystery. I want my readers to feel and smell Louisiana. I want it to be a combination of Flora Coombe, Mary Roberts Rinehart and Frances Parkinson Keyes.'

'You shouldn't overburden yourself with your first effort, dear. When you first came to me you said you felt that I would be an inspiration. Have I been an inspiration?'

'Yes, if you spell it i-n-t-i-m-i-d-a-t-i-o-n.'

'I'm sorry, dear. Would you like me to read what you have written so far?'

'Oh, no, Miss Coombe. It's not anywhere near ready yet.'

'I promise to be kind.'

'Not yet, Miss Coombe. I'd die if you saw it now.'

'Very well, when you're ready. Now I must get through this mail.'

I must admit that I do enjoy the mail that finds its way to my study from all over the world. Some letters are even addressed to Inspector Hecate, asking him to solve some disappearance or a theft. There was a letter as well for Miss Hewitt from her father. She tore it open eagerly, I think in hopes that a cheque would fall into her hands, but none ever did. He didn't approve of what she was doing with her life. He would not support it. He had given her money for her European tour. No more was forthcoming.

She began reading. 'My daddy's still after me to come home. Won't he be surprised one day when my book is published? Then he'll take my writing seriously. When I think of most of my girlfriends back home stuck in some boring finishing school... Here I am working for one of the most celebrated lady mystery writers in all the world.'

'One of? Who are the others?' Why did I have to remind myself? The woman's name was a cankerous sore that would never heal.

'I thought I wasn't allowed to mention her name in your presence.'

'You may mention her. Just don't bring any of her books into this house.'

'Very well then. There's Agatha Christie, too.' Did I detect that she appeared to take unnecessary delight in saying the woman's name?

'Inspector Thaddeus Hecate precedes Hercule Poirot by at least five years. Even though Agatha made her man Belgian does not alter the fact that his powers of deduction are far too similar to my own inspector. I forgive her for Miss Marple, but never for Hercule Poirot.'

'But she has written mysteries without her Inspector, and so have you.'

'As far as I'm concerned Hercule Poirot is not a real inspector and I'm surprised you didn't turn up on her doorstep. Did you go there first and get turned away?'

'Nothing of the sort. She would always be my second choice. You are the very best in the English-speaking world. I can't speak for the other languages. I don't even know where Agatha Christie lives.'

'I believe she has moved to Wallingford. You wouldn't like it at all. It has a poor railway service and is much too far from London.'

'I like it here just fine.'

I busied myself with perusing the mail. Even now, as I write this in the cold winter of 1972, Agatha is still alive and turning out mysteries like the complicated sausages they are. Now she is Dame Agatha Christie as I am Dame Flora Coombe. No doubt she will outlive me. Enough of Dame Christie. Dame Coombe must get on with her story.

The mail completed, I spied a copy of Miss Hewitt's hometown newspaper, which she had dropped on the floor beside her desk. 'Is that your New Orleans newspaper?'

'I don't know why my momma sends it,' Mary Beth replied, not removing her eyes from her typing. 'I think she hopes it will make me homesick.'

'May I see it?' How I enjoyed the colourful accounts in the *New Orleans Times-Picayune*, the fanciful French names of many of its citizens, for instance. I had even jotted some down for future use. The local British paper was much too prim and proper in the depiction of the news – murder – for instance.

'You know, Mary Beth,' I declared to her

as she handed over the newspaper. 'Right now this is your territory, but one day I should like to write about your home myself. Perhaps send Inspector Hecate there for the Mardi Gras.'

She made no response as she continued with her typing. 'My, my,' I exclaimed as I read, 'a memorial service for Huey Long. Look at all those people. You would think it was the Pope who had passed away.'

'My father wasn't there. You can be sure of that.'

I turned to the book reviews. 'This new book on the South sounds interesting.'

'Is it a mystery?'

'No, it is about the Civil War. Have you ever heard of Margaret Mitchell? It says she's from Atlanta.'

'No, but if she's southern, I'm sure she is a fine writer.'

'Do I detect chauvinism, Mary Beth?'

'It's just we feel things more intensely, that's all.' I read further. 'It says this is Miss Mitchell's first novel.'

'What's it called?'

'*Gone With The Wind.*'

'My, what a dramatic title.'

I recognised the quote immediately. 'It's Ernest Dawson. "I have forgot much, Cynara! Gone with the wind. Flung roses, roses riotously with the throng".' How strange then that it was just a title to me without any story attached. Soon the book would be the rage of not only America, but Great Britain as well. How peculiarly satisfying to me that two of our most celebrated British performers, Vivien Leigh and Leslie Howard, appeared in the wonderful film and made it a success.

Am I straying? You must forgive an older woman her recollections. I must turn the page of the newspaper so that I can see that face once again, staring out at me. Was it his youth? His handsomeness. The tawny colour of his skin? Or was it the arresting eyes that seemed to be beseeching me for my help. I thought out loud, 'Such a wonderful face!' I read quickly through the story. 'He couldn't possibly be guilty of murder. Not with a face like that.' I glanced up at the framed photographs around my study. 'Those are the faces of people who could kill.' My eyes were drawn back to the handsome young face in the newspaper. 'Not this man.'

Mary Beth had ceased her typing and stepped over to me so that she could peer over my shoulder. 'Who does it say he killed?'

I was eager to relate the facts of the case. My pulse had already quickened and my blood was running faster than usual, the same way it did when I was writing. 'A woman ... a rather wealthy woman, I gather. It says here that he was a fisherman in the bayou. Have you been to the bayou, Mary Beth?'

'My daddy used to take me down there fishing.' She made a face. 'All those 'gators.'

I continued to peruse the newspaper account. 'The woman who was murdered was one of his customers, one of the people to whom he delivered fish. They found his fingerprints on the murder weapon. On a hammer!' I was shocked by the description. 'What an awful way to be murdered! I would never kill anybody with a hammer.'

'You've used worse than that in some of your books.'

'But those were made up.' I spoke the young man's name. 'Robin Thibodeaux. How fanciful.'

'That's pure Cajun.' She studied the man's photograph more closely. 'He looks Creole to me. That's French and a little bit of everything,' her eyes remained fixed on the photograph, 'especially coloured.'

'They describe him in the story as octoroon.'

'One-eighth is pure Negro where I come from.'

'I know how you feel about the coloured, Mary Beth.' We British had abolished slavery. It took the Americans somewhat longer. If Mary Beth was any indication, they were still regretting Abolition.

'I've got nothing against the coloured,'

36

Mary Beth reacted. 'They're entitled to every right we white folks have – just as long as they're kept separate from the rest of us.' I must have tisked, because Mary Beth continued her defence. 'And anybody who treats the East Indians the way I hear you people do, has no right to cast stones.'

There was some truth to her accusation. I decided to return to the matter at hand. 'Tell me, Mary Beth, if a coloured man like this had witnesses who say that he was somewhere else at the time of the crime, would these witnesses not count for much if they were coloured as well?'

'You're sounding just like Inspector Hecate.'

'Answer the question.'

'The woman he murdered was white, wasn't she?'

I turned the page to reveal the victim's picture. She was not a young woman and she was far from pretty. If it was a recent photograph the victim appeared to be somewhere in her fifties, the hair piled atop her small head flecked with streaks of grey. Mary Beth studied the photo carefully. 'Well, it wasn't a crime of passion. That's for sure.'

'You haven't answered my question.'

She spat it out begrudgingly. 'If all the witnesses were coloured, an all-white jury wouldn't take much stock in them.'

'That's what I thought.'

She was determined to defend her compatriots. 'But you said they found his fingerprints on the murder weapon.'

'Yes, it does say that,' I admitted, reading through the story again for further details. 'I wish they'd be more specific. I wonder if there were other prints as well? Someone else's besides Robin Thibodeaux?'

Mary Beth's eyes were drawn back to the photograph of the putative murderer. 'I must admit he doesn't look like somebody who would do something so awful.' But then she dismissed him. 'Probably uppity. They're all getting that way. When is he going to swing?'

'Swing?'

'Hang. We hang them in Louisiana. And if he's coloured, they don't waste much time before they do it.'

I read further. The story continued to the last page. I was dismayed to discover the date of his execution. 'He's scheduled to die on January 1st.'

'He's lucky they haven't already lynched him.'

'That doesn't leave us much time.'

'Time for what?'

'To save him, of course.'

'Save some nigger from swinging?'

I knew how sensitive that word was to coloured people. 'Mary Beth, I forbid you to

use that word while you are in my employ.'
I returned to the front of the newspaper and studied the young man's photograph once again. If the truth be told – and that is what this book is about – I couldn't take my eyes off him. 'Such a pretty neck,' I whispered to myself. 'I should like to save such a neck from hanging.'

'Where did they try him?' Mary Beth asked.

I glanced through the story once again. 'It says he's from Lafayette. Call the Lafayette Court House, or whatever you have over there, and find out who is representing this man.'

'You want me to call long distance?'

'Do you have a better way?'

She turned and moved to the phone. Her southern voice poured even thicker into the receiver. I almost expected the apparatus to be sticky with honey after she had placed the call. 'I'd like the overseas operator please. I am making a long distance call for Miss Flora Coombe.'

THREE

It is so much easier to place a long distance call now in the 1970s than it was back in 1936. It seemed to take forever for Mary Beth to reach the County Court House in Lafayette County, Louisiana.

Fortunately I was distracted by Bertie, who pushed into the office. She knew better than to interrupt me when I was writing, but assumed that since Mary Beth had been typing, I was not yet composing. 'There's a gentleman to see you, ma'am.'

'What sort of gentleman?' My curiosity, as usual, was immediately piqued.

'A gentleman, ma'am.'

'Can you describe him to me, Bertie?'

'I can't say that I can, ma'am. He's all sort of ordinary. Nothing like a film star or somebody like that.'

'You'd never make a good writer, or a detective, Bertie. You must develop your powers of observation.'

'I'm sure I wouldn't want to be either of those things.'

'Did this gentleman give you a name?'

'Yes, ma'am, he's an inspector.'

'An inspector?'

'Inspector Hanlon. He has something for you.'

'Is he anything like my Inspector Hecate?'

'I wouldn't know, ma'am. You know I don't read those scary books.'

'Well, show this "all sort of ordinary" man in, Bertie.'

'Very well, ma'am.'

Mary Beth, meanwhile, waited on the line. 'Miss Coombe, would you mind handing me the newspaper, please? I've forgotten the nig–' She dared not complete the inflammatory word. My cold eyes forbade her to continue. '–the coloured man's name,' she finally concluded.

'Inspector Hanlon, ma'am.'

As I rose to hand her the newspaper, Bertie ushered the inspector into the room. I dare say that at a quick glance, he could be considered ordinary, but it was clear to me that there was more there than immediately met the eye. This was a man of steely determination as evidenced by the cold cobalt of his deep-set eyes, the coiled curl of his wiry hair, the firmness of his jaw and the tightness of his thin lips. He held a brown fedora in one hand and some sort of paper in the other. I surmised that this was a man who could prove to be a formidable adversary – as indeed he did. My Persian kitty, who has a sixth sense about these things, stood up, arched her back, hissed, and demanded to be let outdoors immediately. How I wish I had heeded my cat's warning and shown the inspector to the door before he had the opportunity to proceed further. I let my precious kitty out of the French windows then took a step or two towards him and was dismayed to observe that I was slightly taller. To this day I do not relish standing over a man, even a man who would prove to be as troublesome as this inspector. At least my first husband towered over me. That I will say for him.

'How do you do, Inspector. I hope this isn't a professional visit.'

'In a way it is, and in a way it is not.' It was immediately clear to me from that one sentence that he was a Yorkshire man, an accent not altogether unpleasant to my ear. 'I've been newly assigned to Oxford. I thought I would take this opportunity to become acquainted with my more distinguished residents.' He handed me the piece of paper that he was holding. 'And to give you this. Usually I don't bother with these trivialities, but...'

I glanced at the paper. I knew immediately that it was a summons. 'If I'd known you were delivering something of this nature, I would not have received you, Inspector.'

'What is it, ma'am?' Bertie, all curiosity, could not help herself.

'That will be all, Bertie.'

'Yes, ma'am.' How she hated to depart; but she obeyed.

I shook my head as I studied the papers more carefully. 'Will these troublesome things never end?'

'What is it, Miss Coombe?' Mary Beth questioned from the telephone.

'Another summons. Another unsuccessful writer accusing me of plagiarism. This one states that the plot of *Murder At Any Cost* was stolen from a book and a writer neither of which I have ever heard. Mary Beth, have you ever read a mystery titled *Murder at Half Past* by Millicent Cotter?'

'No, I haven't, Miss Coombe.'

'Have you, Inspector?'

'I don't read mysteries.'

I took that as an insult, crunched the paper and tossed it onto my desk. 'The case rests.' I was becoming more and more peeved. 'This means more work for my solicitor. He scarcely has time for anything else.' The inspector persisted in just standing there – beneath me. 'Very well, Inspector,' I snapped testily, 'you have done your duty. I am sure my parlour maid is outside the door and will show you out.'

'It is my understanding that you are a writer.'

'Yes, I am.'

'Are you similar to the Yorkshire sisters?'

'The Brontës?'

He nodded. 'They're the ones.'

'Have you read them, Inspector?'

'We had to in school. I grew up in Keighley. They're the local saints there.'

'I simply love the Brontës,' Mary Beth swooned from the phone.

'As you can surmise, I write mysteries, Inspector.'

'Do you now? I read one of those Poirot books. You're not the lady who writes those, are you?'

He couldn't have asked a more infuriating question. Mary Beth took a deep breath at the phone and waited for my response, which was not forthcoming. Mary Beth came quickly to my defence. 'Miss Coombe created Inspector Hecate years before Inspector Poirot was ever even published.'

'You don't say? Inspector Hecate, is it? Perhaps I should read one of those.'

'It certainly would help you with your job,' Mary Beth volunteered.

'Which one should I read?'

'I'm sure I don't know, Inspector.' I had reached the end of my patience. 'Now, if you don't mind, my secretary and I are at work on one of those books you don't read.' I called out loudly, 'Bertie.'

'Yes, ma'am.'

'If I do buy one of your books, would you autograph it for me?'

'I'm certain you'd be much happier with

Hercule Poirot, so Miss Christie could sign it for you. Good day, Inspector.'

He turned in the doorway, lifted his hat as a farewell gesture and finally was gone, Bertie closing the door after him. Almost immediately, Lucretia was scratching at the glass to be let back inside. 'But I just let you out,' I informed her as I opened the door. She glanced around hesitantly. 'It's all right, darling, that nasty inspector has gone.' I picked her up and stroked the long soft fur before replacing her in her warm basket. She whirled round and round to get comfortable, nestled deeply, and went back to sleep almost immediately.

Suddenly something came over the phone. Mary Beth spoke loudly. I'm sure Bertie was savouring every word from behind the door. Mary Beth's speech became even more southern because she was speaking to somebody from home.

'Hello...? Yes, I'm calling for Miss Flora Coombe... Yes, *the* Flora Coombe.' She smiled at me in triumph, pleased that her natives had heard of me even if the inspector hadn't. 'Yes, I imagine that we are lucky to catch somebody there at such a late hour. It's morning for us here in England... Well, I'm glad you're working so late... Well, Miss Coombe would like very much to contact the lawyer who is representing the Robin Thibodeaux case... No, for the defence.' She shot me a conspiratorial look. 'Well, Miss Coombe has other ideas on the matter!' She began to write upon a piece of paper. 'Mr Eben Friendly...? Would you have his phone number there by chance?' She wrote it down quickly. 'Thank you so much for your help. Now if I can just get the operator back...' Somehow magically the operator returned to this line. 'Yes, operator, would you please get me a Mr Eben Friendly at 9879...? No, no, I'll be very happy to wait.' Mary Beth leaned back in her chair a moment as if to take a breather from the phone. 'I can't believe that we're getting through so quickly. When I've called Daddy, sometimes it seems to take forever.'

'It must be because that poor man needs us.'

FOUR

Soon Mary Beth had Mr Eben Friendly on the line. She had obviously awakened him from a deep sleep and it required a moment of convincing before he accepted that we were calling from England and that 'Miss Flora Coombe was going to speak to him'.

I was eager to take the receiver. 'How do you do, Mr Friendly?'

'Are you really Flora Coombe?' His voice was low and gravelly and even more regional than Miss Hewitt's. As is a writer's wont, I immediately created a picture from the voice. His thick dark hair was flecked with white and his striped nightshirt had been slept in for weeks. He was in need of a shave and his unruly eyebrows were as thick as caterpillars.

'Indeed I am.'

'Is this some sort of hoax?'

'No, this is not a hoax.'

'You sound English all right.' There was still the trace of sleep in his voice. 'I've read a heap of your books.

'I've always been pleased with my reception in America.'

'*The Chimes Ring Murder* was my favourite. I've learned a helluva lot from reading your books.' He apologised for the 'hell' but I permitted it to pass. *The Chimes Ring Murder* was one of my many non-Inspector Hecate books and more intricately plotted.

He rambled on with praise for my writing, always a tonic to my hungry ears, but I was anxious to move onto the matter at hand. 'Mr Friendly, I am most interested in the Robin Thibodeaux case.'

'How'd you find out about that way over there?'

'My secretary, to whom you were speaking, receives a newspaper from New Orleans.'

'I did what I could for the boy. The facts were stacked against him. I'll have you know I'm not too popular with the white folks hereabouts for taking on the case in the first place.'

'I'm sure your representing Mr Thibodeaux was most admirable.'

'Are you planning to write a book about this or something?'

'That certainly is not my motivation. I am interested in proving the young man's innocence.'

'Way over there in England, how do you know he's innocent?'

'You can call it a writer's hunch if you like. I pride myself on my hunches.' Indeed they have almost never been wrong. I shall remain mute concerning the few times they were. 'If you could kindly relate to me the pertinent details of the case.'

His speech was maddeningly slow, I wanted desperately to hurry him along. At times a southern drawl can be charming but not when one is in need of facts, which were the following:

1. Although Robin Thibodeaux swore that he never once in his life touched the murder weapon – a hammer – the only fingerprint definitely remaining was his. Even though it appeared that the hammer had been washed clean of blood, this one incriminating

fingerprint remained.

2. Several coloured witnesses swore under oath that Mr Thibodeaux was with them at some sort of 'jambalaya' party at approximately the same time as the murder, but these witnesses – several of them relatives of the accused – were not believed by the white jury.

The third fact was so intriguing that I could scarcely wait to hang up the receiver and relate it to my secretary. Instead I handed the receiver to her. 'Mary Beth, Mr Friendly would appreciate an autographed copy of my latest Inspector Hecate that has not yet been printed in America. Would you please write down his address?' She took the receiver and as she did as bidden, I once again studied the photograph of the handsome coloured man in the newspaper. After Mary Beth disengaged, I was anxious to reveal what had actually done the poor coloured man in. 'It was that American invention of yours – Scotch Tape.'

'Scotch Tape?'

I proceeded with the facts. 'The hammer had begun to splinter. Some tape had been put over the handle to protect it. Robin Thibodeaux's fingerprint was caught underneath the tape.'

Mary Beth was as anxious as ever to find him guilty.

'Well, then he did do it. You can't believe the testimony of his fellow darkies. They'd lie for the price of catfish.'

'Although Mr Friendly didn't say so, I assume he feels exactly the same as you.' I began to pace about the room as I did about the garden in warmer weather when I was agonising over the plotting of a new book. 'Now, how would Inspector Hecate go about this?'

'He'd book passage on the first boat, sail over to America and probably solve another crime during the crossing.'

'There's no time for that. The man is scheduled to hang. But it is easier in my books, isn't it?' I continued to pace, my sensible brown Oxford shoes digging into the carpet. 'If Inspector Hecate was called onto the case he would examine all the evidence, even recreate the crime if need be.'

'We can't do that over here, Miss Coombe.'

'No, we cannot. If that poor man hadn't testified that he had never seen or used that hammer before.' I pictured the murder scene as I spoke, as I did when I was writing. I could see the Bayou kitchen and smell the fresh fish, hear cranes flying overhead and even imagine the victim. 'All he had to say was that in delivering his fish he had used that hammer one day, and that would explain his fingerprint.'

'Sounds to me like he was just plain stupid

– like most of them over there.'

I felt that perhaps an afternoon soak in the tub after lunch would improve my reasoning, but then something occurred to me. Inspector Hecate *was* taking over. 'Mary Beth, let me have your Scotch Tape.'

She dug into her desk drawer which she always kept too cluttered. 'It's here somewhere. I just used it for our mailing yesterday.' She finally produced the metal dispenser and the tape that had been packaged in a bright red Scottish tartan pattern. 'Here it is,' she said as she handed it to me. 'Do you need a hammer too? If you do, I refuse to play the victim.'

'No, the tape will do just fine.' I studied the dispenser admiringly. 'Sometimes you Americans can be so ingenious. What a clever invention.'

'Not to mention the cotton gin.'

I put my theory to the test. I snipped off a portion of the tape and pressed my thumb against the shiny outer side. Mary Beth left her desk to watch me curiously. 'Just as I thought,' I related. 'A fingerprint scarcely shows up on the outside of the tape, and if it did, it could easily be wiped off just like this.' I took my handkerchief and wiped away the slight indication of a print so that it was no longer there. I now pressed my thumb against the sticky side of the tape. My print adhered to it perfectly. I held it up

51

for Miss Hewitt's examination. 'See how it captured my thumb print?'

'Well, I suppose it did the same with his.'

'This shows that for Robin Thibodeaux's fingerprint to be on that hammer inside the tape, either he put the tape on the handle himself...'

'Just before he murdered her,' Mary Beth insisted.

'Or his fingerprint was already there when the tape was stuck on.'

'But he said he never touched that handle, so you can see what a liar he is.' She glanced at his photograph. 'He may be handsome all right, but you don't know these darkies the way I do. They can't be trusted. My own mammy once stole from us, although we could never prove it.'

I was determined to prove his innocence. 'There has to be a reasonable explanation.' I didn't want to wait until I soaked in the tub. I wanted to solve the case then and there. I can sometimes be very impatient. I started out of the office, calling over my shoulder. 'Mary Beth, bring that tape with you.'

Bertie was dusting in the parlour. She looked up, startled to see me, for it was not yet time for lunch. 'Is there something wrong, ma'am?'

'Bertie, where haven't you dusted?'

'I beg your pardon, ma'am?'

'Have you dusted the entire house?'

She went immediately on the defensive. 'I'm working as fast as I can, ma'am. I haven't had time to do the entire house!'

'What room would be the least likely to be dusted, Bertie?'

She hesitated a moment, as if this was some sort of trick question. 'I suppose ... well, I always leave my own quarters for last, ma'am. I won't even let Rosalie in there because I like to do it myself. But I'm that tired at the end of the day, so...'

'What about the scullery, Bertie? When was the last time you cleaned there?'

'Oh, ma'am, I should think that should be Cook's duty, but she always leaves that for me.'

'Then you haven't cleaned there today?'

'I left that for Cook this week, but...'

I turned to Mary Beth. 'It's to the scullery we shall go.'

Bertie was taken aback. If she had the effrontery to physically detain me, she would have held me back. 'Oh, ma'am, you didn't tell me there was going to be an inspection today.'

'This isn't an inspection, Bertie.'

She hurried after me, her hands fluttering about her like agitated wings.

We trooped through the kitchen, where the aroma of leeks filled my nostrils with anticipation for lunch. Cook had also baked bread and was nibbling on a piece herself when I startled her. 'Carry on,' I ordered as I sallied through the kitchen into the scullery. Indeed it was very much in need of a cleaning. Fortunately the sink had not been wiped clean and there was evidence of dust. I pressed my thumb print onto the least clean area of tile. It was clearly in evidence. 'Now, Mary Beth, cut off some tape and place it over this print.' She did as she was asked. 'Now lift the tape.' She peeled it back carefully. When we examined it, my fingerprint was clearly embedded and decipherable. 'Just as I thought.'

'What?' Mary Beth questioned.

'Is this evidence against me?' Bertie wailed.

I held up the tape. 'Don't you see, Mary Beth? This proves that a fingerprint can be lifted off one surface by this tape and placed somewhere else.' My mind was racing faster than my words. I sped up as much as possible to convey the information. 'Robin Thibodeaux, in delivering fish, must have rested his hand against the kitchen sink. The victim must have been as careless a housekeeper as Bertie.' My maid whimpered at the accusation. I continued. 'Then she or her maid or somebody in tearing off strips of this Scotch Tape to stick to the handle of the hammer, must have stuck them first against the sink, hence lifting Robin Thibodeaux's fingerprint from the sink and imprisoning it on the hammer.'

Mary Beth did not accept this, but she was excited at my discovery nevertheless. 'It's right out of one of your books, Miss Coombe! Will you call it *The Scotch Tape Murder?*'

'That would be giving it all away in the title, wouldn't it?'

'I suppose so, but it still makes a thrilling story.'

I started out of the scullery. 'Mary Beth, we must get this Eben Friendly back on the line.'

'Yes, Miss Coombe.'

I turned back in the doorway and looked down on Bertie with the coldest eye I could muster. 'Bertie, if Cook doesn't clean the scullery, then it is your daily responsibility. After all, our food is prepared here. We can't leave everything to Rosalie.'

'Yes, ma'am,' she replied feebly. But my mind was already on another matter. If Robin Thibodeaux didn't kill that poor woman, who did?

FIVE

'April is the cruellest month, breeding
Lilacs out of the dead land, mixing
Dull roots with spring rain.'

Even though Thomas Sterns Eliot's stanza from *The Waste Land* was written in 1922, it could just as well have applied to that month of 1937. The monster Adolf Hitler had been in power since 1933 as head of his notorious Third Reich. How little we knew then of what was really transpiring in Eastern Europe and how much we ignored.

I realise now that during that April I was the lilac lying dormant in the dead land. It is only in hindsight that I can write that it was perhaps the cruellest month of all, because it was the beginning of what was to end so very tragically.

That particular day there was not a trace of sun in the mournful sky. It was the song of the lark that brought me to life and drew me to my window where I noticed it had begun to rain. I rang for Bertie. She appeared with my breakfast tray and paper. My Persian kitty, Lucretia, changed sleeping position on my bed so as not to be disturbed while I ate. I devoured my poached egg and toast and the newspaper as well.

I was soon at my desk. I remember distinctly that I was well into the first chapters of a new mystery, without the benefit of Inspector Hecate. *Murder in Mandalay.* I had visited Mandalay with my officer husband the previous decade. I knew of what I wrote. Now that the celebrated author is no longer with us, I feel free to admit that the novel was somewhat influenced by Somerset Maugham's wonderful story, *The Letter.* Although I hadn't quite worked out the fine points of the series of murders, I was forging ahead nevertheless. Sometimes, things do work themselves out if you just forge ahead. I attempted to explain this to Miss Hewitt on more than one occasion. Usually she just stared at the typewriter and a blank piece of paper, 'completely blocked' as she described it, while my fingers flew across the page no matter what I was writing.

I shall now advance immediately to the introduction of the major protagonist in my story. It was Bertie, as usual, who introduced him. She knew that I didn't like to be disturbed when I was writing, but somehow always managed to do so nevertheless.

'I'm sorry, ma'am,' she half whimpered, 'I know how you hate to be disturbed when you're writing one of your murders, but there's a very odd gentleman out here to see you.'

'Odd? In what way odd?'

Bertie hesitated. I have already written that her powers of observation were poor. 'Well, ma'am, his colour for one thing.'

'What colour is he?' Mary Beth interjected.

'You don't get that colour in our English sun,' Bertie responded. 'Of that much I'm sure.'

'What colour, Bertie?' It was I who persisted.

'Like a goose after Cook takes it out of the oven.'

That was better than Bertie's usual lack of detail. My curiosity was definitely piqued. 'What else is odd about this man?'

'The way he talks.'

'What way is that?' I was becoming impatient because she volunteered so little.

'French ... like Charles Boyer in *The Garden of Allah*, but not really French either.'

'Did he give you a name, Bertie?'

'Yes, ma'am, but it's that hard to get onto my tongue.'

I was becoming more impatient. 'Try, Bertie.'

'Robin ... like in Cock Robin ... or Robin Redbreast. I know I got that part right.'

'Does he have a last name?'

'That's the hard part, ma'am... It's French like. There's a "bow" in it somewhere.'

Mary Beth was as startled as I was. She pronounced it first. 'Thibodeaux!'

I spoke the entire name. 'Robin Thibodeaux.'

Bertie was pleased that we had understood her. 'That's it ma'am.'

I turned perplexed to Miss Hewitt. 'He's here?'

Mary Beth was adamant. 'I don't think you should see him.'

'Why not?' My curiosity was definitely aroused, both to see this handsome man in person and to discover why he had sought me out.

'If this was Louisiana, he'd be delivering fish to the kitchen where he belongs. Not in your office or parlour!'

'But if he's come all the way from America, Mary Beth. I saw you when you came from America.'

'I came first class!'

This hardly seemed to me to be an argument. I got to my feet. 'Bertie, I will receive him in the parlour.'

Mary Beth stood up as well. 'Not without me you won't!'

SIX

The man was wet on the edges from the rain. My first impression of Robin Thibodeaux was that he towered over me. I actually felt petite in his presence, a sensation that was both rare and pleasing to me. I don't think he was any taller than six feet two, but it was his long elegant leanness that conveyed even more height. My readers know that I usually don't stint in my descriptions of characters which were the figments of my imagination, but here, with Robin Thibodeaux, who was a living and breathing presence, I am at a loss for words to describe him.

How do you depict an energy, a life force, that sweeps like a giant wave into a room and lifts you with its tide? Such a man was Robin Thibodeaux. Indeed he was the tawny colour of an overcooked goose, a warm tint that radiated sunshine. His eyes were lost somewhere between the world of brown and green and the darkness of his lashes made them smoulder beneath the strength of his brows. There was symmetry to his cheeks and lips and a shiny darkness to the sturdy hair that curled about his head. I think, though, that it was the voice that captured me like a helpless butterfly beneath his fingertip. It resonated about the room with warm blood from the depths of his bursting heart.

'Bonjour, Madame and Mademoiselle,' he smiled with singularly white perfect teeth.

Mary Beth put an immediate pin in his French balloon.

'We speak English over here.'

'In my country, where I am from...'

She was having none of it. 'It's my country, too, Mr Thibodeaux. In fact, if my momma didn't send me the *Times-Picayune*, you'd be hanging right now with a noose around your neck.'

He flashed Mary Beth a dazzling smile. 'Then it is you I must thank for–'

'It is Miss Coombe you must thank. If she hadn't seen your photo in my hometown newspaper...'

He shook his head. 'Such a bad picture they take of me. They make Robin look as black as pitch.'

Mary Beth looked at me out of the corners of her blue eyes. 'It served its purpose.'

'I must kiss the hand of the lady who has saved Robin's life.' He took my right hand and devoured it with kisses.

'Mr Thibodeaux, I write with this hand.'

'All the more reason for me to love it.'

I somehow managed to pull my hand free.

61

Bertie was standing in the doorway, as fascinated by our exotic visitor as I was and not wanting to quit the chamber. 'Bertie, perhaps Mr Thibodeaux would like some morning tea and cakes.'

He smiled down at Bertie. 'Mademoiselle, that would be most delightful.'

Bertie was taken aback. 'No one's ever called me that before.'

I was becoming impatient with her. 'Bertie, just tell Cook to prepare the tea.'

She mumbled, 'Yes, ma'am,' and backed unwillingly out of the room. Although I relished the gentleman towering over me, I did not forget my duties as a hostess. 'Would you care to take a seat, Mr Thibodeaux?'

He nodded gratefully. 'Robin has walked all the way to you from the town of Oxford. He now has tired feet.'

Mary Beth shot me an impatient look as he sank into a sofa. She was obviously not used to a coloured man making himself so comfortable in her presence. When I took a seat myself, she sat reluctantly beside me on the flowered sofa. 'Why are you here in England?' she demanded immediately.

'I have business with Miss Coombe.'

'Business?' she asked suspiciously.

'Oui, Mademoiselle.'

'You may address me as Miss Hewitt.'

'Miss Hewitt.'

'What sort of business?'

His eyes fastened on me so that I was compelled to look away. 'I wish to thank Miss Coombe for saving my life.'

Mary Beth was not having it. 'You could have written a letter to do that.'

'Robin is not so good with the paper and the pen.'

She was definitely suspicious. 'You came all the way to England to say "merci" in person?'

His eyes fastened on me. If I had permitted myself I would have got lost in their colour. 'Oui, "merci beaucoup".'

'How did you afford the passage? Even steerage costs money.'

I should have told Mary Beth to stop her impertinent questions. I was too mesmerised to speak.

'That is what Robin wishes to discuss with Madame Coombe.'

'*Mademoiselle* Coombe,' Mary Beth corrected. 'Miss Coombe uses her maiden name when she writes.'

'Oui, *Mademoiselle* Coombe.'

'And you can drop the Cajun French. I didn't like it any better back home.'

I had had enough. 'Mary Beth, really! I don't know how you treat your guests at home, but this is unforgivable.'

Mr Thibodeaux did not appear offended. He was obviously used to this kind of superior behaviour from the southern belles of his native country. 'You don't enjoy the Cajun even on Robin's tongue?'

He actually rolled his tongue over his teeth. Mary Beth turned to me, incensed. 'Uppity! I knew he'd be uppity!'

I couldn't help but be amused at her reaction. 'I'm sure Mr Thibodeaux meant no offence.'

He chose to ignore Mary Beth. 'Even Robin, who only reads the tides and the rings on the trees, has heard of the famous lady of the mystery books. Robin's mother had some of these books in her house.'

'I'm flattered.'

'I will be forever grateful, Mademoiselle. Without the great mystery writer, Flora Coombe, Robin would be swinging like the bell.' He bobbed his head back and forth in the most charming way.

Mary Beth was feeling left out. 'What about me? If my momma hadn't sent me the newspaper...'

'You, too, Mademoiselle.' But he did not even bother to look at her.

Even though he was looking directly at me, I no longer felt uncomfortable. There was a gentleness about him that promised a safe harbour. 'Mr Thibodeaux, if I may ask you a question ...'

'I am Robin,' he interrupted.

'Robin,' I continued. 'I ask this as a writer – for future reference. When it seemed that all was lost, and you believed that you were going to die, to be hanged for something you didn't do, what were your thoughts?'

'I prayed that in heaven I would have the same things that I have on earth, my pirogue for fishing, my home in the bayou and the beautiful birds flying above. Heaven can be no better than this.'

I marvelled at the simplicity of his response. 'How terrible it must have been for such a free spirit to be locked away in prison.'

'Only when they take away Robin's music. When Robin does not have his guitar, it is like cutting the throat away from the songbird.'

'How sad for you,' I commiserated.

'Thanks to Mademoiselle Coombe, they give Robin back his guitar and set him free.'

'And what of the actual culprit, Robin?' My mind always reverted back to the crime.

Mary Beth wondered herself. 'Momma hasn't been very good about sending the paper lately. If there was something about that one in it, we missed it.'

'It is only a month or so ago that she finally confess.'

'She?' I was more than intrigued.

'It was Essie, Mrs Carruthers' maid.'

'Would she be by chance a woman of colour?' Mary Beth questioned, as if only coloured people committed murder.

'Essie is a Negro, but three shades blacker than I.' It was obvious that he was proud of the tawny tint of his skin. Caucasians spend a lifetime baking in the sun and never achieve it.

'What was the woman's motive?' There was always a motive to murder – at least in my mysteries.

'Essie is famous in the bayou for cooking up très bon cuisine. She has worked for beaucoup fine people. Essie doesn't like nobody to tell her how to cook the meal, especially her jambalaya. Mrs Carruthers is a very hard woman to please.'

I couldn't believe my ears. 'Do you mean to tell me that over a pot of some southern stew she actually took a hammer and...?'

'Those coloured have killed each other over a lot less.'

Robin let Mary Beth's jibe pass as he did all others from her mouth. It seems to me that the coloured people of America, especially in that period before the advent of civil rights, had to develop a hide as tough as an elephant's, so that such verbal poison darts could not penetrate. Robin, in fact, responded to her derogatory statement. 'Sometimes this is verité. What temper Robin has, I think, is from the eighth part of him.'

I shook my head. 'My, my, over a pot of... what do you call it again?'

'Jambalaya.' Mary Beth informed. 'It's very popular in Louisiana. It's pure Creole and has ham and rice and sausage, tomatoes and onions and all sorts of spices. I can only eat a little at a time. It gives me indigestion.'

'You have forgotten the most important element of all – the fish. The shrimp must be caught the same day or it does not taste as good.'

My mouth was watering at the description of it. 'It certainly doesn't sound like a premeditated murder.' I wondered what Inspector Hecate would make of it. 'But over a pot of stew ... and with a hammer.'

'It must have been the first thing Essie picked up. It could have just as easily been a skillet.'

I shook my head. 'I must remove all possible weapons from the kitchen. Cook does have a mind of her own when it comes to Shepherd's Pie. I always feel it's undercooked, but she likes it runny.' I turned to Mary Beth. 'Perhaps I should obtain a photograph of this Essie for my gallery.'

'What is this gallery?'

'Miss Coombe collects photographs of some of the famous murderesses in history, but I don't think this Essie is famous enough, Miss Coombe.'

'They got beaucoup confession out of her by keeping her in the cell and not letting her eat until she tell the verité. Now, since she confess, they not hang her but make her cook in prison.'

At that moment Bertie entered with a tray of tea and cakes. She placed it on the long coffee table in front of the sofa. 'Will there be anything else, ma'am?' She eyed Robin curiously. No doubt both she and Miss Hewitt would have preferred my guest to have tea in the kitchen with the help. She stole one last look at him before departing. I lifted the pot of tea (at least she had brought out the silver service) and began to pour. 'How do you take your tea, Robin?'

'Robin take it black.'

Mary Beth corrected. 'Over here we say "plain", which means without sugar or milk. The English love their sugar and milk.'

'Plain then?' I questioned.

'There is nothing plain about you, Mademoiselle,' he smiled, 'but I shall take it so.'

I relished his compliment, even if it wasn't true. I was plain. I have always been plain. Even though I powdered myself and used lipstick and rouge and shadowed my eyes, it still did not disguise the fact that I was never beautiful. 'Will you be taking your tea as usual, Mary Beth?'

She pretended not to worry about her figure, but she always took her tea plain with a little lemon.

'I'm not taking any at all.'

I poured my own tea with both sugar and

milk – as a civilised individual always takes it – and proceeded to play the proper hostess, perhaps to over-compensate for the rudeness of my secretary. 'We have the Duchess of Bedford to thank for teatime here in England, although we are having it a bit early today. In 1840, I believe it was, the Duchess started serving tea with cakes at four o'clock in the afternoon to assuage a sinking feeling she always felt at that hour. Now all of England gets depressed at four o'clock.'

Robin sipped his tea and devoured more than one cake.

'Most beaucoup delicious, Mademoiselle.'

'If you had your guitar you told us about, we could have some music with our tea.'

'But I do have.'

'Here with you?'

'I leave it outside the front door.'

I turned to Miss Hewitt. 'Mary Beth, why don't you fetch it?'

I could see that she was incensed at the suggestion. Mr Thibodeaux leaped to his feet. 'Robin will fetch. A man does not want his guitar touched by any other hands.'

As he hurried outside the door, Mary Beth voiced her disapproval. 'Miss Coombe, how can you invite a man like that, a man of colour to actually sit down and have tea with us? Where I come from...'

I had heard enough of her complaining.

'This isn't where you come from. This is a civilised country. And as long as you remain in my employ, I expect you to act accordingly.' I must admit that I come from probably the most class-conscious country in the world, but I was tired of her blatant prejudice.

'But, Miss Coombe–'

I was firm. 'Not another word on the subject. If you don't wish to have tea with us, you can leave the room.'

She reached for a cake and munched with her jaw clenched. 'I will stay here and keep an eye on him. Somebody has to keep him in his place.'

Robin returned carrying a worn guitar that wasn't even in a case for transport. He displayed it proudly. 'This is my spider box.'

I was intrigued. 'What an odd name. Whatever for?'

'Set it aside for one night and a bayou spider spreads her gossamer web across the strings.'

How poetic he could be. I could see both the spider and the web in my imagination. 'What are you going to play for us, Mr Robin Thibodeaux?'

He tuned the guitar with his long delicate slender fingers. I still think coloured men have the most beautiful hands of all.

'I thought that Robin would play a song about his people. There are many Thibodeaux all over the bayou, and all of us of different shades of colour.' He slapped the belly of the guitar. 'This one I shall play is about "Papa Thibodeaux".'

He kept rhythm with the tap of his foot. His singing voice was an irresistible extension of his speech, a dusky black velvet tone that to this very day still rings in my ears. I don't remember the words exactly, but I do recall that they concerned a Cajun fiddle player who played on Saturday night when everybody sailed their pirogues to town.

Mary Beth sat stony-faced. I remember that I applauded appreciatively and demanded more. He sang another song about a Cajun country boy, but then I insisted that he sip his tea and finish the cakes, for I could see that he was hungry. He gobbled them all down. Cook could certainly have been a pastry chef. Her assorted cakes were incomparable. 'Robin was beaucoup hungry.'

Mary Beth could not resist a pointed observation, but I must admit, one that was on my mind as well. 'Why do you always refer to yourself in the third person?'

'The third person?'

'As "Robin" rather than "I" or "me"?' Mary Beth persisted.

'There is a word describing that eccentricity,' I added, 'and it is called "illeism".'

'It is the way of my people,' Robin explained. He touched his heart. 'Here it is I.' He then indicated his entire body. 'The rest is Robin.'

'What a charming explanation!' Indeed I had been charmed by few men in my life other than my late father. Certainly my departed husband had little of what Robin possessed. I know he was a different man with his fellow officers and at the Club, but with me... But I must stop. I shall not disparage his memory any further.

Mr Thibodeaux had more to say on the subject. 'Also, as is with my people, in my story Robin is always the big character.'

'I see,' I responded, but I don't think I really did. I never put myself in any of my stories. I never was a character, although I must admit many of my murderesses could be considered an extension of me. If I hadn't been able to take their heinous revenge through my writing, no doubt I would have been in the kitchen with a hammer myself.

'Now, because of the great mystery lady, Mademoiselle Flora Coombe,' Mr Thibodeaux continued, 'they know about Robin all over America. I think perhaps the world even.'

I could not contain my curiosity any longer. 'What brings you to England, Robin Thibodeaux? Surely not just to thank me.'

SEVEN

Robin Thibodeaux glanced unsurely at Mary Beth. I sensed that he did not want to reveal the reason for his trip abroad in her presence. 'Perhaps ... it is something that...'

'Is this something you wish to discuss with me in private, Robin?'

'Oui, Mademoiselle.'

I turned to my secretary. 'Mary Beth, I doubt that I will get back down to work until after lunch. Why don't you take what I've already written this morning and transcribe it?'

'But...' It was painfully obvious that she did not want to leave me alone with the coloured man. 'That will be all for now, Mary Beth.' Sometimes I had to remind her that she was in my employ. She got up slowly from the couch and departed. If looks could kill, Robin Thibodeaux would have died instantly.

Now there were just the two of us. 'I must apologise for my secretary, but she is your countrywoman rather than mine.'

'Robin is used to being treated mal by such women, unless they are alone with him. Then sometimes it is a different story.'

73

I chose not to pursue that subject any further. Curiosity over his sudden appearance at my home was killing this cat. My own, incidentally, Lucretia, took this opportunity to wander into the parlour and rub against the long legs of my visitor. I blush even now as I admit I would like to have done so myself. Why were these feelings that had lain dormant for so many years bubbling to the surface? Soon the Persian was snuggled safely in the man's lap and purring contentedly. This seemed a good omen to me. Lucretia was very particular about who was worthy of her company. She had taken an immediate dislike to the inspector, for instance.

'What is it you wish to discuss with me, Robin?'

He produced a small notebook from underneath his shirt. 'This.' He set Lucretia gently onto the carpet and stepped over to me. He shook his head at himself. 'All the books I know you have written. How do you write so easily all these books?'

I could have protested and replied that it wasn't easy, but that would not have been true. 'It is my profession.'

He opened his notebook and read aloud. 'Life good. Pirogue good. Fish good. Happy days until police come one day and say I kill rich lady. Robin not happy behind bars.' He shook his head again. 'Is not bon like in your books.'

I had to agree. 'I wouldn't exactly call it literature.'

'That is why Robin come to you, so you can help me write the story.'

'What story?'

'It is the one the big magazine pay big money for.'

'What magazine?'

'It is called *Life*. They give Robin money now, big money when I finish. Only Robin is not bon writer like the great lady of the mystery books.'

I glanced at his notebook again. 'I'm afraid that you are not.' It was becoming clear to me now as I am sure it is to you. 'Is this how you could afford this trip to England?'

'Oui. First I get passport, then I buy the passage. Now no money left to live...'

It was becoming even clearer. 'I suppose they want you to write about my interest in your case.'

Robin nodded hopefully. 'They say that is the best part of the story.'

The sound of Mary Beth's typing from my office reminded me that I had more important work to consider. 'I am in the middle of writing a new mystery. I couldn't possibly–'

He did not appear daunted. 'Robin can wait. There is much for him to do in your garden.'

'My garden?'

'Robin loves spring the best of all. Soon all the flowers reaching for the sun. In the bayou, when fish not biting, Robin helps tend garden of famous old actor gentleman, Joseph Jefferson.' The American actor was well known to me. In fact I had thrilled at his famous portrayal of Rip Van Winkle when I was a young girl. 'The bayou is bon for les fleurs. Very damp. Very moist. Here garden needs more work. Robin has way with flowers. The garden of Mademoiselle needs beaucoup work.'

'I'm sure it does. I have only really begun to... My gardener has other gardens to worry about, and during the dormant months...' I considered his notebook again. Perhaps if I did help him immediately with the story, he would be on his way, but I must admit, part of me already did not want him to depart. 'No doubt your story would be an interesting one. I suppose with a lot of photographs...'

'Oui, of Mademoiselle.'

'No, not of Mademoiselle. I detest having my photograph taken.'

'Mademoiselle would take a beaucoup lovely photograph.'

'Thank you very much, Robin, but it is not so.' I read his first sentences again. 'Before you start out saying that "Life is good", I think it would be important to establish where you are writing about. How do you actually feel about the bayou?'

'It is my home.'

'Well, that is better actually.' I repeated what he had said. "The bayou is my home". We must write that down.' Robin handed me a small pen from his pocket. I flipped to a fresh page in his notebook and began writing. 'Now describe the bayou. I want to feel it and see it and smell it. That's what good writing is all about.'

Robin plunged ahead. 'I am the bayou. I am warm and the bayou is warm. My smell is the bayou's smell – the smell of moss and blossoms and shrimp creole bubbling in my momma's cook pot over the fire.'

I was writing it all down, word for word. 'That's very good. It is very important that your story has your own style. They must never suspect that Flora Coombe had anything to do with writing it.' I was eager to hear more, as if I was simply a reader of *Life* magazine. 'Now what else?'

'When Robin strip naked and sink into the water of the swamp, he is like the snake, weaving in and out between the trunks of the cypress tree.'

'Now that is all very good, Robin, but in writing a first person account like this, you must not describe yourself in the third.'

'No more Robin but "I".' He said it as a statement. This was clearly a man desiring to learn. After that first meeting he seldom referred to himself in the third person, although I must admit, I had found it rather charming. 'I must be careful when I swim in the bayou beyond my momma's house. There is danger of the 'gator suddenly bobbing to the surface and smiling at me with all his teeth.'

'Why couldn't you have sat down and written this well yourself without spending all your money coming to England?'

'I can parler – not scriver.'

'You parler very well.'

'For instance I could not scriver that the famous lady of the mysteries is not as I expected. She is a most lovely Mademoiselle with hair the colour of the red hibiscus.' He reached out to stroke my hair, but I pulled quickly away. Even though I was pleased with his compliment, I never let anybody touch my hair. It was red then but certainly not as flaming as he described. I had grown up with mousy brown hair piled atop my head in true Edwardian fashion. Now it was red and wispy and covering my too large ears that, in my dotage, are still better to hear with than most.

'Robin, he ... *I* am sorry to have offended the lovely lady.'

'I am not offended, Robin.'

'Ii n'est pas bien for a man with the skin the colour of an almond to touch the lady with skin as white as the China doll my

78

sister kept as a child.'

'No, no, Robin,' I protested. 'It is the nicest compliment I have received for a very long time – if ever. I am most flattered.'

'Robin always speaks from the heart.'

'Yes, I believe you do.' My skin had turned redder than my hair. I turned to glance out of the French windows. 'It has stopped raining. Perhaps the sun might peek through.'

'Robin brings the sunshine from home.'

I felt so flushed and overheated, I had a definite need for some fresh air. 'You mentioned your interest in my garden,' I stammered. 'Would you care to have a look around?'

'It would be an honour to have Mademoiselle show me.'

I slipped into rubbers and a mackintosh.

When Robin opened the front door, the crisp spring air blew like the vapour of ice against my burning cheeks. I breathed deeply and got my bearings. As I stepped outside Robin immediately took my hand as if we were sweethearts. I pulled my hand free immediately, although his touch was deliciously warm and my fingers wanted to linger there.

EIGHT

Something was stirring in the garden. Small sprigs of green had suddenly poked their dewy heads out of the rich English soil. When I had meandered through the garden perhaps a week earlier, before the advent of showers, there was no sign of life. Now the promise of flower was everywhere. Was Robin some Merlin who had merely to wave his tan fingers and the flowers would obey?

'Sweet April showers do spring May flowers,' I quoted from Thomas Tusser's *A Hundred Good Points of Husbandry*, written centuries before. It wasn't quite May, but there was already a sprinkling of lilac beginning to flower, the pale reddish purple resembling dots of paint against a brown palette.

He spoke without looking at me. 'Robin was wrong to be familiar and take the hand of the great lady. I just wish you to lead me through your special garden.'

How old was he? He seemed like a boy in the body of a man. He was actually in his late twenties but was none the worse for wear in the Louisiana sun.

'Perhaps if I took your arm, Robin. That's what a proper English lady does. She takes a man's arm.'

His face lit up with the light of a lantern and he opened his arm so that I could slip my fingers inside. How pleasurable to feel the warmth of his manliness. Just a simple touch and I was a schoolgirl again, being asked to waltz at my first dance, perhaps because he towered over me, as boys used to when I was young and had not achieved my full growth. 'Now, Robin, I shall show you my garden, or what it will be when everything is completed.'

I shall not make that tour now, although everything that I envisioned came to fruition.

Mr Thibodeaux immediately understood what I had in mind for the property. What took endless repetition to my often cantankerous gardener, with his small staff of Spaniards, Robin grasped at once. Apparently the vast gardens of Mr Joseph Jefferson, although of a different country and clime, were similar to what I hoped to achieve, a mixture of cultivated and wildflowers, for instance wild honeysuckle growing amidst an assortment of Canterbury bells, dog daisies and cornflowers.

Robin could see it all, even though so little was yet in bloom, but there was something that I had not even considered on which he was insistent. 'The garden must be more than pleasure for the eye. There must be the herbs for Cook to season the food.'

'A herb garden! Of course!' I quickly led the way to where I thought it would grow. 'Come, I will show you. There is an area beyond the kitchen that might be perfect.' I recited the names of herbs. Robin nodded his approval. 'Chives, rue, sage, marjoram, basil, borage, parsley...' There was certainly room for these and more. Cook would only have to step outside the kitchen door to pluck the appropriate seasoning.

'In the bayou we grow the vegetables as well. Around my momma's house we grow everything she needs for the stew.'

I didn't want to disappoint him, but a vegetable garden did not fit into my master plan; practical, yes, but not a thing of beauty. 'I don't think...'

He pointed to the gentle slope beyond the kitchen that disappeared finally into the woods. At the beginning of this decline I had already planted a line of scented evergreens, which, unlike almost everything else in the garden, had been in bloom since the middle of March. It was not a showy plant, but even at a distance, I could catch a whiff of its pure vanilla scent.

'First flowering fruit trees. Beyond that the vegetable garden that no one but Cook will see.'

'Fruit trees?'

He nodded affirmatively. 'There is no spring without the flowering fruits – apple –

peach – plum.'

'And in green underwood and cover blossom by blossom the spring begins.' I couldn't resist quoting a little Swinburne. 'Well, I suppose.'

How prescient he was, although I did not plant an entire orchard. Instead each flowering tree is at a gentle distance from the other. As I write this, I move to an upper window to view these trees, nude and desolate now in this winter of 1972, but how they will flower in the spring, my reliable precursors to what my summer garden will bring.

We returned to the front of my lovely stone house. Below us was a panoramic view of what was already garden or soon to be. My home was reached by a twisting gravel road that was lined with Lombardy poplar trees planted by a previous owner. These tall towering trees were as durable as the countryside itself. At the beginning of this drive at the entrance to the property was the stone caretaker's cottage. Robin's eyes fastened upon this. 'Who lives here?'

'No one at the moment. I have no need of a caretaker. I thought I might turn it into guest quarters. The previous owners were away so often that they had a caretaker who lived there to watch over things. But I am not gone that often. This is my permanent home. It's a charming little cottage actually.'

'If Robin is to make the garden grow, he

needs a place to lay his head and sleep.'

'Have I hired you as a gardener?'

'Robin, he – I – is not for hire. He works for free for the great lady who saved his life while she writes his story for the big magazine.'

'I'm not sure, Robin. I...'

'You put me in the garden, the flowers will grow as never before.'

'I'm sure they will, but...'

'There is only one thing that is missing in your garden besides Robin.'

'What is that?' He certainly knew how to pique my curiosity.

'In the bayou we are never far from the water. Robin will make you a pond in which the swans will swim and the birds will come to drink.'

'And where would you put this pond?'

He pointed to where the weeping willow trees were beginning to grow. 'The willows will surround it, and it will be protected.'

It was too much for me all at once. 'We shall see.' As we turned to the house, Robin's eye was caught by the dovecote at the edge of the structure. 'This is older than the house, no?' he pointed to the small tower.

'It's all that's left from the original castle. It's called a dovecote.'

'For doves? For the birds?' He was excited at the thought of it.

'Yes, for pigeons. We have none now.'

'I will find the pigeons. I will bring them to their new home.'

'I have thought of bringing the birds back, but...'

'The pigeons will return for Robin.'

'We shall see, Mr Thibodeaux, but meanwhile, perhaps you would like to stay for lunch.'

NINE

Robin Thibodeaux and I became immediate partners in the enterprise that is my remarkable garden. Growing up in Brighton, I had such dreams of what my marriage would be, the partnership I would forge with the man I chose to love. Such was not the case with Reginald Campbell. I realise now that I was swept away by the striking figure he presented in his dazzling crimson uniform. Reginald, a Scotsman through and through, was one of 'The Long Red Line', the Argyll and Sutherland Highlanders, the personal regiment of Princess Louise, the sixth child of Queen Victoria, who had married the Duke of Argyll.

Out of uniform, Reginald was not the same man. He only came to life with his fellow officers and his men. At home he drifted into suspended animation. Perhaps it was his disappointment in me that I did not provide him with any children. Since he came back to life when I entertained, I gave as many dinner parties as possible. My mother had been a celebrated hostess in Brighton, so entertaining came easily to me, although I found it a frivolous activity – even though I became known as 'the Hostess of Delhi'.

Is it any wonder that in despair I was driven to my writing desk? If my older brother hadn't read Sherlock Holmes to me when I was a young girl, would I have ever dared to create my own inspector? I attempted writing at first simply to keep me busy. Soon it became my consuming passion. I find it quite astonishing now that my first effort was published at all. I think that Reginald was proud of my instant writing success and of my abilities as a hostess, but he had little use for me as a woman. I shall stop herewith any more talk of Reggie. There are nieces and nephews still about. I shall not tarnish the image of a brave soldier who died in service to his King, not in battle, but from cholera.

No, Reggie and I were never partners, scarcely man and wife. I never truly shared an enterprise with a man until I joined forces with Robin Thibodeaux to create the beauty that became the most celebrated garden between Oxford and High Wycombe.

Robin required very little but I spruced up his cottage nevertheless. I saw that his small kitchen was fully equipped. He rose so early to begin work on the garden, Cook wasn't even awake. Lunch and dinner, however, he enjoyed in the dining room with Mary Beth and with me. My secretary obviously did not approve of his appearance at my table, but she had enough good sense to hold her tongue. Besides, Robin and I were so full of talk of my garden, we scarcely knew that she was there. We were partners in the creation of floral beauty. The summer of 1937 was to be the happiest summer of my life. I suppose one summer of happiness is better than none at all.

I made quick work of writing Robin's article and we sent it off to *Life* magazine. A photographer was assigned to photograph the protagonists, but I refused. Robin was willing, but the publication would have to make do with an unattractive snapshot of me caught at some official function. The important thing was that Robin was paid handsomely, as he was for working so diligently in my garden. Most of the money he sent home to his mother. He was a dutiful son. I could not have asked for better if I had had children myself.

As I suspected, my previous gardener would not tolerate a 'foreigner's' presence in my garden. Hardly a week passed before he presented his ultimatum. 'Either that darkie goes or you will never see hide nor hair of me again.' What could I do but offer him his severance pay? It was really no contest at all.

For Old Barnabas gardening was a job; for Robin it was a vocation. He achieved single-handedly what Barnabas and his staff could only attempt. A world of new flowers danced like butterflies under Robin's green thumb.

Wasn't it John Whitcomb Riley who wrote about being 'knee-deep in June'? It is the best way to describe Flora Coombe and Robin Thibodeaux working side by side in this rich English soil. How idyllic the days. If you could catch a summer like a firefly and contain it in a bottle I would have done it without the slightest hesitation. Mornings I spent with my breakfast in bed and the *Times* and the local Oxford daily, writing at my desk until lunch with Robin, then an afternoon spent surveying his morning labours, working alongside him until it was time to prepare for supper. How handsome he looked with his shirt off in the summer sun. His brown muscles grew with the garden. In many ways he was the most beautiful flower of all. If he held my hand then and stole a kiss beneath the arbour of climbing roses, I did not discourage his advances. Reggie had scarcely kissed me at all. I didn't even know what a kiss was until Robin engulfed my mouth in his own. Will it suffice to say that my mouth opened like eager petals and welcomed this brown bee into her midst? We were like the turtle doves with which Robin stocked my dovecote. Was any bird in love as much as I? For the first time in my life – since I was a young girl in love with my older brother's schoolmate – I was besotted.

TEN

During the summer of 1937, the sun seemed never to falter. The clouds stayed politely away like uninvited guests. Rain fell on other countries; not in England. Flowers bloomed brighter and bigger than ever before – or since.

July was the month of roses. The Madame Plantiers grew to cover the trunk and branches of a dead elm, its white blossoms a bower of celestial beauty. Paul's Lemon Pillar scampered across the entire brick wall that separated one part of my garden from the other. Its blossoms burst like fireworks, leaving a sweet-smelling carpet of pale yellow about the wall.

Even now I wish to write pages describing

those summer roses that still bloom in great profusion, so many planted by Robin; but I shall resist the temptation and, as a good author does, move my story along.

It was a day of celebration: the completion of Robin's Pond. Even after all these years I still call it that. The workers that Robin had hired in the village to help him had done a skilful job. The clear bubbling water was diverted from Sir Knight's Brook which ran year round through my property. It had been named centuries before for the mystical builder of the first castle including the remaining dovecote. The running water could be started or stopped at will by an ingenious sluice gate that Robin had cleverly fashioned and that is still functioning. If the pond chose to overflow in the eventual rains, the overflow was caught and channelled to the extensive flower gardens alongside.

Mary Beth, Cook, Bertie, Rosalie, Robin, the workers and I watched as the water slowly filled the large pond. The weeping willow trees planted sparsely around it were already growing. A carpet of white daisies covered much of the bank. Robin had scarcely put them in the ground and they spread like fire in anticipation of this serene body of water.

Soon the two swans were released: a young couple already so devoted to each other that I immediately named them Heathcliff and

Cathy since, as Emily Bronte's characters in Wuthering Heights, they were joined together for eternity.

Robin had constructed a white pergola on a small island in the centre of the pond to the shelter of which the swans could flee for protection and to nest. Even to this day, when I wish to be entirely alone and contemplate a new murder, I still have the strength to row myself to that small pergola where nobody can disturb me.

As the swans swam contentedly about their new home, we sipped champagne and nibbled the special cakes Cook had prepared for the occasion. My neighbour, Lord Chester Westmoreland, affectionately known as Bunny, who represented our district in the House of Lords, had been invited as well. A portly gentleman somewhere in his sixties, sporting a walrus moustache and grey hair entirely too long and unkempt, he seldom intruded upon my privacy nor I on his. His sickly wife, Lady Agnes, had been invited as well, but as usual, she was 'under the weather'. I suspected that she drank and that she was 'under the bottle'. I wore a large bonnet to protect my fair skin from the sun and had discarded my gardening clothes for something more flowery and appropriate. Mary Beth had dressed in a similar fashion for the occasion and on this particular afternoon was the essence of a beautiful southern belle.

'Capital! Capital!' Lord Westmoreland boomed his approval as the swans glided like skaters through the water. He toasted Robin and his pond and devoured Cook's cakes. 'Of course,' he added, 'it is only an iota of what I have planned for Penmark.' His estate was indeed extensive. It covered much of Aston Tirrold. My property was only a fraction of its size.

'And what is that?' I enquired.

'You know the swampy area at the lower edge of my property that pushes into the Thames where the geese sometimes stop and the grouse and partridge nest?'

'Yes.' He and his wife had shown me proudly around their property, which included Easley House, a massive Georgian structure that is now a summer haven for tourists, Bunny's remaining son living in the guest cottage and off the income from the paying visitors. The estate was made famous in 1937 by something that befell this author. The reader shall find out soon enough.

Lord Westmoreland continued. 'This will become the beginning of a man-made lake, a nature preserve, if you will, that I hope will attract many species of bird life. Hopefully one day soon, all my hunting parties will take place in my own back yard.' He always spoke as if he was addressing the entire

House of Lords. In the large space of my garden, it somehow seemed appropriate.

'But how can you call it a nature preserve if you wish to hunt the very nature you are preserving?'

'I shall carefully follow the limit. While I am busy pushing through the permit, I have already engaged a gamekeeper to begin seeking many of the species I shall require.' He eyed Robin approvingly. 'Perhaps I can hire this young man here to assist in the construction.'

'That is entirely up to him,' I responded, secure that Robin would not absent himself from my garden or my presence.

Robin smiled broadly, delighted to be desired, his teeth gleaming in the sunlight. 'How do you say? "I am happy to be big fish in smaller pond"?' He had indeed become more articulate in my presence. He seldom referred to himself in the third person. If nothing else, after all that has happened, at least Robin Thibodeaux improved his vocabulary and his mode of expression – but at what cost?

ELEVEN

In honour of the completion of our pond, Robin invited my secretary and me for a special dinner at his small stone cottage. Although Robin usually had dinner at my table in the main house, sometimes he felt too tired or dirty from a day's work in the garden and chose to cook for himself in his own quarters. For this special occasion he was preparing his native dish, jambalaya, his mother's special recipe, which I longed to sample. Mary Beth, who did not appreciate Robin's presence at our dinner table, refused his invitation. I accepted with pleasure and I looked forward to the evening with both anticipation and trepidation. Realising that we would be alone together in the small confines of his quarters, I trembled like a schoolgirl.

July wafted through Robin's small cottage, a perfumed breeze that stole through the garden and blew gently through the open windows, rustling the curtains I had ordered especially to spruce up his cottage. I was still wearing my afternoon dress, the flowered silk that fell to my calves and accented the length of my figure. I was not fat. I have never been fat. If one's taste was for a rather boyish build in the body of a woman, I suppose I might have satisfied. I remember I wore a sole strand of my pearls (a gift to myself) and some white daisies from the garden in my hair. Robin wore the rose-coloured silk shirt I had given him as a reminder of our gypsy roses. His trousers were as black as ink and clung to him.

It was probably just the wine that Robin served with dinner that made me feel girlish. The wireless was playing. I remember Fred Astaire singing 'A Foggy Day in London Town' and thinking that the fog in my own life had lifted forever. Every day had become sunny.

The dinner was a savoury mix of rice, sausage, ham, shrimp and other shellfish, blended with tomatoes, peppers and spices. Robin had driven into town early in the morning to purchase the ingredients. As we ate, he spoke of his beloved bayou. All the ingredients were either produced on his mother's farm or caught in the Gulf. He described a typical jambalaya party which all his relatives attended. There would be game playing and singing and dancing. After a succulent bread pudding dessert which Robin also created, he scooped up his 'spider box' and began to sing. I don't remember the words. They were Cajun and full of pronunciations I did not understand, but the melodies linger so many years after the songs ended so badly.

When Robin took my hand and said that, 'now we shall dance,' I fell comfortably into his arms. The wireless played once again. It was one of those songs that Tommy Dorsey and his Orchestra used to play and were very popular in England before and all through the War. I wanted the song to go on forever. When it was over, Robin scooped me up in his arms as if I was a floating dandelion and carried me into the small bedroom. I don't think I had been carried since my father transported me about the house when I was a little girl. Certainly Reggie never attempted it, but for Robin I was so much air. I almost felt as if I had wings.

He laid me so gently onto the bed that I felt as if I had descended onto a bed of rose petals. Before joining me against the pillow, he shed his clothes as naturally as a snake does his skin. How magnificent he looked towering over me – my bronzed Adonis – this statue come to life solely for my pleasure.

He had no trouble removing my clothes as well, peeling them away like petals. When he lay down beside me and buried me in his strong arms, we both smelled sweetly of the garden. As the brown soil hungers to foster new growth, I desperately wanted his seed. Even if it would never bloom, I desired it nevertheless.

I suppose I could go on as is the fancy in many books nowadays, to describe the glorious act of love-making that transpired that night in the cottage: but I cannot write in the style of Mary McCarthy, Grace Metalious or this Jacque-line Susann. Certain things must be left to the bedroom or to the imagination of the reader. Perhaps I can say that with Reggie love-making had always been a rather unpleasant chore – not only for me – but I believe for him as well. With Robin ... how can I say it and remain discreet? With Robin, for the first time, I tasted the exquisite pleasure – the satisfaction – of love. In contrast with Reggie, I never wanted it to end.

I have said more than I wish. I must move on to the aftermath of love, when two people hold onto each other because one of them never wants to let go. I even remember what was playing on the wireless. It was a song from the glorious Walt Disney film, *Snow White and the Seven Dwarfs*. I don't remember who was singing it, perhaps the woman from the cinema. 'Someday My Prince Will Come.' How true it seemed to me during that evening of magic. When Robin whispered in my ear that he wanted to marry me, my heart must have stopped for a moment, suddenly afraid to beat. How did he phrase it? I think he slipped back into 'illeism'.

'Robin loves the great lady who has been

so good to him. I do not want to leave her kind presence and go back to America. Will Mademoiselle Coombe marry Monsieur Robin Thibodeaux?'

'Yes,' I responded immediately, gasping for air. Soon he would be in the main house with me, as my husband in my own bed.

We would go on forever.

How our garden would grow.

Or so I foolishly believed.

TWELVE

I shall not deign to relive the many arguments presented to me against my marriage to the man I loved even better than myself, which, for Flora Coombe – if you know me at all – is an extraordinary thing to say.

That was the first time I was happy that my older brother was not alive to remonstrate with me. My beloved Jimmy lost his precious life in 1916, in the Battle of the Somme, that senseless slaughter of World War One which produced no strategic gains and over a million casualties. I will never forgive our British Commander, the taciturn Scotsman, Sir Douglas Haig, for so blithely committing my brother and so many others to an early grave. What was achieved in that battle? Absolutely nothing. There was still no break in the Western Front. The Somme, which was once a peaceful river in northern France, will forever be a Valhalla, a place where blood still runs to the English Channel.

Although I was a patriotic young lady and supported England's entry into the war, I realise now that we British should have stayed home and let the Serbs and the Germans and the Austro-Hungarians and the French and the Russians fight it out among themselves. Perhaps a little territory would have gone from one country to the other. That would have been the end of it. So many American lives would have been saved as well. What did Rupert Brooke write in *The Soldier* before he, too, was lost to the War?

'If I should die, think only this of me:
That there's some corner of a foreign field
That is forever England.'

Better that Jimmy had grown old on his own soil, that one day he would have been buried alongside Mummy and Daddy instead of in Flanders fields, 'Where the poppies blow, Between the crosses, row on row.'

Those poppies blow over my brother Jimmy's grave even now. I will always remember him as young, so handsome in his uniform, his dark moustache and brows and flashing blue eyes. He aged in a grave so that I did not have to see the ravages of time upon his face as I see them upon mine when I screw up enough courage now to glance in the mirror.

Yes, if my brother had remained alive, he would not have approved of my impending marriage, although I doubt if he could have persuaded me to abandon my plans for matrimony. I have always had a mind of my own, ever since I was a little girl and he could not influence me to lie on his behalf. How many lies I have told since, as you will soon see! Neither of Jimmy's two children, Jack and Rosalind, nor their respective spouses, could alter my plans. Nor could my diligent solicitor, David Chasebourne, nor Mary Beth, or any of my friends, who, I realise now, were just concerned for my welfare.

I was determined to marry so that Robin could legally share my Chippendale bed and I could awake in his arms and not slink away from his cottage in the dead of night to awaken in my own bed so that nobody would be the wiser: but, of course, everybody in the household was.

If I couldn't be a June bride, I would be an August one. We went to Gretna Green.

Our drive north to Scotland, to the village where we would be married, was through a blaze of purple heather. I sat close to Robin in my yellow Aston Martin, my head against his shoulder, purring as contentedly as my Persian cat, who had sensed that I was going away and had leaped into my suitcase while Bertie was packing. I suppose the car was a bit sporty for me, but Robin looked perfect behind the wheel.

Reggie and I had been married in a High Episcopal ceremony with a matron of honor and bridesmaids and family and friends in attendance. In Gretna Green it was simply Mr Robin Thibodeaux and Miss Flora Coombe. There were two witnesses brought in for the occasion. I can scarcely remember their names or what they looked like. I suppose I only had eyes for Robin that day, but I do remember the justice of the Peace, though, because he reminded me of Dan Leno, an actor I had seen in pantomime at the Drury Lane Theatre when I was a young girl. There was something similar in his speech and gestures and features... In one of the pantomimes Dan Leno had portrayed Mother Goose. I remembered that fantasy above all the others he essayed. It seemed in Gretna Green that Mother Goose was marrying us. I assumed that from that day forward my life was going to be a fairy tale, Wendy and her chocolate Peter Pan growing old together in the Neverland that was their magical garden. The Brothers Grimm would have been more appropriate. Those German tales are much darker, and even the happy endings are suspect – such as mine.

'Do you promise to love, cherish and obey as long as you both shall live?'

I certainly did! Robin Thibodeaux had a much shorter span of time in mind.

THIRTEEN

How do I describe my blissful honeymoon in August? We crossed the English Channel into France. I saw the continent for the first time because it was viewed no longer through my experienced eyes, but through Robin's. He savoured every morsel of a world that was new and strange to him. The French immediately understood his Cajun way of expression. They loved him as I loved him. They did not stare, but accepted us together as they had not in England. We devoured France whereas I had only had a taste, a 'soupçon' of the territory before. We drove through the entire country stopping anywhere at our whim, holding hands in a pavement café, picnicking with cheese, wine and sausage in the countryside, delving into the history of the exquisite country on the actual sites of its making. Little did we know that in only a few years beautiful France would be occupied by the Nazis.

How Robin loved to sit behind the wheel of my sturdy yellow Aston Martin that I had bought a few years earlier. I sat as close to him as propriety permitted. I hoped that Frenchmen would not assume that he was just my driver, which happened on too many occasions. Often the top was down and I would wear a scarf against the French wind.

We take the motor car for granted now. During the early part of this century, when I was becoming an eligible young lady, an excursion in an open car (which was all we had then), was a momentous occasion. We equipped ourselves as if we were journeying to the North Pole. We took baskets of provisions and furry rugs and extra scarves and clothing. The women wore the new motoring caps which resembled a military headgear and were tied down with veils. The safe driving speed was considered to be 20 miles an hour and a car always broke down several times before we reached a destination.

Such was never the case with my Aston Martin. It was as reliable as its driver. The French countryside whizzed by us like a series of picture postcards, but it was the nights I enjoyed best of all, when the sun had set and the lighting was more flattering to a woman of a certain age. We would retire to the bridal suite in a small country auberge or a luxurious Paris hotel. The world went away. I was lost in strong brown arms, treasured in a four-poster bed in which anything else but pleasure was forbidden.

I foolishly kept a diary of that trip. When I glance through the pages now, I blush at many of the things I so girlishly transcribed.

Soon I shall destroy this diary of a honeymoon in France so that it does not find its way into improper hands to be published after my death and become an embarrassment to me even in the afterworld. How it pains me now to turn these pages and remember the happy bride I once was – if even for a month. If love is blind, was I the blindest of all?

FOURTEEN

The description of an older man involved with a younger woman as being a 'May-December' romance might have applied to Robin and me as well, although in our case the roles were reversed.

Where did this expression originate? I have searched my extensive library, and although I am not positive, I think it began, naturally, with the great Bard himself. There is a speech in *As You Like It* that I believe is the origin:

'Men are April when they woo,
December when they wed:
Maids are May when they are maids,
But the sky changes when they are wives.'

I should have realised that day when we returned to England in September and the sky was no longer sunny, that the weather was an indication of the gloom that was about to overwhelm me.

The assistants we had hired to watch over the garden in our absence had not failed us. Flowers still appeared to be blossoming in great profusion, especially the garland roses that crept like large snowflakes up the tree branches.

The servants were waiting for us outside my home, lined up as if we were Lord and Lady returning to our ancestral manor, although I wasn't even yet a Dame and Robin was only the lord of my heart. Each one: Bertie, Cook, Rosalie and even Miss Hewitt appeared delighted to welcome us. I had bought Robin his new travelling suit in Paris. It was a light tan material for summer, a perfect complement to his skin. The servants couldn't help but notice how handsome and elegant he looked, which filled me full of newfound pride.

How wonderful to be back inside my own home. The French provided us with wonderful places to stay but yes, forgive me, I have to say it: THERE IS NO PLACE LIKE HOME.

I have always taken that phrase for granted. I have just looked it up, never before knowing its origin. It is from the opera *Clari*, written in 1823. The full lyric reads:

"Mid pleasures and palaces, though we
     may roam,
Be it ever so humble, there's no place like
     home.'

My sentiments exactly.

'We have wonderful presents for each one of you!' I exclaimed, taking my servants' hands. 'And my husband has brought gifts for the sub-gardeners as well.'

I couldn't help but notice Mary Beth's intake of breath when I referred to Robin as my husband. It was something to which she would have to accustom herself. I supposed to many I appeared as some silly love-besotted older woman, but I didn't care. If they only knew what happiness Robin had brought me.

We swept into the house and it enveloped me in its familiar arms. 'My! How spotless everything looks!' I commented.

'Rosalie and I worked ever so hard for

your return, ma'am,' Bertie advised.

'And we gave the silver an extra turn,' Rosalie offered.

'I haven't planned the menu yet, ma'am,' Cook advised. 'I was thinking of something in the Frenchie style, but–'

'Certainly not!' I laughed, sharing my mirth with Robin. 'Something simple. We have been drowning in sauces.'

'And the pastries and the cakes and the eclairs,' Robin added, patting his stomach, which in my estimation, was still as firm as ever. I was the one who had put on weight. Happiness does that to you. 'I must work beaucoup hard in the garden,' he continued, 'to get back my old size.'

'And I will help,' I added, patting my own extra girth. 'October and November, the great planting months, will soon be upon us.'

Robin had set down our bags and was already starting outside. 'I must see our garden now.'

I was as eager as he was. 'If I can just change into something more comfortable, Robin, I shall join you.'

He considered this. 'Perhaps I should change first, too. My work clothes are in my cottage.'

'But, ma'am,' Bertie protested, 'we've brought all of Robin's...' she corrected herself, 'Mr Thibodeaux's things up to the house.'

Robin and I shared a conspiratorial smile. 'This is your house now too, darling.'

He lifted the suitcases once again as if they were no heavier than cotton candy. 'Then I shall carry our bags and change in our room.' He hurried off.

'I'm coming, too,' I said, starting out, but Mary Beth called me back.

'Miss Coombe ... I mean, Mrs Thibodeaux...' she appeared flustered. 'I don't know what to call you anymore.'

'As far as my work is concerned I will always be Miss Coombe.'

'Your solicitor just rang off before you arrived,' she advised. 'He must speak to you immediately. He says that there are some papers that if you don't sign and post this afternoon... If you come in the office, they're right on your desk.'

'Very well,' I replied, following her. 'Get Mr Chasebourne on the phone. I'll talk to him immediately.'

We stepped into my office and I realised that I had scarcely given a thought to my workplace the entire time I was gone. Lucretia, at the sight and sound of me, leaped from her basket and rubbed her furry body against my leg. I scooped her into my arms. 'She waited for you every day beside your desk,' Mary Beth informed. I stroked the pussy who purred contentedly. 'My darling puss. I even have something for you.'

I glanced over at Miss Hewitt's desk and noticed her own manuscript stacked neatly by her typewriter. 'And how has your writing been coming, Mary Beth?'

'I finished it.'

'Why, Mary Beth, that's wonderful!'

'And it's already been rejected by your publisher. I hope you don't mind my going to him first, but we have had such a nice phone relationship. I suppose that's why I got such an immediate response. "No"!'

'What did he say?'

'That it was too American and wouldn't go over here at all.'

'Have you tried an American publisher?'

'No, but I'm compiling a list.'

'It's not easy selling your first novel. Some of our most successful novelists...'

She would hear none of it. 'You only had to make one submission and you were published.'

'I never should have told you that. Perhaps if you let me read your book now...'

'You won't like it. The way it turned out, I'm afraid the mystery isn't the most important part.'

'I'm sure that makes it a much better book.'

She looked reluctantly at her own manuscript. I must say that it looked much too long for a first effort. 'Let me make some more changes and then I'll show it to you.'

'Very well.'

'Now let me get Mr Chasebourne on the phone. He sounded most anxious.'

'Yes, please do.' I sat down at my desk. Lucretia made herself comfortable on my desk and stretched out atop my papers. I dropped my handbag and pulled off my gloves. Strange now that nobody wears gloves anymore when there was a time when I would not have been caught dead without them. Is it because the coal dust is no longer a factor to blacken our British air? I suppose that has something to do with it, although the Queen and her mother still sport them.

Sitting back at my desk returned my mind to work. A new Inspector Hecate was waiting to be written. My mind had not been entirely idle in France. My inspector would holiday there as well, and join forces with a French inspector of my imagination. They would solve a series of murders that begin with jewel thievery on the French Riviera. If my French Inspector worked out, I would feature him in books of his own. If Agatha Christie could have her Belgian, I could have my Frenchman. He would be a connoisseur of fine French food and wine and art. Those of you who were introduced to my French Inspector Pierre Ronnard in *Murder on the Riviera* know that he appeared in several books of his own and rivalled that smug Hercule Poirot in popularity.

While Mary Beth fussed with the telephone, I glanced over the papers to be signed, pulling them from beneath Lucretia's warm body. One moment later and my solicitor was on the line. It was always good to hear his high-pitched voice because he always had my better interests at heart. On this occasion he was concerned with the overseas rights to my latest book. He had also heard from my British publisher, who feared that with my new status in life, I would not buckle down to work and complete my new Inspector Hecate in time for publication. They needed to have no fear in that matter. I would not neglect my work – even for my beloved husband.

I promised to sign and send the papers immediately, then found an excuse for Mary Beth to leave the room so that I could discuss something that was even more important to me. 'Mary Beth, would you be good enough to ask Cook to make some tea?'

She started for the door reluctantly, wishing to linger but departing after I stopped talking into the receiver until she closed the door behind her. 'Yes, David,' I said. 'I have glanced at the papers and I will sign them immediately, but I don't know why we bother with these Russians. They never seem to pay any royalties anyway.' He went on about the principle of the matter, but that was really not what I wanted to discuss. I quickly changed the subject. 'David, you haven't even asked about my honeymoon.'

It was obvious that he still didn't approve of my marriage and really wasn't interested in that side of my life, but he managed a question nevertheless. 'Did you have a nice time, Flora? They say that Paris is dead in August, but...'

'I was alive and that's all that matters, David. It's true what they say. Paris is for lovers, David. All of France for that matter.' I rattled on. I must have been as much in love with love as I was with Robin. When I finished and David waited patiently to hear more, I broached the subject that I knew he would find displeasing. 'David, I want to change my will.'

'What?!' He knew what was coming and he didn't like the sound of it.

'I want all rights and monies pertaining to the Inspector Hecate series to go to my husband on the event of my death.'

'But these royalties were to go to your niece and nephew!' he protested loudly. 'You can't just...'

I would hear none of his arguments. The bloom was not off this blushing bride. I would not wilt under his legal pressure. 'You heard me, David,' I persisted. 'I will make some other provisions for my niece and nephew, neither of whom, by the way, sent me a wedding gift.'

'And your charitable bequests?'

'They will stay the same.'

'I see no reason to hurry into this, Flora. If you'll just–'

'There is every reason to hurry, David. Next Sunday is Robin's birthday. He is my Virgo, which appears to be a very compatible sign for me. Robin's people are avid believers in astrology. I'm bringing him down to London to celebrate. I expect you to have the new will drawn up so that I can present it to him as a gift.'

'How old is he going to be?'

'It doesn't matter!' I shot back vehemently. 'Age does not enter into what we have found together.'

'But–'

I cut him off immediately. 'You will have the new will ready for me to sign on Friday?'

'Flora, I must–'

'Would you prefer I turn my affairs over to another solicitor?'

'No, Flora. I value you over all my other clients.'

'Good. You can expect me in your office some time on Friday afternoon.'

'As you say, Flora.'

I rang off as Bertie hurried in with my tea followed by my secretary. I took a quick sip and quickly signed the remaining papers. 'I think you had better post these immediately, Mary Beth.'

Bertie hovered over the tea service. 'Cook wondered if you would like cakes with your tea.'

'No,' I said, getting to my feet. 'I had my fill of cakes in France. I must change and hurry out to the garden.'

'Did ma'am say something about gifts?'

'Later, Bertie,' I advised. 'Right now Mary Beth has to run to the post and–' I was interrupted by the ringing of the doorbell. 'Would you get that please, Bertie?'

She hurried out. Mary Beth stood a moment in the doorway. 'Speaking of the mail, I took care of everything I could while you were away, but some of it needed your personal attention. It's all there in a basket by your desk.'

'Let's not think about that now. I'll face that tomorrow,'

She was scarcely out of the door when Lord Westmoreland burst into my study.

'Flora! Flora!' he boomed from the cellar of his throat. 'You are here. They informed me that you would be back today.'

'Bunny!' I exclaimed, surprised to see him. He was dressed for roaming the countryside or perhaps a shooting party. His baggy tweeds were gathered at the ankle over muddy boots that I hoped had not dragged dirt across my carpets. His equerry's cap was pulled low across his forehead, but he suddenly remembered his manners and pulled it

114

off to reveal grey hairs lying flat against his skull. 'Is something the matter?'

'Thank God you've come home. We've been waiting and waiting.'

'Waiting for what?'

'Your permission. They said I had to have your bloody permission.' He realised what he had said. 'Forgive my profanity, Flora, but it's bloody red tape nowadays no matter what you do.'

'What sort of permission?'

'To begin constructing my lake.'

'Your lake?'

'The nature preserve. I'm not ashamed to admit that it took a great deal of greasing of palms, but I secured all the permissions to begin except your permission.'

'Why do you need mine?'

'Because a small portion of the lake will dip into the edge of your property.'

'What edge?'

'You needn't worry about your precious garden,' he reassured. 'By the by, I must say it is looking capital. That boy of yours has done a magnificent job.'

'My husband,' I corrected. 'Not only with the garden,' I added boldly, but Lord Westmoreland was not unobservant. I knew for a fact that I looked better than I had in my awkward youth. Love can work marvels – even on me.

'Don't think I haven't noticed the remarkable change in you. Maybe my Agnes needs something like this Thibodeaux fellow to bring her back to life. By the by, the newspapers were full of your wedding. Biggest bit of news since the abdication. Rather skimpy on the photographs though.'

'I saw to that.'

'When Agnes meets her maker, I may go after a young one too.'

'I highly recommend it.' Not wishing to pursue the subject further, I brought him back to the matter at hand. 'Now, of what portion of my property are you speaking?'

'It's the edge of the woods separating your estate from Penmark. I have the paper for you to sign, but I think it's best if I show you where I mean.'

'Yes, it would be best.'

'I am most anxious to start construction before the autumn rains come. I hope to begin flooding by the end of the year.'

'My gracious, this does sound serious, Bunny. Let me just change into something more comfortable and we'll have a tramp around. I'm sure my husband will be most intrigued.'

'Capital!'

FIFTEEN

Robin, Lord Westmoreland and I walked swiftly beneath a blanket of fir trees and pines, the area which I referred to as the forest, far behind Dovecote Cottage and at the rim of my property.

'I hope you are not planning to tear down any of my trees,' I said. We had reached the clearing that became his property, an endless stretch of underbrush that finally reached another run of forest.

'Certainly not, Flora. Not one single pine. These trees of yours, this small forest, will serve as the east end of my lake. If you see the stake there, that indicates the end of your property line, so you see your property will only bear a very small portion of the lake.'

'What do you think, Robin?' I asked, taking my husband's hand so that Lord Westmoreland could observe how strongly we were joined to each other.

'Will I be able to fish in the lake?'

Bunny was anxious to win us over immediately. 'You may have all the privileges of the lake as if you were to my manor born. Certainly it shall be stocked with appropriate freshwater fish to attract our feathered friends.'

I looked up at my husband. 'Well, I see nothing wrong with having a lovely freshwater lake on the edge of our property, do you, Robin?'

'I grew up on the water. Perhaps the Lord will allow me to keep a pirogue on our part of the lake.'

'What is a pirogue?' Bunny demanded suspiciously.

'A fishing boat.'

'Most certainly.'

'Are you sure there is no possibility of flooding? I would hate to think that–'

'Absolutely none. We are arranging that any overflow will be channelled back into the Thames, from which much of the water will come in the first place.'

'But if there were...'

'There is absolutely no possibility of this, but if such a calamity ever befell us, it would be my responsibility to repair all damage.'

'I would like that in writing, wouldn't you, Robin?'

Robin nodded.

I squeezed my husband's hand tightly and smiled at my neighbour. 'You add that as an addendum to that paper you are holding and we shall sign.'

He was taken aback. 'Both of you?'

'Yes,' I stated firmly, 'both of us.' We

started back hand in hand through the woods, Lord Westmoreland following. The air freshened my lungs. It was a different air from what one breathes in France – somehow more bracing. 'My husband and I were about to inspect our garden, Bunny. Perhaps you would like to join us.'

'I glanced at it as I drove in. I especially want to see how your pond is progressing. I am planning on a flock of my own swans.'

'You must see that they are suitably mated,' I advised, 'as are our pair. As you know, a male and female swan are faithful for life.'

'I'm not crazy about that part.'

I had to laugh. When one was as deeply in love as I was, the thought of a lifetime commitment was very pleasurable. 'I'm sure Agnes expects nothing less.'

Lord Westmoreland wished to change the subject. 'You're the literary lady, Flora. You must come up with a suitable name for my preserve.'

'Surely Agnes could...'

He would hear none of it. 'She's deathly afraid of anything with feathers. She doesn't even like my goose-down pillow. That's why I started my small aviary. Now my lake will give me another place to get away from her perpetual whining.' He stopped to look at me.

'Flora, have you ever visited Lake Swansee

119

in Bavaria near where Mad King Ludwig built his fairy-tale castle?'

'Oh yes, I have!' I thrilled in memory of its pure magic. 'We shall go there one day, Robin.'

'Do you remember the swans swimming about the lake?' Bunny asked me.

'As I recall, the swan was the theme of his castle.'

'I should like my lake to resemble that.'

'Then why don't you call it "Swan's Way"?'

He thrilled at the idea. 'Capital! Delightful! How clever you are. How ever did you think of it?'

'I'm not the clever one, Bunny,' although I have to admit that I usually thought I was. 'We have Proust to thank for that.'

'Wasn't he that queer French bird?'

I allowed that to pass. Great writing transcended any sort of perversion as far as I was concerned.

'With a nickname like yours, Bunny, I would think that rather than swans, you would be creating a warren for rabbits.'

'Bah!' he bellowed his disapproval. 'They're only good for shooting and eating. You start with two and pretty soon they'd be overrunning the property. They breed faster than the wogs.'

I had had many pleasant encounters with 'wogs' as he referred to them, when my husband was stationed in New Delhi. I was about to protest but we had reached our own small body of water, Robin's Pond. Heathcliff and Cathy, expecting to be fed, swam to the edge of the water and fluttered their snowy wings. 'You see how they are, Bunny, faithful to the end.'

He emitted a resounding 'Bah' and shook his head so that his drooping moustache vibrated over his lips. I had locked my arm inside my husband's and was smiling up at him. He was my Heathcliff. I was his Cathy. I soon discovered that *Wuthering Heights* wasn't the only story with an unhappy ending.

SIXTEEN

I was determined to make Robin's birthday a memorable occasion. He had only passed through London on his way to seek me out. It was difficult for me to believe that only six months had transpired since the fateful April day when he appeared – as if from some other world – on my doorstep.

I had booked the bridal suite at the Savoy Hotel because I thought Robin would delight in the building's large opulence. Although such a hotel did not usually accept guests of colour, I insisted that they make an

121

exception in the case of Robin since he was my husband. While I busied myself at my solicitor's, Robin went on a walking tour of the city, following a map marked clearly by the helpful concierge. How Robin loved to walk. He had tired me out during our perambulations throughout France.

On Saturday evening, after a scrumptious meal in the River Restaurant of the hotel, I took Robin to the theatre. Apart from some school productions, he had never actually seen a play. Since he loved singing so, I thought a musical would be appropriate. I selected *Me and My Gal* at the Victoria Palace Theatre with the wonderful Lupino Lane as the Cockney from Lambeth who turns out to be the eighth Viscount of Hareford. What delightful music by Noel Gay, especially 'The Lambeth Walk', which we hummed as we left the theatre. Robin almost danced along the pavement as we moved away from the theatre in search of a taxi.

The only drawback to being in London was that people were staring at us. There had been much too much made of our marriage in all the newspapers; *Life* magazine had even run a follow-up. I hated them staring and whispering, but I suppose they would have anyway, even if they didn't know I was famous. I suppose they were intrigued by my husband's colour. He was that handsome, especially in the new blue linen suit I had purchased for him in France.

An almost imperceptible change had come over Robin since we had returned to England. He had seemed freer in French hotel rooms than he was in my master bedroom at Dovecote Cottage. I felt that he was somehow uncomfortable beneath the canopy of my four-poster bed. After theatre and drinks in the Grill Room of the hotel, when we took the lift up to the bridal suite, he once again became the Robin I remembered in France. I am tempted to describe that evening, but I shall leave it to my reader's imagination.

'Happy Birthday, darling!' These first words on the next morning were sealed with a kiss. We luxuriated in bed, munching a scrumptious breakfast and perusing the *Times*. There was a new exhibition of an American artist at the National Gallery. I thought that perhaps Robin would enjoy the work of a fellow countryman, so we walked hand in hand along the Strand to the Gallery. The day was as clear as a crystal amulet; the sun shone with late summery glee.

The artist in question was Winslow Homer. I had seen photographs of his work before, but in this exhibition I understood the genius of his simplicity. He seemed to me to exemplify rural America. I had been in the United States once before on a book tour but visited only the large impressive cities. It would take my new husband to show me the kind of world depicted in Winslow Homer's paintings.

Robin was particularly taken with a work titled 'Gulf Stream', in which a terrified coloured man in the Bahamas sits defenceless in his damaged skiff as sharks menace him during a storm.

How did we spend the remainder of the day? Sometimes my memory does fail me. It seems we walked about the city and had tea and sandwiches in some small tea room. Did I arrange for Robin to glimpse a changing of the guard at Buckingham Palace? It seems a dash of the bright red of the guards' uniforms are buried somewhere in the recesses of my mind.

Our brand new King George VI had scarcely been on the throne five minutes, but was going about his tasks in a most professional manner. With the sinister rise of the Hun from Germany he would soon be sorely tested. Our future Queen, Elizabeth, was only ten years old at the time. I wonder if she was in residence at Buckingham Palace that glorious Sunday afternoon in September. Did she spy my tall dark handsome husband from a window of the palace? Did she wonder about his relationship with the lady standing beside him, no doubt clutching his arm or holding his hand?

It was this beloved Elizabeth who would make me a Dame of the British Empire in 1960. Although the Empire perhaps isn't what it used to be, I am still delighted and proud of this singular honour and my few meetings with the Queen have been most pleasant. May she reign long after my death, longer even than her distinguished forebear, Queen Victoria.

I sometimes ate at The Mirrabel on Curzon Street when I came to London, especially when I kept a flat there before I moved permanently to Dovecote Cottage. That evening I took Robin there.

After the cake and ice cream I slipped Robin's present onto the table in front of him. 'But you have given me so much already,' he protested.

'As you have given me.' I suppose I was a little tipsy from the champagne.

'What is this?' he questioned, looking at the paper I had presented to him.

'Just turn to page nine and read aloud. Your birthday present is on page nine.'

He did as instructed. I can still hear his voice, so velvety deep and hypnotising. 'Upon the event of my death, I will all rights and royalties of my Inspector Hecate series of books, both past and present, to my beloved husband, Robin Thibodeaux.' He stopped reading and looked at me. I wasn't sure he realised what this meant.

'Do you have any idea of the revenue I derive from these books?'

'Beaucoup. Beaucoup,' he replied finally. 'And what of our garden? Of Robin's Pond?'

How I cringe now, in my older age, that I said it, but I was drunk and desperately in love. 'Read on, Robin,' I cooed. 'Everything I have is yours because you have made me so blissfully happy. Dovecote Cottage will be yours forever.'

He took my hand that had signed that document and kissed it hungrily. He read on slowly. He was not quick with the printed word.

'Happy Birthday, Robin!'

How old was he then? I know very well and it still shames me to publish it. He had just turned twenty-nine. I can't even remember when I was that age.

How old was I at the advent of someone else's very special birthday? Even now – so many years later – I cannot bring myself to tell you. If you are that interested you can look it up somewhere. 'Old enough to know better.' I know that is what you are thinking and you are right.

SEVENTEEN

The atmospheric novelist, Thomas Hardy, in his *The Mayor of Casterbridge,* writes that, 'Happiness was but the occasional episode in a general drama of pain.'

Why is it so much easier for a writer to describe the days of misery than those of happiness?

Happiness is like a field of golden daffodils. It is difficult to separate one bloom of golden sunlight from the other.

Such were the days of October. Winter had not quite descended. The garden still welcomed husband and wife. Spent flowers understood that they had already had their bloom and permitted us to cut their sturdy stems back to their roots so that they could be born once again in the spring, as I had been born again: but unlike the blossoms in my garden, I would never bloom again.

I suppose I should have suspected something that October when Robin no longer touched me in the way in which I had become accustomed. I was busy at my writing table all morning, then crawling about the garden all afternoon so that I scarcely noticed anything different when I fell exhaustedly into bed after a full meal and a bit of reading against my pillow. I knew that honeymoons end. I should have been more suspicious that mine was ceasing too soon. It was simply enough to have him beside me at night, breathing softly, as beautiful in sleep as he was in life.

Yes, October was a happy month.

It is the next chapter and the next month – cruel November – that moves my writing hand rapidly across the page; for I have much to tell you; and strangely enough, it is easier to describe than my bliss.

I had accepted too many book-signing engagements before I knew that Robin was to be my husband. I never enjoyed them. Now I found them to be an even greater intrusion because they took me away from the man who preferred to remain home and take care of our garden.

The Mysterious Disappearance, the Inspector Hecate mystery upon which I was labouring when I first learned the existence of Robin Thibodeaux, had just been published. My books usually came out in the autumn in hopes that in addition to my faithful reading public, others would purchase it as a convenient Christmas gift, especially if a copy happened to be signed by the author.

A week of appearances would terminate with the biggest book signing of all at Hatchard's in London. They expected a large turnout. I would be sitting at a table for hours until I could no longer write my name. Then I would have an early dinner with my publisher at the Connaught Hotel (where I usually stayed), and fall exhausted into bed.

Bertie was waiting with the others to have her book signed. She had taken the opportunity of my being away to come down to London to spend a week with her mother. 'Sign it over to my mum,' she requested. 'She's much better at reading these scary things than me.' I remembered her mother's name and inscribed it to her quickly.

'When are you going back home, ma'am?'

'Tomorrow, I think, Bertie. My publisher wants me to stay on but...'

'I'll be coming back on the Sunday train if that's all right with you, ma'am.'

'That will be fine, Bertie.' I had to hurry her along because the line behind her seemed to stretch for miles.

Somehow I worked quickly through the crowd. I missed my husband terribly. His voice over the telephone hadn't been enough. I longed for his presence. I wanted his arms around me. I never enjoyed being in a crowd. He was the only other person I needed. I decided to forsake dinner and my room at the Connaught and return home a day earlier than expected. My publisher accompanied me to Victoria Station. We had a quick bite to eat and then he saw me safely into my compartment.

It was night when the taxi deposited me at the doorstep of Dovecote Cottage. The house stood like a foreboding shadow with nary a light streaming from any of the front windows. It was not that late, but it appeared that everybody had gone to bed. I stole quietly inside and listened before I switched on a light, suddenly as suspicious as my Inspector that something wasn't quite right. I heard a thumping coming from upstairs. At first I wasn't sure what it was. I followed the sound and moved noiselessly upward. This thumping, this rhythmic banging of furniture against the wood floor was accompanied by the creaking of the springs in a bed. Now another sound was audible as well, not quite human. This was a sound my husband never made with me. This was a man moaning like an animal in a wild frenzy of passion. Soon a woman's voice matched his abandon. It was Mary Beth's. I could never imagine that she could sound like that. I was reminded of cats tearing, clawing at each other. I wanted to scream as they were doing, but suddenly I had no breath.

Finally the bed seemed to crash against the wall and the caterwauling ceased. I was transfixed outside the partially open door, unable to reveal my presence or retreat. 'So this was the sound of lovemaking,' I thought.

'Two ferocious creatures screeching in their own private jungle.' With me Robin had only hinted at his passion. I felt humiliated, frozen in my spot on the landing outside Mary Beth's room, my body burning with the stinging fever of betrayal.

Mary Beth was purring with contentment. 'I must have a cigarette,' she said finally. 'They always taste best after you've been in my mouth.' I heard the striking of a match. In the silence of my dark house each little noise became greater than it was.

'I don't like these cigarettes,' my husband complained to her.

'Miss Coombe doesn't like them either. That's why I only smoke in my room.'

'She is Mrs Thibodeaux now.'

'Yes, and you are the heir to her throne.' She smoked a moment in silence. I could imagine their naked bodies entwined together, the black narcissus wrapped around his white lily.

'All right, you can have your cigarette, and then Robin must have his southern flower once more.'

'But we haven't left this bed for hours. I have to get something to eat.'

'Madame returns tomorrow. There is plenty of time for you to eat then.'

I could hear that he was kissing her. Lips that felt so warm and loving against my own were now giving her the pleasure that I had so desperately desired that I had returned home early.

'Robin, please,' she giggled. 'Let me at least finish this cigarette. You're insatiable!'

I wish they had gone immediately back to making love rather than lying there together in each other's arms and talking. It was their conversation that hurt the most of all. Things were said about me that even now – decades later – I can only reveal through their lips.

'It is si bon to hold a beautiful young body in my arm once more. With Madame I close my eyes and pretend that she is you.'

'You pretend that she is me?'

'You and beautiful black-skinned women home in the bayou, women with their own...' But he stopped himself.

'With their own what?' Mary Beth was as curious as I was listening outside the door. I feared and dreaded what he was going to reveal.

'I must not speak disrespectful of the kind woman who saved my life.'

'Tell me, Robin. Women with their own what?

'Their own...' Again he did not complete the sentence. She must have started to tickle him because he laughed. 'Women with their own what?' she repeated.

'Women with their own teeth and hair.' How I detest to repeat what he said about me, but if I leave this portion out, you will never understand or forgive what transpired later.

Mary Beth laughed uproariously. 'I knew about the hair. I mean after a while I could tell that she wore wigs, as good as they are, but her teeth too?'

'The first time when we make love, when I tell her that I love her, she starts to pull my hand away when I begin to run my fingers through her hair, but it is too late, half of her hair has come down over her forehead.'

Mary Beth continued to laugh cruelly. 'How awful for you.'

'Robin learn his lesson. Never go near the hair. It is the forbidden place.' He was obviously running his fingers through her luxuriant mane. 'Such beautiful blonde tresses,' he chortled. 'With you it is a different story.'

'Have you ever actually seen her without any of her hair?'

'I have walked in on her, but I pretend that I have not noticed, that there is still a full head of curls beneath these colourful nightcaps she wears to bed to cover this bald head I have seen.'

'She doesn't have any hair at all?'

'There are some strands. Not enough to cover her scalp.'

'The poor thing.'

I did not want her pity. I have always had

thin hair. Even as a young girl I could never compete with the profusion of locks bequeathed to other young ladies of marriageable age. It was fashionable for young women of my era to wear the 'pastiche' attachment, an assortment of additional curls which added untold lustre and which enabled me to hold my own.

I do not know if it was the heat in India, or a fever contracted while my first husband was stationed there, but my hair fell out in great profusion and never grew back. I suppose that is something else that Dame Agatha Christie can hold over me besides her continuing success. Even in her older years she appears to have a lustrous head of grey hair. As far as her teeth ... well, we British are not known for taking very good care of our own. But I shall let my second husband and his paramour tell you more about that. They were not finished with me yet.

'What about her teeth?' Mary Beth questioned. 'I never suspected anything about her teeth.'

'Once while we are in France, I walk naked into the bathroom without knocking because I know Madame likes to see me without my clothes and she is holding her teeth in her hand and brushing them like they are naughty children.'

'How awful for you! How did she look

without her teeth?'

'Like an apple that is half eaten and left to rot in the sun.'

'The poor thing.'

'Madame always goes to bed with her teeth. Then when she thinks I am asleep she slips them into a glass she keeps in the drawer beside her bed and puts them back in before I wake up.'

'You poor thing. No wonder anybody else looked good to you.'

'You looked good to me the first day I come to this house, even though you were not nice to me and treat me like her manservant.'

'You still are and don't forget it.' They must have kissed or something even more intimate. I think if I had had a gun at that moment, I would have burst in on them then and there and shot them both. Would any jury of women blame me? 'Oh how I resisted you,' she moaned as he must have touched her where he never wished to touch me. 'I didn't want to desire you.'

'Desire? What about love?'

'I am afraid to love you. I can't let myself love you.'

'Because coloured blood runs in my veins?'

'Let's start with the fact that you are married to my employer.'

'Madame saved Robin's life. She has given me a good home. She took me to France

135

where everybody loves the way I parler Francais. I no longer have to worry about my mother and sisters at home. I send them good money. Only when I kiss Madame, I keep my tongue inside my mouth so that teeth not fall out of her mouth and embarrass her. In France Robin learns not to kiss like the French.'

'The French kiss like this, don't they?'

It seemed an eternity before they ceased devouring each other and spoke once again. 'When I kiss my southern flower, my tongue goes as deep as the throat.'

They were kissing again. I hated her for enjoying – for taking away – what was rightfully mine.

I visited the deathbed of a schoolgirl friend recently. 'At least I'm dying while I still have my teeth and hair,' she said, not realising that I had neither. Even so, I would still rather go on living without both as long as I can write. I still have my pad and pen. They are my most valuable assets.

'Oh, Robin,' Mary Beth sighed as she broke free of him to speak. 'It isn't England I will miss when I go home to America. It is you.'

'My Mademoiselle is planning to go home?'

'If I've learned one thing at the foot of the great mystery novelist, it is that I don't have what it takes to write a decent one myself.

There is a fiendish part to that brain of hers that I will never have. It's all in the plotting. I don't have the gift. The people who have read my book say that they like the romance stuff best, so that's what I'm going to try to write when I get home. I'm going to write historical romances. They're all going to take place down south. Damn Flora! It's so easy for her!'

There was movement on the bed. Were they beginning to make love? I could not listen again. I could not. Mary Beth began to whimper. 'Well, I can't have Flora Coombe's career, but I've had her husband.'

'Not often enough.'

'What are you going to do, Robin?' Mary Beth asked after gasping with pleasure. 'She has just about left you everything.'

'I will go on as I promised the preacher and pretend that I love her and one day she will die.'

'The English women may lose their teeth and their hair, but they live to a ripe old age. Just look at Queen Victoria.'

'Robin must be patient.'

'And how patient are you?'

'I am not patient at all.'

EIGHTEEN

When they made love again, even louder than before, I crept silently along the hallway and down the stairs. This time, after a decent interval, I came home all over again, slamming the door loudly to announce my presence and turning on many of the lights. Soon Robin appeared in a robe as if he was emerging from the area of our bedroom. I knew that he had slipped down the back stairway. 'I wasn't expecting you till tomorrow.'

'I missed you so ... I was so tired from signing all those books that I just wanted to come home and sleep in my own bed.' What an actress I am. No one would have suspected what I had just overhead.

He came across the living room to embrace me. Everything must appear as normal as possible. Some sort of revenge was fermenting like a plot in my head. I would act as if nothing was wrong until I put something into effect. 'Has Cook left anything in the oven?' I questioned after accepting the pressure of his lips against mine. I could smell Mary Beth on him.

'Cook was called home yesterday. Some

sort of problem with her family.'

'Not a death?' I was truly concerned.

'No, sickness. Her mother is very sick.'

'Dear me.'

'Not to worry. Robin will cook for his lovely lady.'

'Jambalaya every night?'

'Robin will fix many things. I will go to the fish market in the morning.'

'If you wouldn't mind starting with a cup of tea, I am going straight to bed. I am exhausted.'

'I will massage your tired shoulders and fingers from signing all those books.'

'That would be nice, darling.' He started for the kitchen. 'Has Mary Beth already gone to bed?' No doubt she was listening at the head of the stairs.

'Every night while you are gone, she goes straight to bed with a different book.'

What a cool liar he was. She was going to bed with something other than a book. I wonder if she snuck into my room when Cook and Bertie were there as well. Those nights their lovemaking must have been of the silent variety. It must have been very difficult for them to curb their frenetic passion. The Americans are a loud lot – in everything they do.

'If you wouldn't mind fetching my suitcase, Robin. It's outside the door.'

'Why didn't you call for me to come to the

station and pick you up in your beautiful car?'

'It is our car, Robin.' Was I being too coy? 'Besides, I wanted to surprise you and it was easier to hail a taxi.'

Surprise him I did! He would never know how much.

Robin fetched my suitcase. I followed him into our bedroom which would never be the same again to me as long as he was there. He had violated it! Only after I had dispatched him would it once again become my private sanctuary. 'If you would just fetch the tea, darling.'

When he returned I was already in bed. He knelt beside me and skilfully massaged my neck, shoulders, back and arms, softly kneading his long fingers into my flesh. I attempted to resist but I was still susceptible to his touch. Finally I fell asleep. He must have extinguished the light and crept beneath the blankets to his side of the bed, no doubt exhausted himself from a day of marathon lovemaking.

When I awakened in the middle of the night and watched him sleeping so peacefully and innocently – no longer mine – the hatred boiled up in me like in a witch's cauldron. To know that my husband literally cringed at my very touch was more than I could bear. I would either die from humiliation or have my revenge. I chose the latter.

140

As my traitorous husband breathed deeply beside me, the plan already began to form in my mind – a new mystery plot that would assuage the pain and humiliation I was feeling; a scheme that even my reliable Inspector Hecate would appreciate.

Besides, hadn't my husband confessed to a lack of patience? Didn't he wish my death? Anything I did was justified.

Somehow I got through the following few weeks without Robin or Mary Beth suspecting that I was on to them. I carried on as if nothing was the matter, as if nothing had changed. I suppose it was the laying of my plan that kept this mystery writer sane in the glare of such terrible rejection, my 'mousetrap', if I must borrow the word from Dame Christie's obvious play that should have closed the night of its opening.

I made no more physical demands on my husband, which, I am ashamed to say, I knew was a great relief to him. My excuse was that when I was in the midst of writing a new mystery, I was too distracted and could think of nothing else. How happily he accepted my explanation.

Even with a living breathing husband lying beside me night after night, I was once again embracing celibacy, the return of my trusted friend who could never hurt or humiliate you. This friend has stood me in faithful stead these many decades hence.

Christmas was approaching, the holiday that I treasure above all others because in the first years of my long life it was a Victorian one. My first Queen's consort, Prince Albert, had introduced the Christmas tree to our country. How ours flickered with blazing candles. My brother's and my red stockings were 'hung on the chimney with care', and the logs in the fireplace crackled like the popcorn we had strung about the tree.

I couldn't bear the thought of sharing this holiday with the two traitors who I knew were somehow still managing to couple out of my presence. I put off shopping because I couldn't fathom buying them gifts. The celebration of the birth of the Saviour in their presence would be a desecration. It was a time to put my plan into effect.

To simply inform my reader of my 'plot', for want of a better word, goes against the grain of a good novelist. Better to show how it transpired – to dramatise, so to speak – how things appeared that bitterly cold night in December when everything changed.

The heart of an actress lurked within me. The stage had been set. The groundwork had been laid. To all appearances I was out of sorts. I had not been eating or sleeping well and I had even heard Bertie whisper that 'Ma'am has not been herself lately.'

On this particular evening I was feigning

illness. As darkness descended like a sinister coal dust upon the countryside, I was already in bed and on the telephone to David Chasebourne, my solicitor. Lucretia was nestled beside me and snoring softly in her most ladylike manner. If I sounded agitated, that was my intent. My conversation: 'David, I know that I am not giving you much notice, but I insist that you take the first train in the morning and be here as soon as possible. Do you understand me, David? I'll expect you sometime after breakfast, not that I will have eaten any. I'm afraid to eat!'

'What is it, Flora? You sound so ... so...'

I cut him off. 'I'd come to London myself, but I'm afraid that ... Robin would insist on driving me, at least to the station, and...'

'What is it, Flora? Are you afraid that he will harm you?'

I lowered my voice as much as humanly possible. 'I can't discuss it over the telephone, David. There's no telling who will be listening. Simply draw up the papers and have them ready for me to sign in the morning.'

'I warned you not to change your will so quickly, Flora. It seemed foolhardy to me, and–'

'I know, David,' I broke in. Even though I was simply acting, I still couldn't bear to hear anyone say 'I told you so'.

'Let me make doubly sure, Flora, that this is what you want.' He was always so precise, even in the midst of my feigned hysteria. 'I've kept Miss Bambrick late so she can record the changes. You want your will to be written exactly as it was before?'

'That is correct, David.'

'And you wish to leave nothing to your husband?'

'Nothing at all. Not one farthing.'

'But he might wish to...'

'You heard me, David. Not one farthing.' I drove my acting into high gear. 'Did you hear that, David?'

'What?'

'A click! There was a click on the line.'

'I didn't hear it.'

'Somebody's listening. Is it your Miss Bambrick?'

'She's sitting right here opposite waiting for dictation.'

'It's here at this end! Somebody's listening in. I must ring off immediately. Please be here first thing in the morning!' I dropped the receiver. I actually did hear somebody outside my bedroom door. I supposed it was Bertie. I shouted loud enough for David to hear through the receiver. 'I know you're there. I know you're listening!'

Soon there was a knocking. 'Who is it?' I wailed.

'It's me, ma'am, with your dinner tray. Cook has prepared her special chicken broth.'

'Come in, Bertie.'

She pushed into my bedroom carrying a tray with steaming soup and bread. The soup smelled delicious. I was dying to devour it. This last bit of acting had whetted my appetite.

'If you'd like, ma'am, Cook is preparing veal and lyonnaise potatoes as well.'

Bertie watched as I glanced at the soup suspiciously. 'Were my husband or Mary Beth in the kitchen while Cook was preparing this?'

'Mr Thibodeaux was, ma'am, fixing them that fancy southern drink she likes so much.'

'Was he left alone in the kitchen at any time after Cook poured this into the bowl?'

'I'm not sure, ma'am. He did send me outside to the herb garden for a sprig of mint for that drink of theirs.'

'He knows all about growing things, doesn't he?'

'Yes, he does, ma'am.'

'I wouldn't be surprised if he doesn't have belladonna growing out there somewhere hidden where I can't find it.'

'I don't know what that is, ma'am. Is that the one with the pretty red flowers?'

'Where was Cook when you were in the garden?'

'I don't know, ma'am. Cooking.' I was dying for the soup, but I pushed the tray aside. 'Take this away, Bertie! Do you hear me? Take it away!'

'But, ma'am, you have to eat something.'

'Not until tomorrow. Not until Mr Chasebourne comes here and I have signed all the papers!'

'Is he coming here, ma'am? Should I prepare a room for tomorrow?'

'He's just coming for the day. I ... you mustn't tell anybody that he's coming. I'm only telling you because I want you to know I am changing my will and as before you will be well taken care of.'

'Oh, ma'am, I don't know what to say.'

'Not a word, Bertie. Not a single word.' I doubted that she would say anything to Robin, but certainly Cook would be told as soon as she returned to the kitchen and they would be overheard. 'Where are they now, the two of them?'

'They're in the parlour, ma'am, playing that funny game she likes so much – backgaming.'

'Backgammon,' I corrected, adding, 'just as I thought. Right by the telephone so that they could listen in. Both of them. I know that he was listening when I was talking to Mr Chasebourne. I could hear Robin breathing.'

'If you say so, ma'am.' She stood there looking at me fearfully, not quite knowing what to make of this new frightened exterior that I was presenting. 'If you're not feeling

146

well enough to eat, ma'am, perhaps I should call for the doctor.'

'What good would a doctor do, except give me some sedative. I mustn't sleep tonight, Bertie. I mustn't sleep a moment. If I do, I am doomed! I will never awaken!'

'But, ma'am...'

'Tomorrow everything will be all right. After Mr Chasebourne arrives. Then my husband can grow all the belladonna he wants and it won't do him any good!'

'Ma'am...'

'You must be alert tonight, Bertie, do you understand? If you hear anything amiss you must come to my aid, do you understand?'

'Yes, ma'am.'

'You must sleep with your door open, Bertie. Tell Cook as well, and you must listen for anything out of the ordinary.'

'Such as, ma'am?'

'Just listen, Bertie. Listen.' I pushed the tray further across the bed. My mouth was about to water from the aroma of the soup. 'Take this away.'

'Perhaps ma'am would just like the tea.'

'Nothing, Bertie, nothing that he could have...'

Probably more histrionics than necessary. 'Just take it all away!'

'Yes, ma'am.'

She scooped up the tray. As she started out, I alerted her one more time. 'If you or

Cook hear anything amiss, you come running to my aid, do you understand?'

She gave me one last curious look. 'Yes, ma'am.'

'And take Lucretia. She needs to go out.'

After she departed, I hopped out of bed and locked my bedroom door. Soon someone was turning the knob, attempting to open it.

'Who is it?'

'It's Robin. Why is the door locked?'

'Go away!'

'You must let me in.'

'Go away!'

'Are you not bien? Bertie says that you eat nothing.'

'I'm sick, Robin. I don't feel well.'

He knocked again. 'Then you must let me in so that I can take care of you. There is good medicine, herbs that...'

'I don't want any medicine! I don't want anything!'

'You have never locked Robin out before.'

'I've quarantined myself. If I've caught something I don't want you to catch it as well. Especially with Christmas coming.'

'I never get sick. I will bring you good warm milk. Milk with honey and melted butter. I will feed it to you from the spoon.'

'No. No! Nothing will set right on my stomach tonight. I have water here. That's enough.'

I could sense that he was hesitating at the door, not wanting (out of guilt probably) to forsake his duty as a husband. Soon there was the sound of whispering, or did I imagine it? Nevertheless. There was a more gentle tapping against the door. 'Miss Coombe, it's Mary Beth. Wouldn't you like me to bring you some nice hot tea? Tea is the best remedy for an unsettled stomach.'

'No! Nothing!'

There was a moment of silence when they must have been talking between themselves. Soon Mary Beth was knocking again. 'Miss Coombe, is it all right if I take the car this evening? I'm thinking of going to the movies. I was hoping that you would want to come too. It's the one we read about – that new thriller, *The Lady Vanishes*. It's playing in Oxford. It's with Margaret Lockwood.'

'I couldn't possibly. But you mustn't go alone. Take Robin with you.' I called out even louder, 'Are you still there, Robin?'

'Oui, Madame!'

'You mustn't let Mary Beth drive alone on an evening such as this. It's dark and cold and misty.'

'Oui, Madame!'

'I'll tell you all about the movie in the morning, Miss Coombe. Maybe you can see it later in the week.'

'You'd better hurry,' I advised, 'if you're going to make the first show.'

'Good night, Miss Coombe.'

'Good night, cherie!' my husband called out. Then he knocked once again. 'Where is Robin going to sleep tonight if his wife is mal sick?'

'Get Bertie to make up the guest room. Just for this evening. Just to be safe.'

There was no response. So far everything was working perfectly. Indeed Mary Beth had spoken of going to the cinema earlier in the day. I wanted them out of the house together, and later if he slipped into her bed, so much the better. Now they were going. My plan had to take place that night or never, for the reason that I shall soon reveal.

The reader will see how appropriate is the title of the film they were driving off to see, that perfect Alfred Hitchcock thriller. In the film it is the superlative actress Dame May Witty who disappears, but in real life, it was I who would portray the lady who 'vanishes'.

NINETEEN

It was well past the time for the cinema to let out. Robin and Mary Beth had not yet returned. No doubt they were parked on some lonely country road making their disgusting animal noises. While they were having it away with each other, with no one but themselves for an alibi, I proceeded with my 'plot'.

I was fully dressed and ready to depart, wearing a warm outfit I had recently purchased in London and then hidden away in my fur wardrobe so that no one had observed it. Even my new walking shoes had been hidden away. I wanted no one to be able to say that one of my usual outfits was missing after my disappearance. My torch was also a recent hidden purchase; as were the dark gloves into which I slipped my fingers.

Bertie had left the front hall light ignited. I crept silently through the house and into the kitchen pantry where I knew the wire cutters were stored. I moved quietly outside to the wires conducting electricity into the house and severed them and the telephone wire as well. I knew that both Bertie and Cook had already gone to sleep, so the only light immediately extinguished was the bulb in the front hall. I put the wire cutter back in the wrong place, knowing this would be noticed.

Soon I was back in my downstairs bedroom, the items I needed to leave behind as evidence of my 'disappearance' stuffed into the pockets of my newly purchased simple dark cloth coat, and into a small satchel that

I had also hidden in the back of my volum-
inous wardrobe.

I screamed and screamed until finally
Bertie was pounding at my door. I didn't
know I was capable of such a volume.
'Ma'am! What is it? The lights! There are no
lights. Cook and I are here in the dark with
just a candle!'

'Help me! Someone help me!' I shrieked
like a banshee. 'Someone's trying to get into
my room! Call the police. Why isn't the
telephone working?' I wailed.

Then with a hammer that I had removed
from the kitchen pantry as well, I broke a
pane of glass by the lock in my French
windows so that it shattered loudly, and
opened the door as if from outside and
tossed the hammer into the hedges where I
knew it would be discovered. 'Who is it?' I
screamed. 'Who are you?'

'Ma'am! Ma'am!' Bertie shrieked even
louder than I. 'Open the door!'

'We have to get help!' Cook shouted as
well.

'Don't hurt me!' I continued. 'I'll give you
anything! Anything!' Then a desperate,
'Where are you taking me?' and one last ear-
splitting scream.

I vanished quickly outside the broken
French windows into the night.

I had already torn my nightgown. I left a
few scraps of the gown as if it had been

152

caught by a twig or scraped against the trunk of a tree. I wish I didn't have to reveal what else I left behind – hidden – closer to the edge of what was about to be the new lake: but I suppose I must, because it was the most damaging evidence of all against my husband. Supposedly lost somewhere in the brush then stuffed out of sight – as if they had fallen off as I was dragged to my death – were my red wig and false teeth.

Needless to say, under an assumed name while on business in London, I had purchased a new wig – a grey one more suitable to my age. I had also gone to one of those cheaper dentists for a new set of teeth. I attest once more to my powers as an actress, for I appeared to these people no more like Dame Flora Coombe than some ageing soubrette. My make-up was atrocious and overdone. I was the most blatant of common cockney tarts. How I enjoyed this performance. I wish more people could have seen it. I don't think our Dame Sybil Thorndike could have done better.

In the early hours of the morning, while darkness still camouflaged, all that was left for me to do – my torch in hand – was to continue stealthily through the woods to Oxford. I had mapped the route before and knew that I could make the morning train to London. I walked quickly, filled with the energy of my deceit, a character in one of my own books determined to realise her vengeance.

Who could recognise the esteemed Flora Coombe – not yet a Dame – who, once so meticulous about her far from beautiful appearance, had abandoned her red locks, her bright lipstick, her rouge and powder, her mascara and green eye shadow? And would the celebrated novelist have travelled second class as I was doing now?

I had tied a drab scarf around my grey head and donned thick glasses that I had also purchased in London, which only served to distort my brown eyes. I had never seen myself look so dreadfully plain. I was startled as I gazed into the mirror in the Ladies' W.C. Now I truly was homely. My only regret was that with these thick glasses, I could not read on the train. I detest to be caught anywhere without something to read, but this time it was a necessity. Sensible glasses were tucked away for later use.

Dawn had broken. The day had begun.

As the train left the station, I knew that cement was already being poured into a great portion of the southern end of Lord Westmoreland's property that bordered onto mine. He had decided to make this a separate pond connected to the lake because it was the area most sheltered by the woods. At my urging, it would be off limits from hunting.

As it turned out, I must have hidden my wig and teeth more skilfully than I believed. They were not discovered until the acres of cement had been poured and dried. The Thames River was diverted to flood the area. Then the rain fell. December weather helped to flood the entire area.

TWENTY

I have always loved living by the sea since my childhood in Brighton. If I hadn't fallen in love with Dovecote Cottage near Aston Turrold, no doubt I would have settled somewhere along the coast, for in truth, England is a large island and there is much land to choose along the Atlantic Ocean or the Irish and North Seas or the English Channel.

I chose Bournemouth, a winter spot on the English Channel far enough away from Oxford so that no one could associate me with the missing novelist. Days earlier I had booked lodging at a seaside residence hotel, The Manor House, under my assumed name of Miss Kathleen Couglin, a retired schoolteacher spinster from County Wicklow, Ireland.

The Manor House was comfortable, but far from luxurious, although the meals served in the small dining room were better than I had anticipated. This was the loneliest Christmas I ever spent. With my grey hair and bland exterior, I fitted in perfectly with the regulars, an elderly lot, mostly women, who had nothing better to do than sit in the comfortable parlour listening to the wireless and working on a jigsaw puzzle or playing bridge in the glare of a rather pathetic Christmas tree. Naturally they were curious about the new boarder. I told them as little as possible about myself except to say – in a perfect Irish accent I might add – that 'I was that weary of County Wicklow, and since I had retired from teaching school, I needed a change of scenery.'

Fortunately I knew something of the area which I described as my Irish home. I had utilised it as the setting for *The Shamrock Murders*, and stayed there while I wrote a portion of that book. I don't wish to brag again about my accent, but it was near perfect. I have always had a good ear for such things. I may not have gone on the stage, but I was giving a superb performance nevertheless – in real life – where it matters.

In the afternoon, as I sat with the ladies working over the large puzzle which depicted a famous John Constable country scene, the news of my disappearance came over the wireless. It was described as a possible abduction with implied foul play. The pesky

156

local inspector was interviewed briefly, but he refused to make any decisive comment 'this early in the case'. He would only admit that members of the household were being questioned and that all would be revealed at the inquest.

The women looked at each other and shook their heads. 'I bet it's that light chocolate husband of hers,' Mrs Portman, a rotund widow said, shaking her full grey head of upswept hair that enlarged her head to gigantic proportions.

'And, sure, why do you say that?' I enquired.

'Well, he didn't marry her for her beauty or her youth, did he?'

I could not but agree. I knew it was what everybody had thought. It pained me nevertheless.

'Have you ever seen Flora Coombe?' As I stated previously, I have never included a photograph in any of my books. This was not so much to preserve anonymity, but because there had never been a photograph taken of me of which I approved. Somehow we fool ourselves with a look in the mirror whereas a photograph cruelly reveals the truth of plainness. Let Miss Christie plaster her photograph on the back of every little book. I would have none of it; however, a bad snapshot of Robin and me together, taken in Oxford, had found its way into the newspapers.

Mrs Portman continued. 'Him with the big white teeth and the flashing eyes and his chocolate skin that I saw in *Life* magazine. I wouldn't half mind one like that myself.'

I hoped that the ladies didn't notice that my cheeks were suddenly stinging as if penetrated by the venom of a bee.

'And that Flora Coombe,' Mrs Portman continued, 'always wearing those big hats so we can't get a good look at her, and I know why – because she can't compete with that beauty of a husband. She looked to me like one of those game hunters who got herself an African tiger – at gun-point.'

The ladies tittered: all except one. I was not amused.

'Have you ever read Flora Coombe?' I ventured to question.

'Every single book,' Miss Hildebrand, an energetic spinster who stood as straight and thin as a hat stand, announced. She was an avid reader of mysteries and took them out of the Bournemouth Library by the half dozen. 'I don't think she's quite as good as Agatha Christie, but almost.'

I couldn't hold my tongue. 'I must disagree. Agatha Christie is certainly skilful with her plots but I think Flora Coombe is much stronger with character.'

'Well, I won't disagree,' she admitted, 'but I find Inspector Poirot cleverer than Inspector Hecate. And of course I love Jane Marple.'

She won points with Jane Marple. I had not yet created another sleuth as perspicacious as the snoop of St Mary Mead. However, as my readers know, that would soon change. My new sleuth would emerge from the experience of my 'disappearance', but I mustn't get ahead of my story.

Indeed most of the ladies had read some of my books. They were full of speculation concerning Flora Coombe's possible demise, as the story filled the newspapers in the following weeks. We must have completed a dozen puzzles while arguing the guilt or innocence of my husband.

What I remember most about these myriad ladies was the stench of cheap perfumes and lilac talcum that permeated the parlour. I didn't dare douse myself with my expensive L'Heure Bleue for fear that would give me away as a woman with too many means. I simply had to try not to breathe too deeply for fear of fainting from the stench.

This was the first period of my life since I had created Inspector Hecate in India that I was neither writing nor planning a new story; other than the one that I was living. Like Miss Harriet Hildebrand, I borrowed dozens of books from the local library. It was such a luxury to while the afternoons away with a good book. Many of the books I read were mysteries, but nothing held my attention more than my own case. I had written the scenario. The police were following my plot as if I were on the premises and directing them myself. I shall lay out the information for you as if I were preparing one of my mysteries.

1. Robin's footprints were found in the dirt outside my window. (I had asked him earlier in the day to step through my French window and fetch a flower which I destroyed later.)
2. Robin's fingerprints were discovered on the hammer found in a hedge. (Robin had utilised the hammer on several occasions during his time with me.)
3. Robin's fingerprints were discovered on the wire cutters that had not been returned to their usual drawer. (Robin had used these on more than one occasion as well.)
4. My solicitor, David Chasebourne, revealed that I was about to eliminate Robin from my will the morning after my disappearance and that on the telephone I appeared to be in fear for my life.
5. Bertie stated that I was most agitated the night of my disappearance and appeared afraid that someone – my husband – was going to poison my food.
6. Bertie, through a locked door, heard someone break the glass leading into my bedroom and heard me scream that I was

being abducted.

7. Scraps of my nightgown were found above my home in the woods leading to the new lake.

8. My red wig and dentures were discovered as well. To quote Bertie: 'Ma'am wouldn't even go to the privy without either of those.'

9. Robin could not account for his whereabouts when I was being abducted. He confessed his liaison with my secretary and that they – as I suspected they would – had parked my car, hidden down some country lane so they could commit adultery. Unfortunately Mary Beth Hewitt was not a reliable witness to this because of her involvement with my husband and the fact that as his mistress she would stand to benefit from my death.

10. My body had obviously been buried beneath the earth somewhere in the midst of this great lake that was covered with a thick layer of cement only hours after my disappearance and was now overflowing with water.

11. Lord Westmoreland refused even to consider draining the entire lake – now a formidable task – beside the fact it would be almost impossible to break apart such a vast area of thick cement. To quote Lord Westmoreland: 'Our feathered friends have flocked to Swan's Way, my glorious lake and especially to the nature preserve where the

belief is that Flora Coombe is buried and which I am now calling "Flora's Mill Pond"; and to think what a desecration destroying it would be to the little fishies that are spawning in great profusion. The late Flora Coombe loved nature and its creatures even more than I do. To disturb them would be against her every wish. Let her sleep beneath the lake in peace.'

Everything fell into place at the inquest. To misquote Robert Burns, 'My best laid schemes did not "gang aft agley".'

Although Robin protested his innocence to the coroner and claimed that he wanted no part of my generous will, the inquest jury did not believe him. My second husband was charged with my murder. He was placed in a London prison. Soon a trial at the Old Bailey would ensue.

I hadn't realised the great extent or the intense fidelity of my reading public. They bemoaned the fact that there would be no more Flora Coombe novels and clamoured for Robin Thibodeaux's head. He had destroyed their greatest reading pleasure. Now they wanted his blood. Even the ladies at The Manor House were demanding cruel justice and a speedy trial. 'He done her in as sure as my name is Norma Portman!'

'I hope they string him up!' Harriet Hildebrand concurred. She believed that she had been robbed of her second favourite mystery writer.

'Until there is not a breath left!' I found myself adding. How desperately I wanted revenge. Betrayal is the unforgivable offence. Hadn't I heard my husband say that he was impatient for my own death? Was that not a threat? I had become even more impatient for his.

TWENTY-ONE

For the first time in my already long life, I was going to have to seek employment. In my desire for revenge, I had not fully contemplated the length of time it would take to bring someone to justice. Before my disappearance, I had only secreted away enough money not to arouse suspicion. I realised too late, while idling away my hours at The Manor House, that I should have set up some secret account under the name of Kathleen Couglin upon which I could draw, although I fear that might have been discovered.

I longed to return to my writing desk, to my own canopied Chippendale bed with Lucretia purring softly beside me – and to my garden, even in the dead of winter when all the flowers were sleeping.

Christmas had been a rather dreary affair at The Manor House. Neither a goose dinner nor a dramatisation of *A Christmas Carol* over the wireless had served to elevate my spirits. Next year I would be home and I would make up for it with an elaborate tree surrounded by a colourful collection of gifts and Cook would prepare a feast fit for the Ghost of Christmas Present, and I would invite my niece and nephew and their children.

I read in the newspapers that Inspector Hanlon, still not satisfied with the circumstances of my 'disappearance', had deemed, in collaboration with my solicitor, to keep Bertie on staff to maintain my residence until my case was solved once and for all. I can't imagine that Bertie enjoyed sleeping alone in my large house. I was to find out later – much to my chagrin – that she wasn't alone.

I supposed that Cook had found another employment where her delectable efforts would be appreciated. I hoped that I could hire her back when the time was appropriate. I was sure that Lucretia was being well taken care of, but she must have missed me terribly, as I did her, especially at night when I wanted my Persian princess beside me. To be honest, I wanted Robin beside me as well. I had got used to his warm presence.

As for Mary Beth Hewitt, she was being detained in England as a witness or accomplice to my murder. She had been asked to vacate my estate and was living in London. Photographers followed her wherever she went. Still attempting to disguise her beauty, she nevertheless was the photogenic creature I could never be.

I supposed she wanted to go home to America until she was denounced from the floor of the Louisiana Senate for bringing worldwide disgrace upon her native state – not so much for her involvement in my 'murder' – but because her 'flagrant adultery' had been with a man of the coloured race. Her parents declared that she would no longer be welcome in their home.

With Robin in prison, to whom could she turn? She was a pariah in two countries; under suspicion throughout the world. She took the way out that I had not anticipated and for which I still feel great remorse.

Her London landlady found her cold corpse in a bathtub of blood. She had not only slashed her wrists but an ankle as well. I had not anticipated this when I sought my revenge. I assumed that she would go back to America and disappear forever from my life. Robin was the true betrayer, but I caught more than one in my carefully laid net.

The ladies of The Manor House thought

she got what she deserved. 'We don't need her kind in England – or that Simpson woman either.' I knew I had done her a great injustice. I have often wanted to turn back the clock. Now it was too late. 'No clock can strike for me the hours that have passed.' Wasn't it John Keats who wrote that?

I had wound the clock too tightly. I couldn't stop it now until every hand had struck its hour. As do my literary personages, characters had taken on a life of their own. There was no turning back.

I began to search the newspapers for a suitable offer of employment somewhere in the area of Bournemouth. I was both excited and fearful at the thought of taking on some legitimate type of work. Who would hire a woman of my age, which I must admit was somewhere past forty. What was I fit for other than dreaming up plots and writing them down in the privacy of my study? Women didn't hire themselves out as gardeners. I had no experience as a beautician, to which my plain state would attest. I supposed I could make a stab at being a waitress or a parlourmaid although I dreaded the thought of being on my feet so many hours of the day. Perhaps they would take me on in a small tearoom. I could manage that. I began to make the rounds of these establishments when I chanced to glance through a Cornwall newspaper. The advertisement called out to me.

GOVERNESS REQUIRED.
EXPERIENCE EXPECTED.
PLEASE SEND REFERENCES
TO THE FOLLOWING:

The address listed was a post office box in London. What was required of a governess but a way with children (I had been most successful with my niece and nephew) and a decent education, which I had as well? Wasn't I raised by a governess myself by the name of Nanny Irene Prescott? When I was a young girl, we were not packed off to school. A proper young lady was educated at home. My nanny swore by *Dr Brewer's Child Guide to Knowledge*. It was her education Bible. It was a variation of the quiz book in which all pertinent questions were asked and answered, e.g. 'What was the date of the Battle of Culloden which was the last encounter to be fought by the Jacobites in Scotland?' 16 April 1746 – for your information. We also dabbled in music and dancing and arithmetic and lastly French. A young lady wasn't expected to learn Greek or Latin.

'Oh, what a tangled web we weave,
When first we practise to deceive!'

No, I am not quoting Shakespeare again, even though many attribute this quote to the Bard. It is Sir Walter Scott who coined the above in his 'The Lady of the Lake', a title that one newspaper utilised to refer to me, since it was believed that I was buried at the bottom of one.

I had deceived the world into believing in my disappearance and murder: now I would deceive a potential employer in believing that I was an experienced governess.

I decided not only to emulate the late Nanny Irene Prescott, but to become her. Nanny Prescott and I had always kept in touch. After I grew up and she moved on to future employments, she wrote to me faithfully at least once a month, her letters filled with details of her new employers and her experiences with her new charges. I saved every letter. Unfortunately they were out of reach at Dovecote Cottage. Nevertheless, I remembered the names of the employers who had succeeded my beloved mother and father. It was easy enough to secure their addresses and to write letters of recommendation in their supposed hands. It took some practising, but I became rather skilled in changing my handwriting for the three different letters of recommendation that I wrote. Naturally it would have been better if I could have written on their own personal stationery as well. I hoped it sufficed that I had purchased three different colours of stationery and wore them down with several creasings and leaving them in my windowsill so that the weather would age them as well. If my potential employer chose to pursue these recommendations further and discovered that Irene Prescott was no longer among the living ... well, I would cross that bridge when I came to it.

I was summoned post-haste to London for an interview. I hesitated to return to the city where people knew me, but who would recognise the plain elderly frump that I had become under a wig of grey curls, old wire glasses (through which I could see) and a grey lamb's-wool coat that scarcely kept away the cold? How I could have used one of my furs hanging warmly in my cedar wardrobe. My complexion, without the benefit of rouge or powder was almost as grey as my coat. I hated to be seen this way, but I had the look of a nanny.

The city was drenched in winter rain. I held my black umbrella low over my head in case I should chance by someone I knew.

The office where I was to report was on Bond Street, a solicitor's enclave, including the offices of David Chasebourne, who chanced out of his office building just as I was passing by! I lowered my umbrella as quickly as possible and stepped into a doorway until he passed. I wonder if he would have recognised me.

The office of a Mr George Maxwell was on the third floor. I soon learned that he was the executor of a celebrated estate. He read my references in studied silence. 'Are you familiar with the late Lord Peter Pemberton?'

I nodded. The story had fascinated me and flashed with newspaper print before my eyes. The handsome polo player had, after the tragic motor-car death of his first wife, the beautiful Mayfair debutante, Vanessa Kenniston, married a lovely American widow, Martha Winston, who had, upon the death of her older millionaire American husband, inherited a sizeable fortune. Speculation had it that Peter Pemberton had mortgaged his family's ancestral home in Cornwall to the hilt, and could no longer afford the upkeep; hence his convenient marriage to the American heiress had bailed him out, so to speak.

Peter Pemberton saved his estate and Martha Winston gained a title. Their marriage, however idyllic, was to be short-lived. Not only an expert polo player, Peter Pemberton was a skilled sailor as well. The Cornwall coast, however, can be treacherous, especially when a summer storm appears from nowhere and smashes an expensive sailing craft against the rocks. Only remnants of the craft were discovered. The bodies were never found. The Cornwall coast is famous for holding onto its dead.

'Such a sad story,' I commiserated after George Maxwell ran over the salient facts.

'Even sadder when there are children involved.' He lowered his head and shook it so that his thin wire glasses fell to the end of his nose. He was a small elderly man with very little hair and a head as shiny as a new shoe. I could see the genuine concern in his eyes. I liked and trusted him immediately. 'I have handled the family's affairs since the days of the present heir's grandfather.'

I wondered if he was going to check the references that he once again studied. He appeared to be studying me as well; weighing a decision in his mind.

'We are in a desperate situation at Tower House,' he said finally. 'For the time being, you will be performing the services as both a governess and nanny. Our previous governess, a woman much younger than yourself, has simply gone off – disappeared.'

'How odd,' I remarked.

'Yes, isn't it? She seemed to get along quite well, especially with young Miss Angela. The little girl has been most upset at her nanny's sudden departure. First she loses her mother, then...'

'I can well imagine.'

'I've sent the boy off to school. He is at

that troublesome age that can best be managed by a stern school-master. For the moment, you will only be concerned with the girl. I am most anxious to continue Miss Angela's education. If she were at home in America she would already be attending some one-room schoolhouse, I suppose.'

'Am I to assume that I have been hired?'

'I think I have come to that decision – at least on a trial basis.' He glanced over my references again. 'These indeed are most impressive. Before you leave I shall get my secretary to copy down these addresses so that we can investigate them more fully.'

'Certainly.' I hoped he wouldn't.

'Ordinarily I wouldn't be in such a hurry, but Miss Angela is a young American girl in a foreign country in desperate need of companionship after the dreadful loss of her mother.'

'Is there no family for her in America?'

'There is nobody immediate. We are investigating that.'

'I see.'

'Now in the matter of your salary...'

I demanded more than I thought I should receive, which was still a pittance in comparison to my previous income. To my surprise, George Maxwell agreed immediately. Room and board, naturally, were included. At least I would be supporting myself in relative style.

TWENTY-TWO

The train to Cornwall transported me to a different part of the English world: the south-west coast where Romans once ruled and pirates roamed. England is so many worlds. Occasionally I glimpsed the sea from my second-class window en route from Bournemouth. It appeared cold and uninviting and in places downright treacherous.

Upon my lap was a book that I was fortunate to locate in a small London bookshop. *The Victorian Nanny's Handbook* was by the late Elinor Leyton, who had cared for more than one of Queen Victoria's daughters. It had been my Nanny Prescott's guide during the years of my infancy. Now it would serve me as well. Everything I needed to know about rearing and instructing a child was within its covers.

When I got off the train in Fowey, where the river of that same name meets the Atlantic Ocean, I felt that I was a character of my own creation off on some mysterious adventure. What was shortly to transpire, however, was more than I could have imagined, even for one of my books.

A mystery writer must dig deeply and look

for the evil in men's hearts. My new occupation would force me to do so. Perhaps Robin's behaviour should have prepared me for the kind of people who are not what they seem. While my husband was at Wormwood Scrubs Prison in London awaiting trial, I was about to enter into a world in which it would take all my skill and ingenuity to survive.

Fowey is a charming and active seaport. Rolling hills dotted with stone cottages slope down to the bustling harbour. I would often spend my free day there away from Tower House, feeling almost as if I had stepped into a seafarer's past.

Little did I know that, at the very time of my arrival, the novelist Daphne Du Maurier was writing her classic *Rebecca* very close by, somewhere along the Cornwall coast. I could never want to take credit for an Agatha Christie, but I would have been proud to call *Rebecca* my own. It deserves to be called a classic.

I hired a taxi to St. Claire, somewhat farther south-west of Fowey, where Tower House was located. There appeared to be few secrets among the local Cornwall inhabitants: my driver was full of tales of the celebrated estate.

'Used to be what you'd call a happy home,' the weatherbeaten man informed me on our way along the jagged coast. 'The old

Lord and his father afore him were popular with the Cornwall folk. This new one that was drowned had little use for people hereabouts. There used to be what you call a May Day Fair on the grounds every year. Never missed it. Ale never stopped flowing. His father wasn't cold in the ground 'fore he announced he wouldn't be holding one anymore. It was for a good cause too – the Fisherman's Fund. The only charity that bloke was interested in was himself.'

'A tragic death nevertheless.'

'That's the sea's way of getting even with you. It's a shame his moneybags wife had to go down with him. The sea plays no favourites.'

'Are you by chance a sailor?' It seemed obvious. He still wore the seaman's cap, faded blue with a brim that cast shadows over his wrinkled eyes.

'Gave the sea up before she took me for good,' he admitted. 'She broke my fishing boat apart, sucked me down so deep I thought I'd never come up for air. When she finally cast me out, I took it as a warning and quit for good. It's that Fisherman's Fund that helped me get this taxi you're sitting in. Just about paid them back.' He studied me curiously through his rearview mirror. 'And what might you be doing at the big manor house?'

If I was still Flora Coombe and had

175

dressed and made myself up accordingly, he never would have ventured to ask such an impertinent question. 'I am to be governess to the young lady of the house.'

'So you're the new one for the little heiress.'

It was more of a statement than a question, to which I chose not to reply. Indeed I had a question of my own. 'Were you acquainted with the previous governess?'

His blue hat nodded. 'Took my taxi all the time. She called for me to come that night she went off and disappeared. I had me a flat on the way. By the time I got there she was gone.'

We had reached St. Claire. I had studied it on the map. It was a long stretch of land that jutted like a disobedient protuberance into the sea with Falmouth Bay on one side and the English Channel on the other. It seemed that there was no escape route but the sea. Was I caught like Ulysses between Scylla and Charybdis?

The Atlantic Ocean beat ferociously against the rocks. As we wove towards the end of St. Claire's Point, the public road ceased. The rest of the land was now the Pemberton Estate. There was a gate and an elderly keeper, Davis, who lived alone in the small cottage at the entrance. He was expecting me. We drove along a long drive bordered with tall cypress trees so that I was reminded of the Appian Way in Rome. I glimpsed a stable, a garage and greenhouses. The road seemed to go along forever, until suddenly we reached a green clearing and an extraordinary house burst forth so dramatically it was almost as if it wished to entrap you. The day was overcast so the backdrop for the imposing house was a panoply of foreboding clouds and the restless Atlantic Ocean beyond.

Tower House was aptly named, for indeed there was a tall stone tower at the very centre of its structure, the last vestige of a medieval fortification against the marauding French. One entered the house by this tower through massive carved wooden doors at its base, with the Pemberton coat of arms – a sword, a red rose and a black cross displayed impressively above. You could weave around the circular stairway to the very top turret which provided a view of all of St. Claire and a world of ocean beyond, or fan out into the commodious rooms of the three-storey house, into the east wing or the west wing or the underground floor where prisoners were once held but where there was now an imposing game room.

Although the fortification had been con-structed sometime at the beginning of the 100 Years War, the castle, added much later, still appeared Tudor in design. The bricks of the structure were still the colour of Tudor rust and the tall narrow windows bore the several panes of Tudor glass. A black and white sheep-dog stood sentinel in the door-way.

As I descended the taxi and paid the driver, I was greeted almost instantly by the kindly housekeeper, who introduced herself as Polly Mears. 'I've been waiting for you, Miss Prescott,' she advised.

The driver removed my bag and deposited it inside the house. He exchanged greetings with the housekeeper and handed me his card. 'You'll be wanting to take trips into town. You call this number. I'll come and fetch you.'

He leaped back into his taxi and disap-peared quickly down the long drive. Mrs Mears helped me inside the house. I assumed that she was prematurely grey, for her round shiny face was as unlined as a baby's bottom. There were no angles to her. Everything about her was round and soft, from her pug nose and liquid blue eyes to her thick ankles and chubby feet. She wore the same lavender water that Bertie wore and the familiar scent made me long for home, and a less foreboding house.

'Miss Angela is waiting for you in the nursery. She's that anxious to see you. She has been most perturbed by her previous nanny going off like that.'

'I can well imagine.'

Mrs Mears sized me up favourably. 'Perhaps the woman was too young for the post.' Should I have been pleased that I looked old enough for the position?

'If you could perhaps show me where I'll be sleeping.'

'You'll be residing on the third floor in the west wing near the nursery.' I reached to pick up my bag but she shook her head. 'You'll not be carrying that yourself.' She called out loudly. 'Deidre!'

Soon a black-haired maiden in a starched white and black maid's uniform came racing down the tower steps. She was young and wide-eyed and almost pretty. 'This is Nanny Prescott who will be taking care of Miss Angela.'

The young maid curtsied. 'Pleased to meet you, I'm sure.' The entire map of Ireland was in her speech and manner.

'Deidre is the third floor maid. She will be watching over you. Her younger sister, Bridget, is second floor and their cousin, Mona, is our parlour maid.'

'We're a regular trio,' Deidre smiled.

'And what county are you from, Deidre?'

She was taken aback. 'Can you tell that quickly that I'm Irish?'

'One glance would suffice.'

She laughed out loud. 'Tipperary. And sure I already know I'm a long way from there!'

It was a good thing that I had dropped my

Irish subterfuge, that my alter ego, Kathleen Couglin, had been called home suddenly to County Wicklow on a family emergency, never to be seen by the ladies of the Manor House again. This Irish trio would probably have found me out almost immediately.

Mrs Mears was growing impatient. 'Would you take up this bag and show Nanny Prescott her room? I will wait for her in the nursery.'

'Yes, ma'am.'

We wound round and round the tall tower until finally we were deposited in the spacious third floor, where a long corridor stretched to the far reaches of the house.

'I suppose there is no lift.'

'I haven't seen one,' Deidre smiled. 'Before I was here, when the previous Lord was too ill to go up and down these stairs, they put him downstairs in the east wing in one of the fancy guest rooms. All the rooms down there are Mona's responsibility, but after the death of the young master, we've had very few guests. Just Mr Maxwell who did the hiring of you.'

My room was spacious and looked off to the English Channel. It was certainly too grand to have been constructed for a servant. My bathroom was filled with mosaic tiles depicting creatures of the sea. Glancing out of the window, I saw that between the rear of Tower House and the sea were acres of gardens, a world of dormant flowers with carefully laid paths carved throughout the bed until just mossy grass descended to the beach and boathouse below. I wondered if there was a boat inside, or was the sailing craft that was dashed against the rocks the only one? I soon discovered it was. The boathouse now remained empty, a sad reminder of the unremitting sea.

I was Nanny Prescott now. I unpacked my copy of *The Victorian Nanny* and turned to the chapter titled 'Your First Encounter.'

1. The first task of the new governess is to meet and assess her pupils.
2. Although you must immediately win the child's confidence, you must let them know, even at this first encounter, who will be in charge.
3. Immediately establish a system and a routine.
4. Instruction must take precedence over every other endeavour. You are an instructor, not a nursemaid. Make sure that the mistress of the house understands this.

What if there was no mistress of the house? There was nothing written about that. At least there was a footnote that suggested that 'a woman's always dependable instinct should serve as her guide'. Mine had served me fairly well throughout my already long life, even if I had misread Robin Thibodeaux. 'Love is blind,' Chaucer said in *The Squire's Tale*. In my case it had rendered me deaf and dumb as well. Now I was seeing clearly again.

TWENTY-THREE

Angela Winston was an incredibly beautiful young girl of seven years of age. Although there was an air of sadness about her little face, she still was a fresh breath of American air upon the remote Cornwall countryside. Her long hair was the colour of the sun and her eyes were as blue as the sky. I had seen photographs of her lovely mother in the newspapers, but this girl would grow to be even more dazzling. Her cheeks were red with youth, as were the delicate lips that framed snow-white teeth. I suppose that it is true that Americans have the most beautiful teeth in the world. Even at such a young age my smile was never as radiant.

Angela was sitting at the piano when Mrs Mears led me into the nursery. The child was playing a simple melody, one of the Mother Goose tunes.

'Miss Angela, I would like you to meet your new governess. This is Nanny Prescott.'

'Just plain Nanny to you, Miss Angela,' I advised, hoping to break any formal ice, although this wasn't specified in *The Victorian Nanny*.

The exquisite girl closed the piano cover over the keys, swung her legs around the bench, moved eagerly in my direction, and executed a curtsy. 'Are you going to leave me, too?' she questioned in a small voice that immediately touched my heart.

'Nannies always have to leave sometime, Miss Angela, when little girls such as yourself grow up, or our employment is required somewhere else, but I would never leave without telling you first, so that you would know well in advance.'

'My last nanny tucked me in and read me a story. In the morning when I woke up she was gone without even saying good-bye.'

'I should never do that.'

'My mommy and stepdaddy went away too. They went sailing and they never came back. My American daddy, too, but I don't remember him all that well.'

'Now, Miss Angela,' Mrs Mears interjected. 'It wasn't your mother's fault that a terrible storm came up when they were out sailing.'

'God took my mommy away,' Angela informed me sorrowfully, a little tear appearing quickly in the corner of her eye and spilling like liquid sugar down her cheek.

'Sometimes God wants us so badly that he takes us away before anyone is ready to let us go. God must have loved your mother very much to take her away so soon.'

'I wish he had waited until I was grown up.' She brushed the tear away from her eye. 'Now my brother has gone away as well.'

'But only to school,' I protested.

'He isn't really my brother,' Angela added. 'He's my stepbrother. But I miss him all the same.'

'Well,' Mrs Mears said, moving to the door, 'I shall leave you two alone to get acquainted. Miss Angela was so lonely after the departure of Nanny Silverton, she has been dining with the staff in the kitchen. Now that you are here, Nanny Prescott, we shall resume serving her meals in the nursery. You must let Cook know if you have any preferences.'

'In due time,' I responded. 'But first Miss Angela must show me around the nursery.'

Mrs Mears nodded her head and departed. For an instant I felt as alone as the young lady in my charge. I was miles away from home. As far as the world was concerned, I no longer existed. I realised, for the first time, how difficult it must have been for my own Nanny Prescott to embark on a new situation; however, as did my own nanny, I had to take matters into hand.

'What would you like to see?' the young

girl asked curiously.

'There is so much,' I responded, glancing about. 'When I was a little girl of your age, my own nursery wasn't half so grand.'

'Mommy called it my pink paradise. After my mommy married my second daddy and we came here to live, mommy had this all fixed up for me. We brought my things from America.' She moved to a weathered teddy bear that sat prominently in a small painted rocking chair. 'This is Mr Bear Bottom, but I call him Teddy. Teddy doesn't go away like the others. He's my best friend of all, because he never goes anywhere.'

'Do you have any imaginary friends, Miss Angela?'

She looked at me very strangely, as if I had discovered a great secret. 'I ... Mommy said I shouldn't... Even Nanny Silverton said ... I shouldn't.'

'When I was your age, I had many imaginary friends because I really didn't have any friends of my own age to play with or to talk to.'

Her blue eyes lit up like Delft saucers. 'You did?'

'Oh, yes, I very much needed my imaginary friends. I had an older brother like you, but he never had any time for me. You know the story of the old woman in the shoe who had too many children?'

'Yes.'

'Well, I made all her children my brothers and sisters. I've always had a good imagination and I had such fun bossing them around and telling them what to do.'

'You did?'

She was warming to me immediately. Her features softened. She no longer looked as troubled. 'May I meet your imaginary friends?' I inquired.

'I suppose I don't have as many as you,' she admitted. 'My favourite is Mitzi Poor House.'

'Is she so poor?'

'Mitzi lives in the bad section of New York and doesn't have any of the things I have, so I have to share with her.'

'She must like that very much.'

'Yes. When something gets broken, it's always her fault.'

'Then we must be careful and not let her play with your good toys.'

'She won't listen. She always does what she wants.'

'And your other friends?'

'There's Maisie Martin.'

'And who is Maisie?'

'She's the pretend daughter of the door-man we had in New York. Maisie is very bad. Her father doesn't have time to spank her. I used to take Maisie to Central Park with me. She would do very bad things. She even wanted me to steal a boy's bicycle.'

'Well, we'll have to keep an eye on her. Is there anybody else?'

'Buckley. He's my boyfriend and always says he wants to marry me, but I just want for Buckley and me to be friends.'

'And so you shall.'

Angela suddenly took my hand without any prompting and began to lead me about the spacious room. 'I'll show you my toys, especially the special dolls. They have names too, but I don't really play with them anymore. They just like to sit on their shelf and watch me. Except Raggedy Ann and Andy. They're my friends, too, only they don't like each other so I have to keep them apart.'

Had I won over the child already? Was it that easy or was she just so desperate for companionship? Certainly there was nothing in *The Victorian Nanny* about imaginary friends or how to deal with them. I would approach the situation delicately.

The nursery was indeed a symphony in pink with snatches of blue, yellow and other pastel colours to complete the bouquet. The walls were filled with pale murals from Mother Goose. There was Little Miss Muffet who sat on her tuffet, Jack Horner who sat in a corner, Humpty Dumpy who sat on his wall and other such characters. These paintings were copied from the illustrations of the storybook I had treasured as a child. Suddenly my own childhood flooded back to me – when I had thought that I would grow up to be like my mother with a loving husband and children of my own. Perhaps if I hadn't married Reggie ... or if I had not helped save the life of Robin Thibodeaux... I never dreamed when I was a little girl that I would grow up to become a writer.

There was an enormous doll's house, a large chest to store her toys, an upright piano, and a round table and chairs in front of the fireplace where we would dine. All the furniture had been painted a gentle shade of green with small clusters of pink roses daubed here and there to add colour.

Angela's large bedroom was joined to the nursery. Here there was flowered wallpaper, a bright depiction of spring flowers that made me long for Dovecote Cottage. The bedroom furniture was also painted green with small flowers and the canopy over the four poster bed was pink.

This nursery in the east wing was a world unto itself – a refuge from the remainder of the house – a retreat from the sea that beat with such intensity against the far cliffs beyond the window.

The last room that Angela led me to, somewhat reluctantly, was the schoolroom, although I think she liked to study and learn – at least with me. It boasted shelves of school books and children's stories and a round table with chairs in the centre of the room where we would work. Instead of murals from nursery rhymes there were famous N.C. Wyeth paintings on the walls, illustrations that the celebrated American artist had made for the childrens' classics, *The Boy's King Arthur*, *Rip Van Winkle* and *Robin Hood*.

Angela's mother must have loved her daughter very much to create such a special retreat for her when she uprooted the child from America. The precious girl kept her mother's photograph beside her bed in a silver frame. It was a wedding photo from her mother's second marriage to Lord Pemberton. What a handsome couple they made. I remember a similar photograph in the newspapers. One would never think to look at them smiling radiantly in their silver frame that the sea had already devoured them.

'Now, Miss Angela,' I spoke, looking out the window to the gardens beneath and the churning English Channel beyond. 'Because this is our first day together, we will not have lessons. Since the sun has broken through the clouds, perhaps we can take a walk and you can show me about the grounds.'

Her face brightened. 'Can Sandy come?'

'Another imaginary friend?'

'My dog. He just came to us one day and now he's my special pet. He's my guard dog.

I'd like him to sleep up here with me, but Roman won't allow him into the house.'

'Roman?'

'My stepdaddy's butler.'

TWENTY-FOUR

We bundled up against the winter wind. Angela, who had an extensive wardrobe for a young lady, looked quite fetching in a thick blue overcoat with gold buttons while I made do with my lamb's-wool coat that befitted my new lower station in life.

Sandy the sheepdog, a melding of black and white fur, was indeed waiting for us outside the house as he had been upon my arrival. He was friendly enough to me, but guarded Angela with an alert ferocity. I took her hand in mine and we walked first around the massive building to where the garden lay, Sandy keeping stride alongside as if we had become a triumvirate.

Angela was not as interested in the garden as I was, but nevertheless she appeared impressed with my knowledge of the beds of flowers and my description of blooms that would return in the spring. Although the boxed hedges remained green all year round, the straight line of white wisteria and the dormant beds of the delicious geranium, 'Johnson's Blue', were not yet in evidence.

Beyond the garden, stone steps descended to the beach at the tip of St. Claire and to the empty boathouse where waves still ran beneath a boat's mooring. The boathouse itself was a stone retreat, a comfortable place to escape from the wind and warm yourself in front of a fire.

The beach was long and narrow. At either end of it jagged rocks burst from the sand and jutted out to the ocean so this tip of St. Claire was a protected harbour, a safe place unless one ventured beyond these rocks and confronted the English Channel.

Angela confided that during the summer she often sat on the beach with her mother, who would read to her daughter from one of her Raggedy Ann books.

'My second daddy took me sailing once, but Momma said it was too dangerous until I learned to swim better, even if I did wear a life vest.' She removed a small stick of driftwood from the beach and threw it for Sandy to fetch. The sheepdog bounded through the water to retrieve it, shaking water over us upon his return.

We left the sea and the garden and the great manor house and walked along the road which had led me to the estate. Tall cypress trees sheltered us from the breeze. Sandy trotted slightly ahead of us as if protecting us from approaching danger.

He appeared suddenly from the trees. There was no avenue of escape. Sandy barked vociferously and stood his ground protectively before us. It seemed that the rider was not prepared to stop. He was dressed as black as the stallion he was riding. Only at the very last minute did he pull at the reins so that the huge horse reared up and whinnied and did not trample us. I was reminded of the Headless Horsemen in the Washington Irving story: however this man had the most handsome head I had ever observed. He swung gracefully off his dark leather English saddle. Angela ran to him and he scooped her up and swung her about in his arms until she screamed delightedly.

'Roman, you scared us!'

'As if I couldn't stop my horse when I wanted to!' There was a foreign tinge to his dark voice, something almost undetectable, for in actuality he spoke perfect English, but it was almost too precise and studied, as if he had a need to impress. He set Angela down and approached me. Sandy moved quickly to the girl's side suspicious that this man would do the girl harm. He took my hand. Even though I was wearing mittens he kissed it.

'Is this the new nanny who will see that Miss Angela learns to be a proper young lady?'

'We will do our best,' I replied, lost in the green of his penetrating eyes. They were the colour of my emerald bracelet locked away safely in a bank vault. The chiselled hollows in his cheeks and the fullness of his lips gave dramatic symmetry to his handsome face. He wore no riding hat. His midnight hair was a tangle of curls that fell like Renaissance brush strokes over his forehead. I envied the length of his eyelashes and the dramatic arch of his brooding brows. He cut a dashing figure in his tight riding togs, from the shine on his tall black leather boots to the stylish cut of his coat. He was over six feet and a perfect physical specimen. Dare I admit that I was attracted immediately to him as I had been to Robin? However, the May-December days of my life were over. I was a middle-aged nanny now. Especially in this disguise, I could never consider such nonsense.

'I am Roman.' He smiled to reveal ivory teeth. There was something seductive about his speech, a smile in his voice. 'I was Mr Pemberton's valet. Now I am in command of Tower House. I am the new master, so to speak.'

'But not of the nursery,' I found myself replying, my dander up already.

His green eyes narrowed, but the dazzling smile returned. 'No, that is your domain.' I could have melted beneath the spell of such a smile, but I resisted. 'I am happy to see that you are walking with Miss Angela. A pretty young lady such as this needs her exercise. Our previous nanny was not so fond of walking. I often had to take Miss Angela and Master Scott out myself.'

'Sometimes they walked so fast I couldn't catch up,' Angela complained, 'and they would go riding without me.'

'Your mother did not allow you to ride?'

'She was going to buy me a pony, but then she...' She trailed off.

'Lady Pemberton had a fear of horses.' He moved beside me and whispered. I could feel the warmth of his hot breath in my ear. 'Miss Angela's American father was killed in a riding accident. He fancied himself a jumper. This is a family of many tragedies,' he continued. His breath excited me. I wanted to pull away.

'What is he whispering?' Angela questioned. 'Is it about my daddy dying on a horse? I don't like it when people whisper. Raggedy Andy has a fit when Raggedy Ann whispers to me.'

'Sometimes adults have to keep things from nosy little children.' He turned quickly and mounted his horse. 'I must bring Caliph back to the stable before he cools down.'

'Surely I cannot address you simply as Roman,' I ventured before he rode away.

'But you have no other choice,' he advised

from his horse. 'It is the only name I have. I could call myself Roman Pemberton, but I fear that would not sit well with the Mr George Maxwell who employed you.'

'No, I don't think it would.'

He studied me, considering something, before finally speaking. 'Has Mrs Mears not told you how I came to be part of Tower House?'

'I'm afraid she hasn't.'

'It is usually the first thing out of her mouth. I will save her the trouble and tell you myself. I am from Romania. Gypsy born and raised. We travelled in a caravan. I was a young boy when we came to England to fleece the British. The senior Lord Pemberton thought he was a bit of a daredevil behind the wheel of his Lamborghini Espada. He ran into my parents' wagon, injuring them both. I have little memory of the event, but somehow I was thrown free. Out of guilt, Lord Pemberton decided that he would bring me here and raise me with his son. We were almost the same age. My parents made him pay heavily for me, but he could afford it. I became the stable boy. I loved those horses. I have a way with horses. I attended classes here with Master Pemberton, although he was simply Peter to me, for we grew up as brothers. When he went off to Harrow, he would bring his books home so that I could study as well. When the old

Lord died, I was brought into the big house to attend to the new Lord's personal needs. I believe you know the unhappy remainder of the story.'

'Perhaps I should call you Heathcliff and not Roman.'

'Yes,' he replied with the trace of a grim smile. 'I know of this gypsy boy Heathcliff from *Wuthering Heights*.'

'Heathcliff became master of the estate as well.'

'But I did not go off like this character to make my fortune. I could never leave Tower House. It is the only home I know.' He started off, but then turned his horse around for an afterthought: 'And at present there is no Cathy in my life to torment me.'

He departed in a canter, suddenly veering through the cypress trees, and was gone. Angela bent low to pet Sandy, who relaxed when horse and rider had disappeared. 'My stepdaddy took me riding with him once. I sat on his saddle and Mommy was furious. When do you think I can get a pony and start riding like Scott?'

'That is something we shall have to ask Mr Maxwell.'

'I don't think Mr Maxwell likes me.'

'Oh yes he does, and he has your best interests at heart.' I took her hand. 'Now I think it's time for some nice hot cocoa.'

TWENTY-FIVE

It was almost twilight when we returned to the nursery. Soon St. Claire would be shrouded in darkness. While Angela practised a piece on the piano, I perused the texts in the schoolroom. Fortunately there was much from which to choose. Although many of the texts were from America, I was pleased to discover a smattering of books listed in *The Victorian Nanny*, such as *Elements of English Education* by Brown, *Mrs Chapone's Letters on the Improvement of the Mind*, and *Tomkin's Select Poems*. Also, for young men, there were such books as *Blair's Grammar of Chemistry* and *A Young Man's Arithmetic*. I was certainly glad that Lady Pemberton's stepson was away at Harrow. It was daunting enough to school a young lady without educating a young member of the opposite sex as well! I was also relieved to see that there was a copy of *Dr Brewer's Child Guide to Knowledge*, which had been my own nanny's favourite.

I was assisting Miss Angela with a piano piece when there was a knocking on the nursery door. I was expecting Deidre with our supper, but was surprised to discover Roman, in proper butler attire, carrying a large silver tray. He looked immaculate and impeccable, to the manner of the man's servant born.

'Since Miss Angela will no longer be eating her meals downstairs with the staff, it shall be my special honour to bring her her tray every evening. It will be one of my few opportunities to see my pretty young lady throughout the day, now that she is once again to be occupied in the nursery.'

'I'm sure that is very kind of you, Roman.'

He made a show of setting the nursery table and removing silver dish covers to reveal a hot meal of roast lamb, potatoes and vegetables.

'Since Miss Angela has the appetite of one of our little Cornwall sparrows, you see that her portions are much smaller than yours.'

Even though I was exceedingly hungry, my plate was heaped too full. 'I certainly do not eat like a Cornwall sparrow, but this is more than I can devour.'

'You must eat what you can, Nanny, to sustain yourself for these long walks.' He moved to the doorway and bowed. 'If you desire anything else, you must ring for Deidre.'

He turned and was gone, his brazen smile lingering in the air like the Cheshire Cat's.

'Why doesn't Roman allow the dog in the house?' I questioned curiously as we began to sample our delicious repast.

'I don't know,' she replied absently, her

mind on her lamb, which she cut slowly. 'I think it's because Sandy doesn't really like Roman.' She held up a morsel of her meat. 'Is this a little lamb like Mary had in the Mother Goose rhyme?'

'Certainly not,' I corrected. 'I'm sure this is full-grown sheep. Some are happy to give us their wool, while others are glad to give us our dinner. We mustn't look a gift sheep in the mouth. We must enjoy it.'

According to *The Victorian Nanny*, it should not be the duty of a governess to pick up after her charges, nor be concerned with a young lady's cleanliness or that of the nursery. That was the duty of the young lady's maid. Blessedly such was the case at Tower House. I watched as Deidre dutifully cleared away our dishes and prepared Angela for bed. A bath was drawn; teeth were brushed; hair dried. It was only left for me to read a bedside story and supervise Angela's prayers before she drifted off to sleep. I chose Langhorne's *Fables of Flora* – my own namesake – which I had enjoyed as a little girl and was also recommended in *The Victorian Nanny*. Just before she drifted off to sleep, Angela opened her eyes slightly and whispered softly: 'You promise to be here tomorrow when I wake up?'

'I promise.'

She must have believed me. She almost

smiled before closing her eyes and falling asleep immediately.

How happy I was to retreat to my own room, decidedly more commodious than my quarters at the Bournemouth Manor House. I relished soaking in the great bathtub, running the water as I unpacked my few pitiful belongings. No one who knew me would ever have believed that I could travel so lightly. When I placed a few trifles on the writing desk, I noticed the corner of a piece of paper protruding from beneath the blotter. I thought that I would throw it away, but when I pulled it free, the single word leapt out at me and startled my eye with its boldness. The word was printed in black ink. DEPRAVED. What did the writer mean? Was it printed by my predecessor, Nanny Silverton? It was something at which I could only wonder.

I never realised how full a day is in the life of a governess! A child believes the world revolves around herself. Growing up, I never once considered that my own nanny had almost no time to herself. From morning to night my world became Miss Angela's world. I had little time to think of myself or of Robin and the trial for murder that was descending upon him.

I awoke at six and entered the nursery at seven after Angela had been dressed and prepared for the day. After we breakfasted in the nursery, I began her lessons.

Although I was raised by a governess and never attended school outside the home, I do not subscribe to the notion that a young woman should concern herself only with needlepoint, dancing and music lessons, and perhaps a light skimming over geography and history and maybe a smattering of the classics. Fortunately my own father assisted in my home education. I learned much of what the young men of my day were learning. Arithmetic was Father's speciality. He led me through fractions and decimals and percentages. Angela knew little of arithmetic, so I started her with simple addition and subtraction. She was a bright young girl. She learned quickly everything I had to teach her.

Our mornings were filled with what I called our 'academics': arithmetic, geography, history, English grammar and composition and French. I was not overly proficient in the latter subject, but I had had enough lessons myself to teach the rudiments of the language. I don't recall who said a teacher learns from his pupil, but it certainly was true in my case. I had forgotten much, or perhaps had not learned so much as I believed.

After lunch in the nursery, we took a long walk throughout the extensive property. This was not only our favourite part of the day but Sandy's as well. He awaited us eagerly outside the front door, his tail a black and white flag waving in the wind. He would trot faithfully alongside Angela, never leaving her side as we roamed the property, often tramping along the cliffs above the English Channel, watching the sea twist and turn beneath us.

After our walk it was time for the more frivolous activities in the young lady's education: music (piano), dancing and needlepoint. I am not bragging when I say that I was somewhat expert in all three, although dancing had changed drastically since the days of my youth. I was not confident of the new steps that had emerged from the recent swing era.

Finally, before dinner, we had our 'reading hour'. I chose the books that had thrilled me when I was Angela's age, such as *The Prisoner of Zenda* by Anthony Hope and the thrilling stories of Jules Verne, such as *Around the World in Eighty Days*. Even though she was too young to read them herself, Miss Angela was advanced enough to delight in hearing these stories.

After supper, when Angela had been prepared for bed, I continued our reading until she fell asleep. I scarcely had time to engage in any reading of my own. I remember that when I crawled into my own bed to peruse the new book by Dorothy Sayers, *Busman's Holiday*, I fell immediately asleep.

TWENTY-SIX

If this were simply another one of my detective stories rather than a memoir, I would probably title this chapter 'The Mystery Begins'. Assuredly it did on a bitterly cold afternoon late in February when Miss Angela and I were in the midst of our afternoon walk, the faithful sheepdog, Sandy, as always, at our side.

We seldom ventured to the edge of the cliff on the far side of the property which ran parallel to the gated entrance to the estate. Here the Channel waves beat ferociously against the rocks and treacherous currents became sinister whirlpools. This was a far cry from the protected beach at the top of the property to which we usually ventured.

I don't remember now what brought us there on that particular day. I don't remember many things at this advanced stage of my life. Perhaps it was a desire to tempt the waves below, to fill our lungs with the sea air and to feel the wind lashing our hair: or in my case, my grey wig.

As we studied the frothy cauldrons of sea water below, Sandy foraged about the area as was his wont. Soon he began to dig, finally producing the handle of a bag. I examined it curiously, and with great effort dislodged it from the soil. It wasn't a hand-bag as I first believed, but a small tattered overnight bag, containing several personal belongings that Miss Angela recognised as belonging to her previous governess.

Why would a woman departing the estate bury her bag?

Had she met with foul play?

It was my nature to suspect the latter.

Upon returning to Tower House I sought out Roman and presented him with the satchel of the missing governess. He did not appear terribly surprised at the sight of it. 'Most peculiar,' he commented at his desk. He had taken over Lord Pemberton's office and was utilising it as his own. 'But then Nanny Silverton was a most peculiar young woman.'

'In what way?'

'She was not a seasoned lady such as your-self. Although she won the confidence of young Miss Angela, she had little success with young Lord Pemberton. She was often reduced to tears and would wander out at the oddest hours. I would discover her weep-ing behind some tree or other. If she hadn't found favour with Miss Angela, I would have had her dismissed long before she departed.'

'Would it be in your power to have me dismissed as well?'

204

'I could certainly make a recommendation to Mr Maxwell,' he responded. Was it a veiled threat against me to mind my own business? Something I have never been able to do. 'So far your work has been most satisfactory.'

'I am pleased to hear it.'

'And you enjoy accompanying Miss Angela to Sunday service, whereas Nanny Silverton was most agitated at the prospect, for she was a Rosicrucian and attempted to proselytise the children, which I strictly forbade. Old Lord Pemberton who was Church of England through and through, must have been turning over in his grave at the thought of it.'

The Rosicrucians, also known as the Great White Brotherhood, are believed to have originated as a secret society in ancient Egypt during the reign of the Pharaoh Ahmose I, who reigned from 1570 to 1546 BC.

The Rosicrucians believe that there are two planes of existence: the earth plane and a higher one beyond our grasp.

Rosicrucians still practise the art of alchemy or transmutation of base metals into gold in many of their laboratories, and offer healing services to those members of their society who choose not to visit a doctor.

The Rosicrucians have always believed that there is but one soul in the universe and that this one universal soul is God. Hence their beliefs have often been described as 'Christian mysticism'.

The main tenet of the Rosicrucian order is that its members claim that they are in possession of 'new' knowledge. What this 'new' knowledge is, I suppose I would have to become a member to discover, a deed which is beyond my curiosity.

Perhaps the appeal of the Rosicrucian Order to a lower class young woman such as Grace Silverton, is that in ancient Egypt, Ahmose, the wife of Pharaoh Tuthmosis I, was the first woman to become a member of the secret society, on equal footing with her husband. Since this time, unlike so many other religions, women have always been on equal footing in this still secretive organisation.

'But to simply vanish like that and bury her belongings. What has that got to do with being a Rosicrucian?' I demanded after considering what I knew of the organisation.

'I agree that it is most mysterious. I am motoring into Fowey this afternoon. I shall bring this valise with me and take the matter up with the police.'

Although I did not trust this Roman, I foolishly left the matter in his hands, for the following day something else occurred to occupy my attention. The London trial of Robin Thibodeaux began at the Old Bailey.

TWENTY-SEVEN

How frustrating it was for me to have to wait until the close of day – sometimes even late at night – to peruse a copy of the *Times*. The local Cornwall newspaper was available earlier in the kitchen, but it was the *Times* that printed verbatim the testimony of the trial. Unfortunately the newspaper went to Roman in the morning and he kept it throughout the day before finally depositing it in the kitchen. Why he kept it so long I will never know, because the only thing in which he appeared interested was horse racing. It is my belief that he often placed bets; however his true interest was simply the horses themselves. 'Someday I shall own a stable of racehorses,' I heard him brag to Deidre and Mrs Mears.

'But where would you obtain that kind of money?' Mrs Mears questioned skeptically.

'I shall have more than enough one day,' he assured her. 'You wait and see.'

Each evening, after Miss Angela had fallen asleep, I would descend to the kitchen to devour the coverage of the trial, sometimes taking the newspaper back to my room. The staff were fascinated with the trial as well and full of opinions. I thanked my lucky stars that the newspaper had no recent photographs of me, at least none without a hat that concealed my face. The photo they utilised most often was my old wedding picture taken with my first husband. I looked nothing like that young girl now: innocent and trusting and foolishly imagining that a lifetime of wedded bliss stretched like a primrose path before me.

Deidre and Bridget, the black-haired Irish sisters, were in agreement that Robin Thibodeaux was a heartless murderer and 'should swing like a pendulum from the gallows!'

Mona, the freckled redhead, their younger cousin, wasn't as sure. She studied Robin's visage in the newspaper wistfully, unable to take her eyes from his handsome face. 'Sure, this doesn't look like the face of a murderer.'

'Then where is Flora Coombe?' Polly Mears demanded, 'if not dead at the bottom of a lake where he buried her.'

'You say you've read some of her books, Mrs Mears,' Mona responded. 'What's to prevent her from pretending to be dead so that she can have her revenge on him cheating on her?'

The redhead was cleverer than I imagined. I hoped that few others shared her opinion.

'What woman would go off without her hair and her teeth?' Bridget demanded. She was the most fetching of the three; the most concerned about her appearance.

'She never should have married him in the first place,' Mrs Mears interjected. 'Pure lust. It was nothing but lust. Lust will do you in every time. You remember that, girls. You've got to find yourselves a good man as I did and forget the lust.'

'Are you saying, Mrs Mears, that Flora Coombe got what she deserved?' Deidre demanded.

'Nobody deserves to be buried at the bottom of a lake. The man that done it deserves the same fate as she. They should bury him at the bottom of the Thames.'

I made little comment, for I was busy reading the transcripts of the trial. Mrs Mears studied me curiously. 'Surely you're taking a particular interest in this trial, Nanny Prescott.'

I glanced guiltily up from the newspaper as if I had been caught with my hand in her cookie jar.

'It's just that I have read all of Miss Coombe's books. I can't imagine that there won't be any more Inspector Hecates.'

Mrs Mears concurred. 'They say that all the old ones is selling big all over again.'

'Fancy that,' was my response. How I would have loved to get my hands on those royalties. At least there would be a windfall waiting for me when I returned.

'Tomorrow when I go into Fowey, I shall stop at the library and check out some Flora Coombe books so you girls can read them for yourselves,' Mrs Mears promised.

'Not if they're that scary,' Deidre cautioned.

I couldn't resist interjecting. 'They're not meant to frighten as much as to puzzle and pique the curiosity. You must examine the clues and think for yourself.'

'If there's murder involved, they're scary,' Bridget insisted.

She reminded me of my own Bertie, who immediately put my book down as soon as someone was done in.

'Once you get started on one you won't want to stop,' Mrs Mears added. 'I'm going to be reading the last one she wrote, *The Mysterious Disappearance*. I read somewhere she hadn't finished her new one before he buried her at the bottom of a lake.'

She was correct. I had purposely left *The Lady Cried Murder* unfinished so as to make Robin appear even more guilty. The story was all worked out beforehand however. All that was left was for Inspector Hecate to make his summation and name the killer. It would be completed in the space of a week after my return. When would that be? How could I leave Miss Angela now after we had become such good friends and she had grown so dependent upon me?

As Robin's court case progressed, I pored over the testimony in the privacy of my bedroom. How I longed to clip the continuing coverage from the *Times,* but how could I explain my inordinate interest in the case? It is only now, as I finally tell this story, that I have obtained transcripts from the trial and will now present snippets that I feel are relevant.

I was sorely tempted to take leave from my position as governess and venture to London and observe the trial first-hand. I would disguise myself even more severely so that no one could possibly recognise me. But what if somebody did? I would be prosecuted myself. No doubt Agatha Christie would feature such a ruse in one of her elaborate plots, a second *Witness for the Prosecution,* but I couldn't be so foolhardy.

Nevertheless, I could well imagine the timid Bertie as she entered the witness box, placed her hand on the Bible, and promised to 'tell the whole truth and nothing but'. I saw a photo of her in the newspaper. She was dressed in her Sunday best, which happened to be my Dior cast-off that she shortened and took in to fit her smaller figure. Her brown eyes looked as big as black buttons in the light of the photographer's flash. If her frightened countenance was any indication, she was not enjoying this moment in the glare of London notoriety. I could even hear her voice, high pitched and anxious, rising by decibels the longer she testified.

BERTIE

She was that weak from not getting any nourishment. She wouldn't touch a bite for fear that Frenchy had done something to it. She kept asking me if he had been in the kitchen. Well, she wouldn't even let him in the room when he asked her to go to the films. She was sure Frenchy had listened in when she told her solicitor over the phone to take him out of her will. Later that evening I woke up to hear ma'am screaming that somebody was hurting her, that they were taking her somewhere. It was pitch black on account of there was no lights. I banged on the door, but it was locked from the inside. I called the police, but I was too late. They'd already spirited her away.

According to the newspaper, Bertie stood in the witness box the entire day. I shall not take the time or space to recreate everything she said. I am too much the novelist to do that. I will simply conclude with her final statement that I found most telling and damaging to the defence.

BERTIE

Miss Flora would never go off without her wig and teeth. Not unless she was dragged

212

off, and they fell off somehow. That's what I say! She wouldn't even be seen in the privacy of her own bedroom without them. Someone would have to murder her before she'd be seen without her hair and her teeth.

Soon Inspector Hanlon was called into the witness box. I could well imagine the importance he was assigning himself as the Chief Detective Inspector upon the case. He had attained considerable notoriety for being the investigator of what was already being called 'The Crime of the Century'.

I must say that, if the newspaper was any indication, he did not overdress for his appearance in court. He appeared to be wearing the same brown twill suit that he wore when he presented himself at my door. His wiry hair appeared a little longer, perhaps for the winter, but other than that he appeared exactly the same. I liked him none the better, even if he gave his testimony exactly as if I had written it myself. I shall present the highlights:

INSPECTOR HANLON
Upon arriving at the premises, I discovered that someone, or somebodies had tampered with the electrical wires and broken into the private quarters of Miss Flora Coombe. Excuse me, Mrs Thibodeaux.

And later:

INSPECTOR HANLON

Upon investigation it was discovered that Mr Thibodeaux and Miss Hewitt had not attended the film at all. Miss Hewitt had rented a room under an assumed name which the two had been known to frequent on more than one occasion. However, the night of Miss Coombe's, excuse me, Mrs Thibodeaux's disappearance, no one in Wycombe appears to have seen them either arrive or depart this location.

He continued by declaring:

INSPECTOR HANLON

Upon careful examination of the property in the morning, footprints, fitting the shoes of Robin Thibodeaux, were discovered beneath the broken window of his wife's bedroom. Also, in examining the premises about the house, not far from Lord Westmoreland's new mill pond, which juts onto the Thibodeaux property, we discovered a wig and false teeth that have been identified as belonging to Mrs Thibodeaux.

Inspector Hanlon added:

The report from Mrs Thibodeaux's dentist in London unequivocally identifies the false teeth discovered by Lord Westmoreland's lake as belonging to Miss Flora Coombe.

How I suffered at this talk of my wig and false teeth! It was almost unbearable – except for the fact that my desire for revenge was stronger than my vanity.

When Lord Westmoreland stepped into the witness box, he looked more the role of a country squire than a Member of Parliament, if his photograph in the *Times* was any indication. I suppose he felt that his costume was more in keeping with the testimony he was about to give, of a country gentleman who loved all of nature and was doing his best to preserve it.

I felt compelled almost to smile at his testimony, although I must admit that I was not overly pleased with the new name that Bunny had chosen for his nature preserve.

LORD WESTMORELAND

The day of Flora Coombe's disappearance, my men were reinforcing the bottom of my nature preserve – my nature lake – with cement. They worked on into the evening, so the cement was still wet. Robin Thibodeaux came over for a visit and watched the men at work. He seemed most interested. I even heard him ask one of my men how long it took the cement to dry. He said something about creating a new pond on his own property, but you see, he'd already made one. It is my belief that Flora Coombe is at the bottom of my nature preserve, that he buried her beneath the cement. The following afternoon, you see, while the search was on for her, we filled my lake with water. The birds came right away, I might add, paddled in so happily as if they found a new home. He's a clever bloke, that Thibodeaux. Flora Coombe suggested I call my preserve Swan's Way, but now I am rechristening it Flora's Mill Pond. They talked about digging up my preserve, but you see, we concluded by diverting a much larger portion of the stream water than we originally intended. I convinced the boys at the home office that digging up my preserve wouldn't be feasible. Not feasible at all. She's gone, Flora Coombe. That's all we need to know. You can't bring up those poor bodies trapped in the Titanic any more than you can bring up Flora. It's almost as if she had a burial at sea. Even if we did destroy my nature preserve, we'd never find her under all that cement anyway.

The defence made quite a to-do about the absence of a body – mine in this case – and Inspector Hanlon was once more summoned to the witness box. At the finish of his questioning he was most succinct in his conclusion.

INSPECTOR HANLON

In reviewing all the facts of our investigation, it is my conclusion that Mr Robin Thibodeaux and Miss Mary Beth Hewitt engaged in the wilful murder of Mrs Robin Thibodeaux, more widely known as the celebrated author, Miss Flora Coombe. This even in the absence of the *corpus delicti*.

I was beginning to believe that I could perhaps like this Inspector after all.

Robin Thibodeaux, the accused, was the last to step into the witness box. When I read the final words of his testimony, my heart almost went out to him, but the wheels of justice had been set spinning. I chose (I am not proud of this fact) to let them run their course.

Perhaps it was out of nervousness or desperation, but Robin once again spoke as if he had just come to England from his native Louisiana. His newly acquired proper use of speech seemed to have deserted him. The 'illeism' had returned.

ROBIN

Once before they say Robin murder somebody. But they find that this is not true. Miss Flora Coombe show that Robin is not guilty. Where is Mrs Robin Thibodeaux now to show that Robin not harm her? She hides.

She punishes me for making love with the younger woman. Robin is sorry... In his own way he love this woman who save him from death. Robin is only guilty of taking young woman into his bed. Robin will always be guilty of this. But in his heart he have great love for the lovely lady who save him from death. Please she come forth to save him again.

Could the verdict have been anything else when the victim was the most popular mystery writer in all of England? No, I am not going to concede that I was the second most popular. Agatha Christie be damned! Certainly I was number one in sales when I was so brutally 'murdered'. Dame Christie's pathetic short-lived 'disappearance' to Harrogate when her first husband, Archibald Christie, confessed that he was in love with another woman, hardly boosted her sales at all. She was an amateur at faking a disappearance and was discovered almost immediately. It was a different story in my case.

If I am digressing, I am sorry. No doubt my readers are much more interested in the outcome of Robin's trial. I shall not delay.

Robin Thibodeaux was found guilty of my murder and sentenced to hang from the gallows. When the defence pleaded for time to mount an appeal for what they characterised a miscarriage of justice – since there was no *corpus delicti* – this was denied. Unlike America, justice is swift in England. It is our way of getting on with it, I suppose. The Americans let things drag on forever.

I must admit that I did not feel elated at the verdict. There was a time when I would have almost cheered. Now, time had passed and my desire for revenge had somewhat subsided. I almost felt sorry. But as the characters take over a story when I am creating a new mystery, so had the events that I had put into motion. The train had left the station. I could not stop it without burying myself beneath the tracks.

TWENTY-EIGHT

The month was March, and what the great William Shakespeare had written in his *Winter's Tale* had come true:

'Daffodils, that come before the swallow
  dares,
and take the winds of March with beauty.'

Indeed the yellow flower had already poked its head above the soil to perform a dance to the cold winds that brought even more colour to Angela's already rosy cheeks. Certainly there were no sign of swallows. They never came to Tower House. Maybe they were afraid to roost in the eaves. There was evil there, as I would soon discover.

It was the faithful sheepdog, Sandy, who led us to the body. He trotted ahead of us, occasionally turning his furry head to make sure that we were following.

Before we realised, we were near where Sandy had unearthed Nanny Silverton's satchel. Soon we were standing at the top of the cliff. Sandy had suddenly stopped and barked at something below. It was a Saturday morning and Miss Angela was not having her lessons. The tide had receded much further than previously. The tides of the English Channel are unlike any other. At one moment small ships are bobbing like corks in the water. Almost instantly the tide has retreated and they are beached like baby whales. I know that this has something to do with the lunar cycles and the pull of the moon, but I have never quite understood it. I don't really believe that my mood has ever been affected by the moon as people claim. Whether it is a full moon or a half moon, I don't feel differently. I think that people simply use this as an excuse for irrational behaviour – such as murder. Do my readers remember 'the lunar defence' in my *The Moon Murders?* Was the body that we were about to discover the cause of some mysterious pull of the moon as well?

Miss Angela saw what Sandy wanted us to see. Her eyes were young and far-seeing and much stronger than mine. She pointed, then realising what she was seeing, she turned away and buried her face in my grey woollen sweater.

I squinted to where she was pointing. At a good distance, in an area that had always previously been covered by the sea, the remnants of a body lay wedged between two rocks. It was both chilling and hypnotic to observe what the sea can do to one who is not their own, to one who cannot survive underwater.

It was a woman. That much was certain. Long tresses of black hair were stretched out along the sand like loose strands of seaweed. From a distance the face was unrecognisable. There was so little remaining of it. It had been eaten away by hungry sea-urchins, clinging to the remains of white flesh like barnacles to the hull of a ship. No mermaid this, for there was the remains of a torso with arms and legs and what was left of a print dress.

Sandy barked again at this spectre coughed up from the sea. How long had he known that it was there and why had he picked this day to lead us to it? Was this the first day the tide had been sufficiently low to reveal its secret?

I quickly pulled Miss Angela away from the site. We hurried away, Sandy following alongside, until Miss Angela spoke what was upon my mind and I was fearful to utter. 'That wasn't my Mommy. I know it wasn't.'

'Of course not,' I reassured, really not certain of the fact.

'My Mommy had long beautiful blonde-hair. It wasn't all black like that. Scott said that my Mommy and his Daddy are sleeping together in each other's arms in the part of the boat they never found.'

'I'm certain they are.'

We walked quickly back to Tower House in silence once again until I could no longer stop myself from asking. 'Did your last nanny, Grace Silverton, have black hair?'

'Oh, yes. Much longer than mine. It fell all the way down her back. Sometimes she would let me brush it for her. A hundred strokes every night, that's what it took.' She stopped suddenly, realising the gravity of my question. 'That isn't my Nanny Silverton back there, is it? Is that why she went away and never came back? She fell into the water?'

'We shall see,' I assured her. 'We shall assuredly see.'

Upon entering the manor house, I did not seek out Roman nor Mrs Mears. I went directly to the telephone and demanded to be connected to the Fowey Police. Who knew when the tide would ever recede so low again?

TWENTY-NINE

The tide had returned before the Fowey Detective Inspector and a rescue squad arrived to retrieve the body, which was once again submerged. Rather than solicit divers, the inspector deemed it wiser to wait until the tide was pulled out to sea once again.

We all waited; each member of the household staff: Roman and Mrs Mears, Mona (the Irish sisters were too frightened), the cook, Hortense, who had eaten too much of her own concoctions and breathed heavily as she walked the lengthy distance to the cliff, Danny, the stable boy, and the police and the younger men who would retrieve the body. Miss Angela had been left behind with Bridget and Deidre. Sandy the dog, however, had come forth to observe as well.

We must have been a peculiar sight, lined up as we were along the cliff, a wind-swept crew, watching impatiently as the tide retreated at a maddeningly slow pace, drop by drop, or so it seemed.

The mysteries of the centuries were buried

beneath these waters, the remnants of pirate ships, British men-of-war, French frigates and Roman vessels. The sea guarded these treasures and was reluctant to release them.

Finally, as the sun retreated with most of its light, the rocks were exposed. The body was gone! It was no longer wedged between the stones! The sea had claimed its victim once again. I was reminded of 'Annabel Lee', the extraordinary romantic poem by the American poet, Edgar Allan Poe, whose love was consigned to 'her sepulchre by the sea, in her tomb by the sounding sea'. Was this true of this victim as well? Had Poe's 'demons down under the sea' demanded her return?

'It was there this morning! A woman's body!' I said it so they all could hear, for they were all looking at me curiously, especially the Detective Inspector, Bertram Hawkins, a man of my vintage, who had experienced more than I had ever written about. I learned soon enough that he had once been part of Scotland Yard. He considered his sojourn with the Fowey Police almost a retirement. He was certainly older than my Inspector Hecate and dressed more in the casual manner of a country squire than a man of the law. There was a suggestion of weight to his ruddy cheeks and stomach. His grey hair was still in great abundance. His moustache and eyebrows appeared to have a mind of their own. I liked him immediately. That he had seen much was made clear by the cast of his avuncular brown eyes. He appeared to swallow life slowly. He was not quick to judgement – as I tend to be.

'Was the sun in your eyes this morning?'

'It most certainly was not! There was hardly any sun at all till this afternoon. I know what I saw and it was a woman's body!' I assumed that he was from the Cornwall region originally. His husky voice had traces of the local pronunciation. Perhaps his father had been a fisherman.

'You say this "body" had dark hair?'

'Long black Lorelei tresses.'

'Are you sure it was a woman?'

'I'm old enough to know the difference, Inspector!' Why did I always get so uppity with the police? I suppose I thought I had sharper powers of deduction.

'I expect you are.' He eyed me curiously. I wanted to protest that with a proper wig and make-up I could appear years younger.

'I wasn't the only one to see the body, Inspector. I'd rather you wouldn't, but if you must, I suggest you question Miss Angela Winston who saw the body as well.'

'And if indeed there was a body, Nanny,' he appeared to enjoy calling me by that name, 'whose body would you say it was?'

'Perhaps my predecessor.'

'And who would that be?'

'Grace Silverton, as you well know. Nanny Silverton to you. Miss Angela has informed me that she had exceptionally long black hair as did the body we saw this morning.'

'That she did,' Mrs Mears intervened. 'Prided herself on it. She must have brushed it 100 strokes a night.'

'And why would this Grace Silverton be under the sea? Is that what happens to the help around here?'

I didn't mind his being flippant. My Inspector Hecate had a similar irreverent manner. My readers enjoyed it.

'As you already know, Nanny Silverton more or less vanished from this estate one evening and has not been seen or heard of since.'

'That's true, Inspector,' Mrs Mears concurred. 'Called herself a taxi, went out to meet him at the gate, but when he finally came, she was nowhere to be found.'

'Surely you've made inquiries yourself after the discovery of her satchel buried on the estate?'

'What satchel?'

'It was reported to your headquarters.'

The inspector turned to his subordinate, a much younger man, who obviously idolised his superior. 'You know anything about this, Carruthers?'

'No, sir.'

I turned to Roman, who had been stand-

226

ing listening to our conversation. 'But you took the valise into the police station yourself.'

'I thought I could make better use of it.'

'And what was that?' the Inspector asked.

'Since she buried her belongings, I didn't think Nanny Silverton wanted them anymore. I turned them over to The Fisherman's Thrift where they could do some good.'

'What?' If I sounded surprised, I wasn't really. I had suspected that Roman would not bring the items to the police, but I had been too distracted by the trial of my second husband to give it much thought.

Roman attempted to explain. 'This is where items are sold and the proceeds go to fishermen's widows.'

The inspector's curiosity had definitely been piqued. 'You found this woman's belongings buried on the estate?'

'I found them,' I boasted. I pointed to Sandy, who appeared to be listening to our conversation with great interest. 'Rather this sheepdog did. I thought it was something that the police should investigate.'

'Investigate it we will,' the inspector promised. He turned back to eye Roman. 'Why didn't you bring this to our attention?'

'I suppose because we were well rid of this Nanny Silverton. I didn't feel that she was a good influence on Miss Angela. I didn't want to do anything that would bring her back to us.'

'I see.' The inspector obviously wasn't accepting this feeble explanation, but I surmised he was the kind of man who watched and waited and allowed suspects – to quote the great Bard – 'to hoist themselves on their own petard'. He addressed himself to his subordinates. 'It's getting too dark to do anything now. We'll have to bring in divers tomorrow and see if they can find anything.' He turned to the man nearest him. 'Carruthers, run a missing person inquiry on this Grace Silverton.' His eyes encompassed all of us who laboured in the Tower House. 'Why don't we go back to the house and you can tell me all you know about this "missing" woman?'

'I know very little about her,' I responded. 'I am her replacement. She departed before I arrived.'

'Well, Nanny,' he looked me in the eye, for we were exactly the same height. 'You're not the only one in the household.'

'I suppose I'm not,' I admitted. As usual, I was placing myself at the centre of the story, when I was just an observer.

Roman stepped forward. 'Perhaps when we step inside, the inspector would like some sherry or whiskey.'

The inspector liked the sound of this. 'I always drink on the job.'

As the inspector learned, between sips of the household's best sherry (nothing but the best for Roman), there was little information to be gained regarding the mysterious Grace Silverton. It was I who suggested that the inspector contact Mr George Maxwell, who had hired Grace Silverton in the first place. No sooner were these words out of my mouth than Roman took over the conversation as if this had been his idea. Roman was seated before the massive fireplace in the great hall of the Tower House. You might have thought he was lord of the manor. The inspector had also made himself comfortable while the remainder of us stood as the servants we were.

Finally Miss Angela was brought down from the nursery into the great hall. Deidre had already dressed her for bed. The inspector kept his seat so that when Angela stood before him, they were almost eye to eye. 'Did you see the same body in the ocean as your nanny did this morning?'

Miss Angela's demeanour suddenly changed in a way that I had never seen before. She pushed her head forward and arched her shoulders and spoke in a slightly different voice. 'Angela didn't see it, but I did.'

The inspector glanced curiously at me before speaking to the child. 'And who are you?'

Miss Angela grew even more defiant. 'I'm Angela's friend, Maisie Martin.'

It occurred to me immediately that the sight of the body that could have possibly been her mother or more probably her governess, was so upsetting to the fragile little girl that she had to assume her imaginary friend's identity to confront it. 'Maisie Martin is one of Miss Angela's imaginary friends,' I explained to the inspector.

'I see,' responded the inspector, studying the girl curiously. 'Did you see the body this morning, Miss Maisie?'

'Yes, I did, but only for a moment, because Nanny turned my head away very quickly before I could get a proper look. She thinks I'm a scaredy cat, but I'm not. It's Angela who is scared.'

'And would you say this body was that of a woman?'

'Yes.'

'Are you sure?'

'Yes.'

'Why?'

'Because it looked like this dolly Angela had. She had long black hair too. When I dropped it into the bath it got all wet and looked just like what I saw on the beach. Angela was very upset with me. She loved that doll.'

I couldn't help smiling a little in triumph. Whether it was Miss Angela or Maisie talking, she had corroborated what I had described.

Angela became herself again. She took my hand and looked up at me in a way that was familiar. 'Can we go upstairs now, Nanny? Can you read me a story?'

THIRTY

I looked forward to my next day at liberty more than I had to any of the others. My curiosity had been more than piqued by the extraordinary disappearance of Grace Silverton. I was determined to discover what, if anything, Inspector Hawkins had unearthed about the missing woman. The divers had not discovered her body. If Miss Angela had not seen the corpse as well as me, perhaps I might have doubted my own sanity.

It was Lord Byron in his *Childe Harold's Pilgrimage*, who wrote:

'Roll on, thou deep and dark blue ocean – roll!
She sinks into thy depths with bubbling groan,
Without a grave, unknelled, uncoffined, and unknown.'

I telephoned for a taxi early in the morning. Toby, my original driver to Tower House, the former fisherman, was there as usual to transport me. He was full of questions concerning the missing body. News travels fast in Fowey, or indeed in all of Cornwall.

'You're not the first one to see a body that wasn't there,' he observed, studying me in his rear view mirror. 'The sea loves to play tricks with you. There were times when I thought I saw King Neptune himself.'

'I know what I saw, Toby. Miss Angela saw it as well.'

'And how is the little heiress?'

'I wish you wouldn't call her that, Toby. We never speak of money and I never think of it and her in those terms.'

'She's keeping her American name, isn't she? She's still a Winston, isn't she?'

'I think that's customary.'

'Since that's where the money comes from.'

I deemed it best to change the subject as we sped towards the coastal village.

'As I recall, Toby, when you first brought me out here, you mentioned something concerning the former governess summoning you to Tower House to bring her into town.'

'That's right, I did. I was just sitting down to supper. They always call when you're just sitting down to supper.'

232

'How did she sound? Was she...?'

'You'd have to ask my wife. She took the call. She always takes the calls.'

'And she wasn't there when you came to fetch her?'

'No sign of her. When I drove up to the house, Mrs Mears says that this nanny was so anxious to get started, she walked to the gate to meet me. That gatekeeper never saw her either. Of course I'd had this flat tyre which delayed me a bit.'

'How odd.' Why was I so certain it was foul play? I suppose it was my fiendish mind at work.

'You know what I think?' Toby offered, as we approached the fishing village.

'What?' I knew that he would tell me even if I didn't ask.

'I think that nanny got so anxious, especially when I was late with that flat tyre, she just walked all the way to the main road and got herself a ride.'

'But the gatekeeper didn't see her.'

'Old Crumpton doesn't see a lot of things. She could've slipped out easy.'

But what about her valise? I wondered. What about the satchel buried in hopes that no one would discover it? I didn't mention this to Toby.

'Where do you want to be dropped off?' he inquired, as the Fowey harbour loomed before us.

'The police.'

The Fowey Police Station, called the Royal Duchy of Cornwall Constabulary, was not part and parcel of the picturesque harbour. It was situated beyond the view of the English Channel.

Inspector Bertram Hawkins was already at his desk. He did not appear surprised to see me. His brows and moustache looked even wilder early in the morning. How I would have loved to have gone at them with my scissors. I even imagined what my life would have been like if I had succumbed to a sensible man of his age, rather than a young man of glorious colour from Louisiana. If I had had my wits about me, I should have married a seasoned gentleman such as Inspector Bertram Hawkins. What a pair of detectives we would have made together.

'Have you seen another body?' he questioned of me as I sat down opposite his desk.

'I know what I saw. If I'd had any sense I should've retrieved the body then and there and dragged it to shore.'

'Have you ever had experience with a dead body?'

'I've seen people dead, if that's what you mean. I was a volunteer nurse during the Great War.' I was going to add that I had seen my first husband dead as well, but thought better of it. I had to continually remind myself that I was not the celebrated Flora Coombe, but the spinster Irene Prescott who had spent her life in service. I deflected attention away from me. 'No doubt you have had your fill.'

'Seeing them I could tolerate. Never liked handling them, though.'

'But isn't that a job for the coroner?'

'If you're lucky.' He offered me a cigarette which I declined. I do not approve of smoking. That is probably why I am still alive today to tell this story.

'What brings you to my station this morning, Nanny Prescott?' He was clearly enjoying his cigarette. If the yellow stains on his right index and middle fingers were any indication, he had been enjoying them for many years.

'I couldn't help but wonder if you had unearthed any pertinent information in regards to my predecessor.'

'Grace Silverton?'

'The very same.'

'If we hadn't tracked down a former employer, I'd say she didn't exist.'

'How so?'

'Her former charge is the only person she kept in touch with.'

'Who would that be?'

'A Miss Natalie Harris of Hyde Park. Grace was sent to care for her directly from the orphanage.'

'She was an orphan?'

'From the day she was born. She grew up in an orphan home that later burned to the ground. As soon as she was old enough, they arranged employment as nanny to a Natalie Harris who was just a young girl at the time. Grace took care of her till Miss Harris turned eighteen, then she worked for another family. She fell in love with the footman who was one of these Rosicrucians. He emigrated to America with promises to send for her, but she never heard from him again.'

'She departed Tower House in such a hurry. I wonder where she was going.'

'How do you know she was in such a hurry?'

I related all that I knew of the mysterious disappearance of Grace Silverton, concluding with my recent conversation with Toby, the driver, and asking why a woman would bury her travelling clothes if she was journeying to London. Inspector Hawkins appeared impressed. 'I would say you would make a pretty fair detective.'

I was pleased with the compliment, but little did he know that I could possibly beat him at his own game. Still, even his suggestion that I might qualify as a colleague warmed my heart in a way that I had not expected. How I wished that he could see me as I truly was: not this dreary nanny, but a younger woman who knew how to dress and make herself attractive.

'If you continue to share information with me, Inspector, I shall be happy to share information with you.'

He stuck his cigarette in his mouth and reached across the table.

'On that I will shake your hand.' He had a firm grip to which I was not accustomed. In a strange way I wished that I was not wearing gloves so that I could feel his flesh pressing against my own. Dear me, I must have been getting over Robin's foul treatment of me if I was actually harbouring such thoughts with another man. He held my hand longer than necessary. Our eyes met in a way that made me blush. He finally released my hand and decided to speak. 'Perhaps I should relate a conversation I had this week with Mr George Maxwell, the executor of the Pemberton estate.'

'It was Mr Maxwell who hired me.'

'He stated that the night Grace Silverton went missing, she telephoned him to say that she was on her way to London to see him.'

'Did she say why?'

'It was something that she couldn't discuss over the telephone. She wanted to tell him in person. Mr Maxwell said that he had the impression that she was afraid that someone was listening in.'

'How very odd.'

'Do you have any idea what she wanted to tell him? Has anybody said anything about this at Tower House?'

'Not to me. Nothing at all.'

'I assume you will keep your ears open.'

'As always.'

He ushered me out of the station in a most gentlemanly fashion. He didn't take my hand again, but he held the door open for me. As I walked the distance towards the harbour I wondered why I hadn't revealed the word that Grace Silverton had slipped beneath the blotter. 'D-E-P-R-A-V-E-D' she had printed. I suppose a good mystery writer always holds something back from her readers or from the police.

When I walked from the police station into town, the cold February wind blowing from the harbour stung my cheeks like freezing nettles. When Robin Thibodeaux was no longer among the living and I could return to my own beloved home, I would begin thinking of spending the English winters in a warmer climate, somewhere in the Tropics, perhaps. In truth, when I did return home, I never wished to leave. I am still braving a British winter at Dovecote Cottage and am none the worse for wear as I am writing this.

Did I feel a sore throat coming on? I would not infect dear little Miss Angela. She was too precious to me. I ventured into the Fowey Chemist's Shop for something to ward it off. I really can't remember now what the chemist prescribed. We didn't have the remedies in the 1930s that are available these days. At that time a doctor didn't even recommend orange juice. I think perhaps just tea with a little bit of lemon was the usual panacea.

I was surprised that the chemist was a woman. I am always pleased when a woman assumes a position formerly dominated by men. Weren't our best rulers queens? Namely Elizabeth I, Queen Victoria and now our Elizabeth II? I have no doubt that one day we will have a female Prime Minister as well.

If I were at home in Oxford and I felt one of my sore throats coming on, my doctor would prescribe a dose of codeine that soothed the pain nicely until the soreness had passed. I certainly did not have the prescription, and even if I did, it would be under the name of Flora Coombe, not the Nanny Prescott that I had become.

The chemist wanted to be pretty. She had done everything to achieve the effect. However, it was a losing battle, her features were sadly all wrong: her nose was too large, her eyes too close together and her lips – overly painted – too thin, as was her figure.

When I had been a nursing volunteer during the Great War, I had actually managed to pass the Apothecaries Hall examination, which enabled me to dispense for a medical officer or a chemist, but I did not enjoy dispensing as much as nursing. As a writer I have such a great interest in people. I found the war-wounded particularly fascinating at the University Hospital in London, where I was assigned. Dispensing medicine wasn't nearly as fascinating as comforting soldiers; however I did develop a knowledge of potions, lotions, ointments, drugs and poisons that has served me in good stead for my writing.

'Are you new to Fowey?' she questioned.

'Relatively speaking,' I replied, glad to be inside the warm shop out of the cold. 'I am newly employed as governess at the Tower House in St. Claire.'

Her expression changed immediately. Her smile didn't quite fade, but it was different somehow. The mention of Tower House had struck some kind of nerve. Why, I couldn't be sure.

'Have you been to Tower House?' I inquired.

'Oh, no,' she replied. 'I'm new to the vicinity as well. This is my first employment as chemist. I'm from Plymouth. I was hired to assist Mr Mellors, who has been under the weather as of late.'

'Oh, yes, I've seen him,' I responded. He

was very elderly and took his sweet time in waiting on me.

'I am to take over entirely when he retires.'

'My congratulations, Miss Lancaster,' for she had introduced herself as Evelyn Lancaster and I had offered my new name, Prescott, which I was by then used to saying.

Back outside, with the wind slicing through me as if I were a thin loaf of bread, I longed for my warm nanny's room at Tower House. I decided to have a leisurely fisherman's lunch at one of the restaurants along the wharf and call for a taxi home sooner than I anticipated. Still, the chemist's reaction to the name Tower House remained behind like a lingering medicinal odour. As I did with my writing, I stored this information away in my mind in hopes that it might prove to be useful.

THIRTY-ONE

A week must have passed. I busied myself with the education of a proper young lady and conquered my sore throat before it became a reality. If the severe winter weather permitted Miss Angela and me to stroll about the property, we never ventured near the cove where we had seen the body.

My young charge pretended it had never happened and I did not wish her to assume the identity of her imaginary friend, Maisie Martin, in order to withstand it.

I think it must have been on my next free day that I chose to visit the isolated cliff alone. I had taken a long walk by myself, although Sandy insisted on accompanying me. I was bundled up against the extreme cold with a woolly hat and mittens and my pathetic 'in service' lamb's-wool coat. How I could have used my beautiful ankle-length mink.

I left the property and walked, it seemed, for miles. I was lost in thought, feeling remorse for the death of Mary Beth Hewitt and some guilt for Robin Thibodeaux, who loved nothing as much as the outdoors, but instead was rotting away in prison.

Upon my return through the entry gates to Tower House, I chose to venture along the cliff. I had no idea of discovering the woman's body once again; still I must have hoped so even to return there. I know that Herman Melville in his masterpiece *Moby Dick*, refers to the sea as a 'shroud'. Perhaps the sea would reveal her booty once more before consigning the body to her final resting place.

It was early evening. The tide that had crept out in the afternoon, was creeping back in like a turtle returning to the beach to lay her eggs. I couldn't believe my eyes. The body had returned! Or what was left of it. An entire leg was missing and there was only a fragment of the other. There was just the torso now and the long black hair, reaching like tentacles towards the shore.

No one would believe me again if this body was once more swallowed by the tide. I was determined to preserve the evidence. I followed the steep path down to the beach and approached the form. I couldn't bear to touch the clammy white remains. At long last I pulled her by the hair. I suppose this was an irreverent thing to perpetrate upon the dead. It was all I could muster. I fought nausea and attempted not to look at the creature I was dragging along the beach. Reaching my destination, I fell into the sand, and in so doing, inadvertently turned over the body. Sand crabs were crawling like ants over what was left of the face. There was a gaping hole where there had once been a nose and small sea creatures were crawling in and out of empty eye sockets.

It was one thing to describe a corpse in one of my mysteries. It was quite different to come in actual contact with one. I vomited profusely and ran from the beach and up to the gate house where I dialled the police. When the inspector came on the line, I blurted it out immediately.

'Inspector, this is Irene Prescott. I have

found the same body on the same beach once again. This time I have pulled it away from the tide. If you come immediately, you will see that I am not as crazy as you believe!'

What would we mystery writers or detectives do about the identification of a decomposed body if it weren't for dental records? What would happen if I were discovered beneath Lord Westmoreland's lake, with scarcely a tooth in my head? What then? Would my false teeth suffice?

Fortunately, this was not the case with Grace Silverton. Her first charge, Natalie Harris, revealed that her parents had sent her nanny to their family dentist. Miss Silverton's dental records were forwarded to Plymouth, where the Cornwall coroner made a match with the pathetic corpse.

Inspector Hawkins generously shared this information with me. I felt almost as if we were becoming associates – partners – so to speak, in solving the mystery of her death.

The question was how did Grace Silverton die? There was more than one contusion about her skull, but the coroner could not ascertain with accuracy if these were from a blow to the head or a fall from the cliff onto the rocks and ocean below. If there were such a blow to her head, who had struck it; and why was her satchel buried in hopes that it would not be discovered? If this were a suicide, had she attempted to bury every trace that she had even existed? Had she hurled herself from the cliff as did Greek tragediennes of yore?

I very much doubted it. If this were one of my mystery stories, murder would have been the only possibility: but who had murdered her and why? My mind was turning over the few facts as if my pen was already racing across a sheaf of paper. Assuredly Roman was the only suspect. He did not turn over Grace Silverton's valise to the police. But what reason would he have for murdering her and why had she departed Tower House so suddenly? Who was 'DEPRAVED'? Why had she printed this word, or was it scribbled by someone else who had long before inhabited that room? Roman's behaviour towards me had been respectful. He did not interfere in the nursery and from what I learned from Mrs Mears and the Irish girls, his relationship with Grace Silverton had been no different. Had they had a secret affair from which Grace Silverton was attempting to escape? Was she referring to herself as 'DEPRAVED'? I felt that Inspector Hawkins had his own suspicions, but he was not the type of man to act unless he had definite proof.

If this was simply a story I was writing, I would manipulate the facts and quickly solve the puzzle to my own satisfaction.

This was not to be the case.

When Mr George Maxwell called me to the telephone soon after the identification of Grace Silverton's body, I picked up the receiver with trepidation. This was the first time he had telephoned me since I had accepted employment. I feared that he had discovered that I was not Nanny Irene Prescott at all, but an impostor.

'Hello?' My voice wavered. I feared what was coming.

'Nanny Prescott?'

'Yes, this is she.'

'I felt that I should alert you.'

'Alert?' My heart skipped a beat.

'Master Scott has been sent down from Harrow. He should be arriving at Tower House this evening.'

'Sent down? But why?' It really wasn't any of my business.

'I don't think we should discuss that, Nanny Prescott. The important thing is, I feel it will be best if he has schooling at home until the autumn. Then we shall see if I should send him off to another school or hire a male tutor.'

'But...' Could I keep academically ahead of a boy of fifteen? With Miss Angela, I managed, but... Mr Maxwell must have felt that I had money in mind. 'I realise that this is an added burden. I will increase your salary accordingly.'

'Thank you very much, but...'

'You have had such success with Miss Angela. I'm sure that you will do as well with Master Scott.'

'I will certainly try.' At least I wasn't being sacked from the first situation I had ever attempted. Nursing didn't really count because I was simply a volunteer.

'There is something very peculiar, Nanny Prescott.'

My heart fell. 'What is that?'

'When I checked out your references...'

'Yes?' My heart skipped another beat.

'We inquired of two previous employers. One gave you a glowing reference. The other wrote back equally highly of you, but they insisted that you were dead.'

'How odd,' I managed to reply. 'Who would that be?'

'A Mrs Hadley Burnett.'

'Oh yes, little Susan's parents. It is a lonely profession, Mr Maxwell. Out of sight, out of mind, so to speak. Some of my young charges kept contact with me. Others, like Susan's parents, didn't. They must have assumed I no longer existed.'

He appeared to accept this feeble explanation. 'I can understand that.' He cleared his throat. 'If you have any difficulties with Master Scott, please ring me immediately. I have instructed him to bring home all his school books so that you can continue as if he were still at Harrow.'

'That will be a great help.'

'I will be in contact with you, Nanny Prescott.' He was about to ring off.

'Mr Maxwell?'

'Yes?'

'It is my understanding that you have been contacted in regards to the discovery of Grace Silverton's body.'

'Yes.'

'Might I pose a question?'

'What might that be?' His voice grew colder. I could imagine his elderly body stiffening at my intrusion on what didn't directly concern me.

'It is my understanding that Miss Silverton departed here on very short notice – as a matter of fact without any notice at all. Did she perhaps telephone you of her decision before leaving Tower House?'

There was a decided silence at the other end of the line. Finally he spoke. 'Why do you assume that she telephoned me?'

Should I betray the inspector's confidence? 'I just thought that perhaps...' I trailed off, not quite knowing how to continue.

He finally broke the silence: 'I have only spoken of this to the police. As you know the newspapers managed to get hold of the discovery of her body and Tower House and the family are once again in the newspapers. There has been enough tragedy in this sad family already. I will not lift a finger to contribute to it. Fortunately what happened at Harrow, of which I will not speak, has escaped the notice of the press; at least Scott's involvement in the tragedy.'

Something else now to tantalise my insatiable curiosity.

'Then she did speak to you?' I had to know. Wasn't it my business to know since I was her replacement?

'Yes, she did telephone me very late in the afternoon just before I left my office.'

'And what did she say?'

'She said that she had something very important to discuss with me, something she was afraid to relate over the telephone. I said that perhaps I could come down to Tower House later in the week, but she said that she could not stay in that house another night, that she was going to leave and that she would see me in London the following morning.'

'How odd.'

'Yes. She sounded ... "frenzied" ... I suppose is the best description. I learned later that her choice of religion was rather eccentric as well. It sounded as if she was having some sort of breakdown. We will never know.'

'You never discovered what she wanted to discuss with you.'

'No.' And he rang off quickly.

THIRTY-TWO

Roman retrieved young Master Scott at the train station. As usual he drove his former master's Rolls-Royce Phantom III, which he considered his own. Only 710 of this model were produced until production stopped in 1939 due to the war. I wonder how many replicas of this extraordinary car exist now, or who is in possession of the one that Roman drove.

Miss Angela had already been put to bed. I was reading her a story when the young man burst unannounced and uninvited into her bedroom. Such a handsome lad of fifteen I have never seen. He bore a striking resemblance to photographs of his father, but his hair and colouring came from his mother. It was of an entirely different hue. Often redheads are referred to as being 'carrot-topped', but the thick tresses of Master Scott's hair were not the colour of that vegetable but of the cherry, as deep red as the fruit. It was parted at the centre of his fine head and fell naturally to either side of his face. There were no freckles upon his cheeks such as redheads often bear. His skin was not rosy as was his stepsister's but the colour of scrimshaw, not so white as to startle you, but a pale hue nevertheless. His eyes were such a deep shade of azure that I thought the lights in Angela's bedroom might be playing tricks on my vision. His long eyelashes and brows were darker than his hair. They accented the power of his penetrating eyes. His jawline was decidedly strong yet was softened slightly by the suggestion of dimples in his cheeks and a small cleft in his chin. His lips were thin and his mouth determined, but when he smiled his face radiated as if bathed in a rainbow. He was deliciously tall for his age as with that thin statue of a boy growing to manhood, all angles and sinew and nary a trace of fat.

'Scott!' Angela exclaimed as he approached the bed. 'Nanny told me you were coming! Did you miss me?'

He bent low and kissed his stepsister on the forehead. His abundant hair mingled with her own. 'I would rather be here than any other place in the world. I was not meant for such a school as Harrow.' He stood up and studied me. I fear I blushed because I have always been a victim to such handsomeness, even in one so young.

'I am Nanny Prescott.'

'I have never seen a nanny who looks so

much the role as you,' he said finally, taking my hand and kissing it in rather a grand manner. He almost sucked my skin with his lips. Goose bumps spread immediately across my flesh.

'Before my father married Angela's mother, I was tutored by a certain Mr Cramer, who insisted on speaking to me in Latin, and then after that, Nanny Silverton, until she left us, and when I was very little, a stout little lady named Nelly.'

'Nanny Silverton drowned,' Miss Angela volunteered.

'So I have been told,' he replied, his eyes still fastened upon me. 'I hope that you are better educated. I fear that I was not as sufficiently prepared for Harrow as I should have been.'

'And is that why you've come home?' I said it before I could stop myself. I had not meant to question. Curiosity would certainly kill this cat.

'I caught up in no time,' he responded, ignoring the larger meaning of my inquiry. 'I hope you can keep abreast with me.'

'We shall manage somehow.'

'I shall bring my schoolbooks to the schoolroom tomorrow.'

'And after we've completed this school year, what then?'

'Perhaps a new school or a new governess. We shall see.' He smiled, but it was more of a smirk as he continued to take my measure. 'I am very tired and longing for bed. I shall see you in the morning.' He kissed Angela once again, this time on the cheek. 'Good night, little sister.'

'Good night, Scott.' She looked up at him as he smiled down at her. 'Now that you're home ... do you think that you and Roman will take me riding?'

'You have to start with a pony first, Angela. The horses here are much too big for you.'

'Will you buy me a pony?'

'I couldn't buy you a pony. You must ask Mr Maxwell. You are the one with all the money in this house and he makes all the decisions.'

'But I don't want to ask Mr Maxwell. He frightens me.'

'Tomorrow I shall crawl about on my hands and knees and you can ride on my back.'

'You promise?'

'Yes.' He made a point of bowing to me. 'Good night, Nanny Prescott.'

His presence lingered after he left the room, something disturbing in the air, something I couldn't yet fathom. One thing was certain. I would have to work doubly hard to keep ahead of him in his studies. Being a governess was becoming an even more difficult task. I was about to earn every farthing of my salary.

Now I had two students with whom to contend. I was able to play the role as a Victorian nanny with Miss Angela. Master Scott was far too precocious for me to hide behind an old-fashioned out-of-date manual. His studies seemed extremely advanced for a young man of his age. In several instances it appeared that we were learning together, rather than my instructing him, although in mathematics, thanks to my father's excellent tutoring, I was superior.

I thought it rather odd that Master Scott wore his Harrow school uniform to the classroom. He certainly was handsome in the long black dress coat and matching tie, which looked somewhat funereal against his spotless white shirt. It was as if by continuing to wear his school uniform, he was not acknowledging that he had been expelled from the institution; nor was he accepting defeat.

Often I felt that Master Scott was challenging me. He loved nothing better than an intellectual argument: over the existence of God, for instance, or the superiority of the Impressionist painters over the Pre-Raphaelites, or the excellence of Wagner and Beethoven over all other composers. His passion was history. He had an inordinate interest in Germany, especially Prussia, which was no longer a kingdom unto itself, but the core of the new German Empire created in 1871, when King Wilhelm I of Prussia was proclaimed Emperor of all Germany. 'If God had been kind and he truly existed,' he was fond of saying, 'he would have made me King of Bavaria. I would have made better use of my kingdom and joined these Nazis early on so they would not take it away from me. Now it is too late.'

'Mad King Scott,' I couldn't resist laughing.

'You may laugh,' he retorted, 'but I am partially German on my mother's side. Rather than Oxford or Cambridge, I should prefer to go to Heidelberg.'

'Before you are old enough to go to Heidelberg, Master Scott, we may be at war with this fiend Hitler. He has already joined forces with Italy and Japan and is talking of annexing Austria. He is your mad king.'

'No matter what happens,' he vowed, 'I will not be prevented from getting my duelling scar.'

Was he serious? Or was he just grandstanding for my reaction? I continually felt challenged. Although he was never quite disrespectful or insolent, he did not quite treat me with the respect my seniority deserved. Was he laughing at me or just being flirtatious? He would sometimes look at me in a way a young man should not look at an older woman. It was not a look to suggest that he found me desirable, but just the reverse – that I was drawn to him – and he understood. There was a danger, a mystery to him that I found fascinating. He would often touch himself in my presence in a way that was not quite proper, and then he would smile mischievously if I caught him doing so. In truth, he was so inordinately beautiful for a young man that I could not stop admiring him. When one is not comely, one cannot help admiring such a trait in others.

When lessons for the day were at last completed, Master Scott seldom accompanied Miss Angela and me on our walks. He often studied on, or if the weather was salubrious, he went riding with Roman. What dashing figures those two cut on their precious steeds, Roman's stallion the colour of his hair, and Scott's horse the colour of his. How Angela longed for a pony so that she could commence riding herself. When I telephoned Mr Maxwell and put Miss Angela on the line so that she could ask his consent, he said that he would consider it as a possibility for the summer.

Looking back now, I think that Scott began to question my background almost immediately. He would look at me curiously and ask a pointed question that might possibly catch me out if I did not take the time to think before I responded. 'Where did you learn that?' 'Have you ever been abroad?' 'You must have had many free nights in your employment to have seen so much theatre.' On several occasions he would demand: 'Have you always been in service?'

'As sure as my name is Irene Prescott.' It was not such a great lie for it was true of my former nanny.

'You don't behave like someone who has been in service.'

'How should I behave?'

'Less full of yourself. You behave as if people have been in service to you.'

'I'm sure I don't know what you are talking about, Master Scott.' Too often the imperious Flora Coombe broke through Nanny Prescott, like foam rising to the top of a glass of ale.

'I think you have many secrets,' he said one afternoon in the classroom when Miss Angela was not in our presence. His blue eyes bore down on me until I was compelled to look away, out of the window, at the tall pine tree tops that were wet with rain.

'Such as, Master Scott?'

'I don't think you have been with children at all before, and that is why I find you interesting because you treat Angela and me as if we are little adults.'

'I have always treated my charges thus.' I had become such an adept liar, I wondered if I would ever be able to escape the habit or even discern truth from fiction.

He was smiling at me. It was a devilish smile, one that not only revealed beautiful young teeth, but something hidden. 'I will tell you a secret, if you will tell me a secret in return.'

I accepted his gaze, looking deep into his unflinching eyes. There was something I very much wanted to know about, something that George Maxwell had forbidden me to ask.

'I shall tell you my secret if the secret you tell me about yourself is something I wish to know.'

'What do you wish to know?'

'Why were you expelled from school?'

His smile faded. His lips were once again tight and drawn. 'I have wondered why you haven't asked me before. I would have told you. At least some of it.'

'You can tell me now.'

'You will share a secret in return?'

'I promise.'

He hardly hesitated. He did not look away when he told me. 'A classmate at school killed himself because of me. He hanged himself from a tree. If he hadn't left a note, perhaps they wouldn't have blamed me so much and let me stay on.'

'What did the note say?'

His smile returned. 'That is two secrets.'

'I suppose it is.'

'Will you tell me two in return?'

'No.'

He considered this. 'I cannot tell you any-way because I was never shown the note. I'm sure that it was very romantic and very tragic – something poetic – as Chatterton might have written before he took his own life. Justin fancied himself a poet, although I think I wrote much truer verse. He fancied that I was his Lord Byron. I had read of the young Lord Byron and his young lover at Harrow, the Earl of Clare.'

'But why would he kill himself?'

'He mistook affection for love.'

'But...'

'You have had your secret,' he interrupted before I could question further. 'Now it is my turn. Tell me something that you would not want anyone else in this household to know.'

I hesitated. What could I tell this erudite young man that was the truth and yet would not unravel my elaborate deception. He had told me his truth. I had to tell mine in return. 'I have written a book that was pub-lished.'

He was taken aback. 'You have?'

'Yes.'

'What kind of book?'

'That is two secrets.'

'In a way I told you two.'

'It was a mystery.'

'Under your own name?'

'No.

'Would I have heard of this book?'

'Perhaps.'

'Was it successful?'

'I am working as a nanny. Does that answer your question?'

'I should like to discover the title of this book.'

I smiled an enigmatic smile, even though it wasn't nearly as mysterious as his. 'One day, perhaps, all will be revealed to you, as they say at the end of such books.'

THIRTY-THREE

An inquest was finally held in Fowey as to the nature of the death of Grace Silverton. Some of the household were summoned to testify, myself included, for it was I who had discovered the body.

I had the distinct impression that this was simply a formality and that very little would come of it. The coroner did not seem overly interested in what any of us had to say. This was not a celebrated writer of mysteries whose body had been discovered under mysterious circumstances: this was a mere nanny. I had become much more aware of our unfair British class system since I had

260

gone into service. As a witness, I was simply another servant at Tower House. My answers were taken down and I was ushered out of the witness chair as if nothing I said held much importance.

It was the handsome Roman who fascinated the female coroner the most, even if he were in service as well. When he smiled his dazzling smile, the coroner flushed noticeably and smoothed down her hair. He succeeded in presenting Grace Silverton as a somewhat unstable woman who delved into the occult and without any reason or warning suddenly departed the estate.

The witness who should have been called was George Maxwell. He should have revealed Grace's desperate phone call before she disappeared, but he chose to stay away. I even believe he had used his influence to get the inquest over with as quickly as possible.

The only piece of information that could not be explained away was the burial of Grace Silverton's valise, although Roman made it appear that it was the irrational act of a woman who either wished to vanish without a trace or take her own life and leave nothing of herself behind.

The coroner's conclusion was that Grace Silverton either fell or jumped to her death. The case was closed.

When I ventured into Inspector Hawkins' office to voice my displeasure, he appeared amused at my ire and invited me to sit down across from him. 'Matters aren't always tied up so neatly and quickly as in mystery novels,' he responded.

I was taken aback. Had he found out about me? Had he discovered my true identity?

'Why do you mention mystery novels?'

'Because obviously you read them.'

I felt somewhat relieved. 'I may.'

'Your whole approach to this case has been as some amateur sleuth, a snoop like Agatha Christie's Miss Marple.'

Could I not escape that woman, even though he had no idea I was her rival? I had no desire to discuss Dame Christie or the character she introduced in *Murder at the Vicarage*, who, by the way, was much older than I at this time of my life, and who I found rather tiresome.

'I should think you could use all the help you could get.'

'A detective never knows who or what is going to solve his case.'

'But there no longer is a case.'

'Sometimes it is better to accept an immediate solution. It is after matters are forgotten and the culprit relaxes that the truth comes out in the end.'

'And you think you have a culprit?'

'This Roman seemed awfully anxious to convince the coroner it was suicide.'

'Why couldn't the coroner see that?'

'She failed to look past the man's obvious charms. How have you managed to avoid them?'

'Let us just say that I learned the hard way to look beyond such things.'

'Will you continue to snoop about Tower House? To be my Miss Marple?'

'I'd rather be Nanny Prescott.'

Soon after the inquest, the promise of an early spring was realised in April.

'Each flower and herb on earth's dark
  breast
rose from the dreams of its wintry rest,'

to quote Percy Bysshe Shelley, as such flowers as the crocus and the daffodil ventured beyond their winter cocoons to test the climate.

Angela, however, became ill so that she was too weak and listless to take our afternoon excursion in the promising spring weather and count each new bud as it stood waiting to blossom.

The young girl began to throw up her supper and had difficulty keeping other meals down as well. I suspected some sort of intestinal flu, but the concerned doctor, a local who doted on the young miss, could find no trace. He was at a loss to explain the reason for her condition. I could not understand it either. Surely it couldn't be the food, for we were all eating the same meals, with Scott dining with us in the nursery on occasion or having his supper in the grand dining room with Roman, who still insisted on serving the nursery meals. Was he the head of the house or merely a servant? I think he no longer knew himself.

Miss Angela often stayed in bed all day long. She was usually too weak even to get up, suffering from nausea and complaining of constant stomach pain.

I must add that her stepbrother appeared genuinely concerned for her welfare. He would often sit and read to her during the entire afternoon after he had finished his lessons, settling on Alfred Lord Tennyson's 'Idylls of the King', explaining any word that Angela did not understand and writing it down so that she could learn it. Soon her young head was full of love and admiration for the Great King Arthur and his knights and their ladies.

How beautiful she looked, even in her illness, a fairy princess, her long blonde tresses pressed against her white pillows, her eyes still as blue as a summer sky.

Her prince of a stepbrother was equally handsome as he read to her in an expressive modulated voice, playing all the roles with great aplomb. He seemed to me they had both stepped out of the pages of storybooks.

I became so concerned with Miss Angela's deterioration that I telephoned Mr Maxwell and insisted he send a specialist to treat the young lady before she grew any weaker.

I won't mention the specialist's name, though assuredly he will be dead by the time this is published – for he was not a young man – but he was little better than a quack. Unable to truly diagnose what was ailing the young girl, he decided that her illness was purely emotional due to the many losses in her family. He treated her with laudanum for the pain and some sort of tranquillizer for her nerves, hardly a healthy remedy for any young girl.

I must admit, however, that Miss Angela did appear to improve temporarily so that we were able to enjoy late April walks again and to marvel at the appearance of new flowers. I could only wonder how my own garden was blooming without the touch of Robin Thibodeaux's green thumb. He was to be executed soon. It was time for me to do something to prevent it. I didn't quite know how to achieve this without exposing myself to prosecution. My long-term plan, after Robin's death, was finally to emerge in a state of amnesia, pretending not to know what I had done or where I had been. To do so now would be to jeopardise my position as governess at Tower House. How could I leave now when Angela needed me so desperately?

Still, the hangman's noose was hanging over Robin's handsome head. How he must be trembling in the fear of the approaching day of his execution. Perhaps he had suffered enough for the wrong he had done to me.

As I pondered this question, Miss Angela once again became ill. Yes, the opium mitigated her suffering, but her strength had ebbed and she became more listless than before. Suddenly Angela Winston disappeared entirely and Maisie Martin assumed control. 'Let Maisie be sick,' Miss Angela said as she assumed the different character.

Beginning to worry concerning my own health and sanity, I finally took my free Saturday and descended into Fowey. Missing my walks with Miss Angela, especially in this more stimulating month of April, I took an extended one of my own in the woods beyond the village. It scarcely mattered where I walked. My mind was on Miss Angela's illness and Robin's impending execution.

I was walking along a lane with small stone houses that looked as much a part of the woods as the surrounding trees. In the distance I saw someone emerge from the farthest dwelling. The sight of Roman was so startling to me that I hid myself behind one of the many trees so that I would not be seen. I suppose it was not the sight of Roman that was so startling, but who was standing in the doorway with him: Evelyn Lancaster, the local chemist, the woman who was remarkable, not for her beauty, but for her unsuccessful attempt to achieve it. Even at a distance I could surmise how dazzled she was by her handsome partner, that she had never achieved the attention of such a dashing gentleman before, and that she was very much in love. When she pulled him back into the shadow of the door so that they could kiss once more, I almost envied her – but just for an instant. No more May-December romance for me. December may be a lonely month, but I now prefer it.

Such a long and passionate kiss! When it was over she quickly closed her door and Roman was on his way, walking so closely to where I was hiding that I feared to breathe, but passing by without a notion that I had observed him.

I knew Roman well enough. I could sense the extreme vanity of the man to know that a homely woman such as Evelyn Lancaster could be of no real interest to him. It would take great beauty or great wealth to entice the likes of such as he. If he simply needed a woman for the pleasures of the flesh, there would be many beautiful women available to him.

I assumed that there was something that he needed from a woman as plain as Evelyn Lancaster, as Robin had needed something from me. If Roman needed poison, who else but a chemist to provide it? Evelyn Lancaster was a chemist – but a woman first; even more susceptible to the charms of a Roman than the average girl of some beauty. Wasn't she new to the town, probably lonely and even more vulnerable than if she had remained home in Plymouth?

The first substance that came to my mind was arsenic. It could be utilised in extremely small doses to kill an infection, but larger amounts could be deadly. Or was he utilising something more sophisticated and venomous? In one of my stories I had featured 'L.S.', which was short for liquid strychnine, used in very small doses to treat illness, but with an ability to kill if given in a larger quantity. Or was Miss Lancaster providing strychnine hydrochloride, which in a generous dose could prove to be equally deadly? If my research had been correct, all these substances were difficult to detect once they entered the digestive system, especially if ingested in minute doses: then it was attrition that finally killed the victim.

Is this what was making the darling Miss Angela so ill? Was he slowly poisoning her until one day she simply weakened and died? Would a medical examiner be able to detect these small traces of poison? And what was his motive in bringing on the dear girl's demise? That I would have to ascertain. I doubt that Evelyn Lancaster would come forward that she had unwittingly provided the poison, for she would lose her licence to practise. However, I suspect that Roman could make almost anybody do anything he desired. Fortunately I was not put to the test.

If Miss Angela died, would her fortune go to Scott, her stepbrother? If so, how would that benefit Roman?

Was I being overly imaginative? Perhaps Miss Angela's illness was in her mind. Was I attempting to create a mystery where none existed?

I was determined to find out.

THIRTY-FOUR

Immediately on my return to Tower House, I telephoned the office of George Maxwell. I would demand his presence in Cornwall at once. How my heart sank when his secretary informed me that Mr Maxwell had departed on urgent business to America only days before! He had flown the entire distance to New York, had concluded his affairs, and had departed on the Queen Elizabeth for a return voyage that very morning. For five days I would not be able to speak to him!

'I wonder if I might ask you something, Miss Simpson?' She was a spinster who appeared to love her position and her employer. She had been extremely courteous to me during our first meeting and had been helpful over the telephone.

'What is that, Miss Prescott?'

'I was wondering ... I suppose this is none of my business ... but Miss Angela ... because she has been so ill ... was wondering as well ... and I said that I would ask Mr Maxwell for her ... or put her on the line to speak with him...' What was another lie more or less?

'What was that?'

'If, God forbid – I hesitate to even voice it – but if Miss Angela did not recover ... would her fortune revert to some special charity or foundation her father set up in America?'

'Certainly not.' She stopped herself. 'I really should not be discussing this.'

'But it would put the child's mind at ease to know.'

She hesitated until finally speaking. 'Mr Maxwell had me retype the will recently. Will this just be between us? I don't think Mr Maxwell would approve if I revealed anything.'

'I will swear Miss Angela to secrecy as well.'

First she cleared her throat, then: 'The will

clearly states that in the case of Mr and Mrs Pemberton's deaths and Miss Angela as well – if they had been in a plane accident, for instance – the bulk of the considerable estate would go to Scott Pemberton her stepbrother. He would be the beneficiary.'

I was silent for a moment. The breath actually left my body. 'I see,' I said finally. 'I am sure that will set Miss Angela's mind at ease. Master Scott has been so considerate and helpful to her through her illness.'

'But I thought she was improving. I doubt that Mr Maxwell would have departed if he believed...'

'Well, she was, but ... at least the medication is making her more comfortable.'

'Should I send a telegram to Mr Maxwell at sea?'

'No, I don't think that is necessary. If there is a change we certainly should, but...'

'He will be back shortly.'

'Thank you, Miss Simpson.'

I rang off. What could I possibly put in a telegram? That I suspect that the butler is poisoning the heiress? For what reason? I doubt that Roman was even mentioned in the will.

I should have gone to the police then, but I was behaving like that silly Miss Marple. There was still more to discover.

Whether my suspicions were correct or false

concerning the poisoning of Miss Angela's food, I was determined that Roman would have nothing more to do with the serving of it.

I announced that for the time being, Miss Angela would be dining in the kitchen. My explanation was that her illness had kept her confined to the nursery entirely too long. At least her meals could provide a change of venue. She could observe the dinner being prepared which should be of interest to her and revive her flagging spirits. In fact, it did.

What could Roman do but agree, although he soon suggested that Miss Angela and I join him and Master Scott in the large dining room. 'Perhaps later,' I replied, 'when Miss Angela feels stronger.'

For the next few evenings I watched carefully as every morsel of Miss Angela's dinner was served directly from the stove to our kitchen table. In truth we enjoyed the company of Cook, the Irish girls, and Danny, the stable boy.

The most amazing result (but not to me) was that Miss Angela made a dramatic improvement after only one night of dinner in the kitchen. The next day she was almost her old self once again. Maisie was moved back to America and Angela once again spoke in her own voice. Her breakfast and lunch were served as usual in the nursery by Deidre, so I had little fear that the food was tainted.

On the fourth day Miss Angela actually desired an afternoon walk. I was beside myself with happiness that she was once again the healthy little girl to whom I had first been introduced.

Miss Angela's dramatic return to rosy health had confirmed all my suspicions. It was only one more day before George Maxwell would return from America. Still, there was no motive for Roman's crime. I simply could not believe that since Master Scott would gain from Miss Angela's death, it was he who had somehow tampered with her meals. It was always Roman who served them. How could Scott obtain the poison on his own? Strychnine is not something that can be readily purchased. Perhaps the gardener had a supply to kill rodents in the garden. I quickly discovered that he had not.

Inspector Hawkins was correct. I was becoming the Miss Marple of the estate, ferreting out information in an attempt not merely to solve a case, but to prevent the murder of a darling little girl. I considered going to the inspector, but I had no definite proof. As he had stated in his office, there was not sufficient evidence to convict Roman of Grace Silverton's murder. I had no tangible proof that Roman was poisoning my charge. The inspector probably would simply have been amused by my suggestion.

I considered going through Roman's belongings in search of the strychnine. I could visualise the tiny bottle as I described it in *The Purloined Poison*, blue glass containing grains of white crystalline powder and labelled 'Strychnine Hydrochloride. POISON.' I imagined Evelyn Lancaster slipping the very same bottle into Roman's pockets after they had made love. I wonder what he told her he needed it for? Did she, besotted as she was with him, even care?

Perhaps I would slip into his private quarters if the opportunity presented itself. Roman had appropriated one of the master suites on the second floor for his own use. I was informed by Bridget that he kept it locked at all times. She was only allowed inside to clean when he could supervise her. How could I obtain the key?

There was certainly more to being a governess than giving lessons. I must admit that I was both thrilled and daunted by what was confronting me. Life is truly more interesting than my fiction.

THIRTY-FIVE

Without my realising it, the 'darling buds of May' had blossomed. We traipsed through the garden like painters collecting colours for a summer palette. We congratulated Angus McPhearson, the gardener and his son, Robert, on the beauty of the late spring blossoms. We promised to return later with baskets to collect the flowers.

Sandy was with us as well. I think the dog had despaired of his beloved Angela ever coming out for a walk again. His black and white tail wagged incessantly as the indication of his joy.

The most beautiful blossom in the entire garden was Miss Angela herself. The colour had returned to her cheeks so that they were almost as pink as the small primroses running along a wall of the garden. Her long blonde tresses, that fell like golden honey down her back, rivalled the yellow chrysanthemums blooming in all their glory. Her eyes were a deeper hue than a bed of bluebells that were slowly invading a corner of the garden. For a moment it seemed that everything was looking up. How could it not on such a glorious sunny day as that?

'Can we walk through the woods?' Miss Angela questioned. 'Maybe we will find some good mushrooms for Cook.'

I was adept at separating the bad from the good fungi, but I doubted that we would discover any on such a glorious day. 'We usually find them after a rain, Miss Angela. I doubt if any have surfaced this time of year, but we shall try. Perhaps we shall find one or two.'

As we moved around to the front of Tower House and reached the stables, we saw Roman and Master Scott, taking advantage of the beautiful weather as well, riding off. Miss Angela called out but they did not respond. I was glad, because I did not wish to encounter them.

At first we walked along the cliff to feel the sea breeze and fill our lungs with sea air. I quoted a line from Ralph Waldo Emerson which seemed appropriate for the day.

'In May, when sea winds pierced our
    solitudes,
I found the fresh Rhodora in the woods.'

'Shall we find any today?' Miss Angela asked curiously.

'I fear it grows only in America where Ralph Waldo Emerson lived. He was the poet who wrote that.'

'What does Rhodora look like?'

'I believe it is a lavender-coloured flower.'

'I should like to see that. Maybe one day when I go home.'

I was taken aback. She had never spoken of home before. 'Do you still consider America your home, Miss Angela? Would you like to go home to America?'

'I think I would. I was never ever sick back home. Would you come with me?'

'We shall see.' I took her hand and we entered the woods.

I think it was George Meredith in his *The Woods of Westermain*, who warned 'Enter these enchanted woods, you who dare.'

We felt little trepidation as we braved the sheltering myriad of trees that prevented the May sun from shining through and cast fairy shadows about the velvety green turf. We did not worry because we had the faithful Sandy with us as protector. We found neither mushroom nor rose-coloured flower, but the search was delicious nevertheless. There is always something new to see in the woods.

It was when we emerged from the dense thicket and began our return to the manor house, that I witnessed something that has been burned forever, a lasting fire, in my mind.

We had reached the stables as the afternoon light had waned to that pristine stillness when day ceases to reign and night is waiting to creep like a long shadow about the land.

Miss Angela desired to pet the horses. I acquiesced. I knew that this was Danny the stableboy's free afternoon and evening to visit his family in St. Austell. All the horses were in their stalls. Roman and Master Scott must have returned from their ride. They had taken off the bridles and saddles and the stallions were munching on hay and nibbling oats.

When Miss Angela had enough of petting the beasts, we exited the stable and walked alongside it in the direction of the great house. There was a window in the tack room where Danny slept. As we were about to pass, I heard a strange sound, almost a moaning. Was somebody in pain? I could not be sure. I must have been more curious than perplexed. As is my wont, I approached the window and peered inside. What I observed shocks me to this very day.

How can I describe what I witnessed without disgusting my readers? A writer wants the reader to see what she saw, but in this instance, dear reader, you must fill in the necessary blanks yourself.

Suffice it to say that both Roman and Scott were naked and making love in much the same manner that a man and a woman do, emitting the same sounds of ferocious passion I heard between Robin Thibodeaux and Mary Beth Hewitt.

Although Miss Angela could not see into the window, she heard her stepbrother moaning. 'Is something wrong with Scott?' she questioned.

At that moment, Roman turned his head on the pillow to glance at the window. I quickly pulled my head away, but I could not be sure if he detected me or not.

'There is nothing wrong with Master Scott,' I whispered, pulling her quickly away. 'Roman and your brother are shadow-boxing in Danny's room. Master Scott is getting the worst of it.'

'Can I see?'

'No, dear. They have their shirts off as men do when they play at boxing, and it wouldn't be proper for you to see them that way. In fact we must say nothing and pretend that we have not seen them at all.'

'A secret?'

'Yes.'

'I love secrets.'

Everything was now clear to me. I understood now why the former nanny, Grace Silverton, had printed the word DE-PRAVED and left it beneath the dresser blotter. She had observed what I had seen. Had she caught Roman and Scott in the barn as I had? Was she walking in the woods and discovered them making love while their horses waited nearby nibbling on the grass? Or had she barged unexpectedly into Scott's bedroom and discovered them there?

This was what she wished to relate to George Maxwell. This was what she could not discuss over the telephone. This was why Roman, and perhaps Scott, would not let her go. She had been murdered for her silence. Was I now in the same danger?

Roman would indeed benefit from Miss Angela's death if her fortune was passed onto her stepbrother. Lovers, especially when they are young such as Scott, will do anything for their intended. I wondered if Roman even cared for the boy. Was he simply seducing the young man for his own financial gain? Was Scott under his spell as was the chemist, Evelyn Lancaster?

When had this unnatural perversion begun between servant and young master? The boy was not quite sixteen. Oscar Wilde was cast into Reading Gaol for much less. I would see that Roman went to the same prison.

If only George Maxwell were back from America.

I could wait no longer.

In the morning I would bring Miss Angela into Fowey with me. We would throw ourselves upon the protection of the local police.

THIRTY-SIX

It was dangerous to stay at Tower House for even one more night. I could tell from the way that Roman looked at me when he strode into the kitchen that he had caught a brief glimpse of my face in the stable window. He did not look ashamed nor fearful nor even threatening. It was a knowing look as if his green eyes were telling me that we understood each other now; as if we shared sexual knowledge. There was a smirk on his sensuous lips, almost a suggestion that there was passion for me as well, if I desired it. I could not hold his glance any longer. I had to look away. When he strode out of the kitchen he did not look back. Nothing had been said. But he knew that I knew that war had been declared.

Miss Angela and I were sitting at the kitchen table when he had entered. The young girl's appetite had returned and she was enjoying the meal of mutton and potatoes and carrots, but I could scarcely touch a bite.

When Cook sat down with us, she brought out the newspaper. I, who had previously been so anxious to devour the news, especially of the trial for my murder, had hardly given it a thought. 'They're going to hang the blackguard tomorrow,' she said.

'Who?' I questioned distractedly.

'The Frenchy bloke that done in that mystery writer.'

Now she had my attention. 'Robin Thibodeaux?'

'That's the one.'

'But ... I thought that wasn't to be until September.'

'He must have confessed or something.'

I buried my nose in the newspaper. There was the familiar picture of my second husband's handsome face. To think that in the morning the life would be choked out of his powerful neck.

I knew immediately that I could not go through with it. His execution had to be stopped. I could delay no longer!

I read the newspaper carefully to determine why the execution had been advanced. It was at the request of the prisoner! I could well imagine that the free Louisiana bayou spirit could not tolerate the confines of an English prison cell. Even if Robin had a window with bars what could he see but the perpetual gloom and rain of a London winter? My Robin was wilting like one of his beloved flowers without sunshine. He would rather die than waste away, becoming a grey shadow of what he once was.

I had had my revenge. It no longer mattered as much that my second husband had violated the marriage vow. Robin Thibodeaux had suffered enough. I had already taken one life in my revenge – Mary Beth Hewitt's – even though that had not been my intention.

After I had got Miss Angela to bed, I would telephone the Prime Minister. I had met Arthur Neville Chamberlain. He had been my dinner partner at an intimate soirée. He would recognise my voice. The noose would be put away. But what would I say after I announced that I was still very much alive? I would be saving Robin Thibodeaux's tawny skin but I had to save mine as well. Would my amnesia be believable? And why had I waited until the last minute as if my life was some suspense film when a phone call arrives to save a prisoner before the stroke of midnight? I was being ridiculously dramatic.

I had not seen Scott at all that evening. I assumed that he had dined with Roman in the dining room. He made no appearance in the nursery. Soon Deidre had Miss Angela ready for bed. The child slipped beneath the covers and placed her weary head against the pillow. She wanted a story. I knew that she would soon be fast asleep. 'This has been a long day for you, Miss Angela.'

'Scott hasn't finished reading *Kidnapped*.

Can you pick up where he left off?' How could I concentrate on the pages of Robert Louis Stevenson when our lives were in danger? Bridget tiptoed out of the child's room. I began to read. I scarcely knew what.

Miss Angela was beginning to nod off. Roman barged unannounced into the room. He was holding a mug. Steam was coming from the top.

'What is this?' I said, perturbed and frightened by his intrusion.

'A treat for Miss Angela,' he replied, approaching the bed.

'What kind of treat?'

'I was pleased to see that Miss Angela had such a long outing today after being so ill. I thought a nice warm glass of milk with Horlicks would help her sleep. I am sure it will bring her the sweetest of dreams.'

'I love Horlicks,' Angela replied. 'We never had that in America.'

Roman approached the bed. 'Now drink up, Miss Angela, before it gets cold.'

'But she has already brushed her teeth,' I intervened.

'A little warm milk with powder won't hurt.'

As he bent low over the bed to give Angela the cup, I took it from his hands. 'Perhaps I should have a sip first. It may be too hot. I wouldn't want it to burn Miss Angela's tongue.'

'By all means,' he said, not happy with the fact, but artfully disguising his displeasure.

I put the cup to my lips. I had no intention of even taking one sip, but he suddenly raised the cup higher so that inadvertently a healthy portion of the warm liquid poured down my throat.

'Is it really too hot?' Miss Angela asked.

I managed to catch my breath. Did I detect a trace of arsenic or strychnine? How could I tell when I had never digested them before? The concoction tasted sweet – too sweet.

'No, Miss Angela, it is not too hot, but...' I purposely dropped the cup so that the contents spilled onto the floor.

Miss Angela was obviously disappointed. 'Oh, Nanny, look what you've done!'

'Clumsy of me.'

Roman's green eyes bore into mine. They were the colour of jade and I could not look away from them. 'Perhaps I should fetch some more,' he suggested.

'No! Miss Angela must get her sleep. We have been learning that sugar is not good for the teeth and that drink was entirely too sweet.' (I am sure that it was my craving for sweets as a young lady that destroyed my own). 'If Miss Angela desires something to drink, I will fetch it from the kitchen myself. Right now I must insist that she goes to sleep. She has not been well, as you know. I shall be sitting up with her all evening in case she needs anything,' I threatened.

'As you say,' he said, but he was not pleased. He simply stared at me. I almost withered under the power of his gaze. He stooped to retrieve the cup. I wanted to keep it as evidence, but I did not protest when he took it and left the chamber.

I hurried into Miss Angela's bathroom and stuck my finger down my throat in hopes of throwing up the amount of liquid poison I was sure that I ingested, but unfortunately nothing came up. I had eaten almost no supper and very little breakfast or lunch. If I had indeed ingested poison, it was finding a relatively empty stomach upon which to work its evil. I removed an eye dropper from the medicine chest.

I returned to Miss Angela's bedchamber and sucked up a portion of the white liquid I had spilled onto the floor. This I hid away in one of Angela's drawers then cleaned away the remainder of the mess.

I stepped to Miss Angela's bedside and pulled the white wicker rocker closer to her bed. She opened her eyes for a moment, murmured 'Good night, Nanny,' and was off to sleep.

Only a night-light burned across the nursery. I hurried down to the maid quarters beyond the kitchen to ask Deidre to sit by Miss Angela's bed until I returned. 'If she happens to wake up and desires water or anything to drink, make sure that you are the only one to give it to her.'

'Yes, Nanny,' Deidre replied, eyeing me curiously. 'And where will you be?'

'I have to make an important telephone call.'

Deidre appeared concerned. 'Is everything all right, Nanny?'

The words would no longer come. A deadening trance had taken over my powers of speech and was descending like an insidious potion throughout my body. Suddenly it reached my intestines. I doubled over in unbearable pain. I sank to the floor. Deidre cried in surprise. That is all I remember.

THIRTY-SEVEN

When my eyes fluttered open it was dark. I didn't know who or where I was. I felt strangely, as if I had died momentarily. Now I was coming back to life. Was I once again home in my own bed at my beloved Dovecote Cottage? For a fleeting moment I believed this to be true. I hoped that Robin Thibodeaux and Roman and all the rest of it had just been a nightmare. Finally, when I reached over and turned on the bedside lamp, I saw that I wasn't safely home at all, but in my bedroom at Tower House.

I focused my bleary eyes on the bedside clock. It read 8:30. Since it was dark outside it had to be the following evening, if not even days later for I remember putting Miss Angela to bed at nine! I had no idea how long I had been in bed. Was Miss Angela even still alive? Had I failed her in her most urgent hour of need?

I struggled to sit up and swing my weak knees so that they could dangle from the bed. As I attempted to stand on my own two feet, everything in the room began to swim in circles. I doubted if my legs would support my weight when Deidre came into the room carrying a dinner tray and switched on the light. 'Oh, you mustn't get up!' she exclaimed. 'You've been that sick.'

'What is wrong with me?'

'The doctor said it was food poisoning.'

'The doctor was here?'

'Yes, Nanny, have you forgotten? You collapsed on the kitchen floor. We telephoned him immediately. He's beginning to think something's the matter with the water here. First Miss Angela and now you.'

My heart almost stopped. 'Was Miss Angela sick again?'

'Yes, and after the nice lunch that Mr Roman served her in the nursery himself. She threw all of it up and wouldn't touch a bite of the dinner he brought her. She keeps asking for you.'

'I must go to her.' I attempted to stand up once more, but sank back onto the bed.

'You'll be going nowhere, Nanny, until you have something to eat. You've had nothing in your stomach for twenty-four hours and Cook has made you a special chicken broth and some toast and tea.'

I was suddenly hungry. 'This came directly to me from the cook?'

'She just now served it up. She sent up the newspaper too, because you enjoy it so, and Mr Roman is finished with it.'

Deidre served me in bed. I took a spoonful of soup. It made me feel better already. I then unfolded the paper. It was on the first page of the London *Times:*

THIBODEAUX HANGS

It was more than I could bear. Why hadn't I saved him sooner instead of waiting for some overly dramatic last minute phone call as if I was Sylvia Sidney saving Henry Fonda from the electric chair in that American film?

Somehow I had to put the thought of Robin's death out of my head. I knew tremendous guilt would haunt me for the remainder of my days. There were now two dead because my precious vanity had been wounded! What started out in my head as the planning of one of my intricate mystery plots had ended in double tragedy. Nevertheless, I had to concentrate on what was transpiring at Tower House. A young girl's life was in danger. It was up to me to save her!

I did feel better after the nourishing soup Cook had provided for me. I felt stronger immediately. As soon as Deidre removed the tray and left me alone to rest, I managed to stand on my own two feet and move unsteadily about the room, growing more confident with each step, so that I was able to dress and prepare for my departure from the house.

Deidre had fallen asleep beside Miss Angela's bedside. I shook her awake and said that I would sit up with Angela. She looked at me curiously. 'And here you are fully dressed as if you're going somewhere.'

It was time for another lie. What did one more matter in the scheme of things? 'I was just out for a breath of fresh air. After being in bed for an entire day, I simply had to go outside.'

'And are you feeling that much better, Nanny?'

'Much.'

'Here I'm not much good if I'm falling asleep myself, but you fetch one of us if you start nodding off.'

'I promise.' I indicated the beautiful sleeping child. 'How is Miss Angela faring?'

'Sleeping soundly, but the poor sick

creature wouldn't take a bite of supper. Mr Roman was that upset with her. He is very concerned.'

'I hope tomorrow she will be better.'

'We all hope so.'

Deidre made a point of tiptoeing quietly out of the room. As soon as I was certain she had descended the back staircase, I gently awakened the sleeping child. Miss Angela blinked her blue eyes. She appeared to be pleased at the sight of me. 'Are you not sick anymore, Nanny?'

'I feel fine,' I lied. 'And what about you?'

'I had a bad tummy again. I'm so sick of having a bad tummy. If I feel like this tomorrow, Maisie Martin will have to be sick instead of me.'

'Miss Angela, I promise you are never going to be sick like this again.' I pulled back her covers. 'Now I am going to get you out of bed and all dressed, because we are going on an adventure.'

Her eyes widened. 'An adventure? What kind of adventure?'

'We are going on a secret midnight mission to London.'

'As if we were secret spies?'

'Exactly as if we were spies. We mustn't let anybody see or hear us depart. We must be very quiet – like mice.'

I dressed Miss Angela as warmly as possible and retrieved my own detested lamb's-wool coat from my wardrobe and before we departed, I slipped the tell-tale glass dropper I had hidden in Angela's drawer into my purse. We moved silently down the great middle stairway, the twisting remnant of the original medieval tower. I took her small hand and led the way because barely any light fell on the circular stairway. For a fleeting instant I began to fall. Fortunately I held tightly to the railing cord to steady myself.

Soon we were on the ground floor. How I prayed that everyone had gone to bed, that our flight would not be detected until morning. All the great rooms were dark. They resembled huge caverns from which monsters and trolls could easily leap forth and waylay you. I wanted nothing more than to leave that house once and for all and never return.

The great door opened with a loud creaking. Had anyone in the household heard it moan on its hinges? Sandy, the sheepdog, was waiting for us, his tail wagging, panting his greeting. How did the dog know that we would be there? Were we his lost sheep that he was sent to protect and guard? I closed the massive wood and iron door without shutting it all the way, for surely it would bang as it was wont to do and wake the entire household.

We were outside! The air was crisp and

filled our lungs with freedom! The sky was clear. There was a panoply of stars that twinkled with celestial music. There was a sliver of moon, a fingernail of silver that lit our way through the woods.

We dared not take the road that led to the gatehouse. If somebody was searching for us we would be found immediately. How dark the woods seemed. Every tree became a black umbrella to blot out the stars and moon. We could scarcely see our hands in front of our face. How stupid of me not to bring a torch. No heroine of mine would have been so shortsighted. At least Sandy was with us. He knew the way. They say that dogs can see in the dark. He strode in front of Miss Angela and we followed as best we could. It was such a great distance to the gate. As soon as we reached it, I would waken Davis and demand that he drive us to town. His old touring car was always parked in the garage beside his cottage. He would have to take us.

. Was somebody following? I heard nothing. Still, the dog would stop suddenly, look back and growl softly, then continue along. Dogs not only see in the dark, their hearing is equally acute. Had Sandy detected soft footsteps somewhere behind? Could he see a figure darting from tree to tree, following us stealthily, a vampire without wings about to swoop and devour us?

We emerged from the woods near where Grace Silverton had either fallen or been pushed off the cliff. Why had the dog led us here? Was it to bring us out of the dense woods so that we could get our bearings underneath the blinking stars?

I kept Miss Angela a safe distance from the cliff's edge. Even though it was a calm night, the sea still sounded ferocious, beating incessantly against the rocks of Cornwall. I wanted to hurry quickly – to get as far away from the treacherous area as possible.

Roman suddenly appeared before us. He was darkness personified, his clothes and his hair. Only the whiteness of his teeth shone in the light of the slim moon.

'And where are you taking Miss Angela, Nanny, at this time of night?' He spoke as if it was a simple question, without hostility or rancour.

'As far away from you as possible.'

'Miss Angela belongs at Tower House with her brother.'

'So you can pervert her as you have that innocent boy?' I didn't want to say these things in front of Angela, but I couldn't help myself.

'Miss Angela belongs with us,' he repeated, advancing, 'but you are dispensable.'

'Another nanny gone missing? Her body found in the sea?' I thought quickly as we all do under such extreme situations. If he was able to dispense with me and say that I disappeared as well, how quickly would the authorities discover that I had assumed the name of a woman, a nanny, who was already dead? Would anyone know who I really was? In truth, Flora Coombe would truly be murdered after all. Could Roman get away with murder once again? If he disposed of Miss Angela that very evening he could say that I – a crazy woman who had assumed another's identity – had poisoned the little girl and then taken my own life.

'Let us pass!' I demanded.

When he advanced upon us, the dog would not allow him near. I had never heard Sandy growl so ferociously. Miss Angela stood transfixed, not knowing what to say or do. Roman retrieved a large branch. He began to wave it threateningly over the dog who would still not let the man approach.

Finally the dog bit into the stick and held it firmly within his powerful jaws. As Roman struggled to free the wood from the dog's mouth, I squeezed Angela's hand and attempted to scurry around Roman and flee in the direction of the gate house. Unfortunately this forced us to be on the side of the cliff. When Roman saw that we were running away from him, he gave up the stick and started after us. Sandy dropped the stick as well. Roman was almost upon us when the sheepdog gained momentum, leaped into the air, bit into Roman's neck and sent them both hurtling over the edge of the cliff!

Angela screamed the dog's name. I peered below into the darkness. For a moment I saw nothing. Then the figure of Roman became visible. He had only fallen halfway. He was gathering his breath and wits about him. He was beginning to crawl up to where we were! The dog was nowhere in sight.

I pulled Miss Angela's arm and sped back into the woods. I had no idea I could run so fast, although I was not as old as I had made myself look. Poor little Angela could hardly keep pace.

Soon we were at the caretaker's cottage. I banged desperately against the door. Old Davis stumbled out of his bedroom and turned on a light. 'What...? What are you...?'

'You must drive us into Fowey immediately!'

'What–'

'It's Miss Angela. She's sick. We have to get her to the doctor immediately!' I knew that this would work on him better than anything else I could say. We had often stopped by his cottage on our walks. He had doted on Miss Angela.

'I'll just get some clothes on.'

'No you won't!' I thundered. 'There is not a moment to lose! Get your keys and come immediately to the car.'

When would I breathe freely? When we arrived in Fowey or London? At least we were being driven away from Tower House; not nearly fast enough! Would Roman reach his car and follow us? Davis drove so slowly I was tempted to shove my own foot against the pedal. 'Faster!' I demanded. 'Faster!'

'This ol' buggy doesn't go that fast!'

We were almost in Fowey. Thank God it was a short distance from St. Claire. As we neared the harbour I made what appeared to Davis to be a curious demand. I had thought of going to the police, to Inspector Hawkins, but at that hour, in a sleepy seacoast village such as Fowey, the station would be closed. 'Davis, do you know where Toby the cab driver lives?'

'Toby Jenkins? I know the cottage very well. I dined there once that many years ago.'

'Take us there.'

'I thought that miss needed a doctor.'

'She's feeling better now, aren't you, Miss Angela?' She looked up at me unsurely. I nodded my head for her.

Toby's taxi was parked in front of a darkened house. I bid Davis goodbye and banged on the cottage door. Toby and his wife answered together. She looked confused. He recognised me immediately. 'Is it Nanny Prescott and the little princess?'

'Toby, I'm about to pay you the biggest fare you've ever earned.'

'And where would that be to?'

'To London. Now. Immediately. As fast as you can carry us.'

He did not appear pleased. 'All the way to London?'

'I'll double your fare!' I added as an inducement. Fortunately I had not opened a bank account in Fowey. I simply cashed my monthly cheque and stuffed the money in my purse. My handbag was bulging with pounds.

'What are you waiting for?' his wife demanded. 'As if we didn't need the money!'

We were on our way: from Plymouth to Exeter to Salisbury; just road posts in the night, but signs that we had left Cornwall far behind. When we reached Basingstoke, dawn was breaking – a new day – a new beginning for Miss Angela – and for me, a journey to my past.

THIRTY-EIGHT

Somewhere south of London we checked into a small hotel.

Miss Angela and I rested and refreshed ourselves and had a healthy breakfast served in our room. After our ordeal it seemed neither of us had ever been so hungry.

'Are we still spies?' Angela questioned, munching a piece of fried bread. 'You haven't told me why Roman came after us like that.'

'Miss Angela, dear,' I replied, choosing my words carefully. 'I think I should wait until we meet Mr Maxwell. He will decide what to tell you.'

'Momma said I could always trust Mr Maxwell and that I should go to him if anything was ever wrong, even though he scares me.'

'It appears that now is a very good time.'

Mr George Maxwell had arrived home in England on my forgotten day when I lay ill in bed with little or no memory of what had happened to me. He had taken the train from Southampton to London, spent a restful night, and had returned to his office only minutes before Miss Angela and I appeared in his waiting room. Miss Simpson was astonished to see us. 'I told Mr Maxwell that you had telephoned the minute he arrived in his office. I was attempting to get you on the telephone.'

'We are here instead.'

'Is there something very wrong?'

'If you could tell Mr Maxwell that we are here. It is most important that I speak with him.'

Miss Simpson rang into the inner office.

'Mr Maxwell, we do not have to telephone Nanny Prescott. She is here in your office with Miss Angela.'

'What?!' His surprise leapt through the receiver. In a moment his door was flung open and he was standing before us. 'What is this? What brings you here?'

'A taxi,' Miss Angela responded as Mr Maxwell took her hand. 'All the way from Cornwall. I slept most of the way.' He looked at me for some sort of explanation. 'We pretended we were spies.'

'Mr Maxwell, I think perhaps I had better speak with you alone.'

'I think perhaps you'd better.' He held his office door open for me. 'Miss Simpson, perhaps Miss Angela would like a cup of hot tea.'

'I won't be long, darling,' I assured Angela and disappeared into George Maxwell's spacious office.

A good novelist does not trouble her reader with information that he has already grasped. What I related to George Maxwell was exactly what I have already described on these pages: what transpired during my sojourn at Tower House, to the disturbing scene I observed through the window in the stable bedroom.

Mr Maxwell appeared to be at a loss for words. I produced the eye dropper filled with poisoned milk. 'I suggest that you have

300

this analysed immediately. There is a very good lab for such analysis here in London.' I had used it in my stories and named it.

'Now how would you know that?' he questioned, eyeing me curiously.

'I am an avid reader of Agatha Christie,' I replied quickly. How I hated to credit my rival as a cover for my own expertise in crime!

'The news you bring is very disturbing.'

'I suggest that you telephone Detective Inspector Bertram Hawkins in Fowey and have Roman detained immediately. He should not only be charged with murder but attempted poisoning as well, and the corruption of a minor, the most unforgivable of sins.'

He hesitated. 'The attendant publicity. The boy's reputation.'

'You can't delay, Mr Maxwell. Roman must know that he is in serious trouble. I doubt that he will simply wait to be arrested.'

He reluctantly reached for the telephone. 'Miss Simpson, would you connect me with Detective Inspector Bertram Hawkins of the Fowey Police.'

As I suspected, Roman had fled. He had disappeared as did Master Scott with him. They had packed some of their belongings and vanished: across the English Channel to France, I assumed. They were nowhere to be found in England.

Mr Maxwell attempted to keep the information out of the newspapers. They got wind of it nevertheless. Fortunately for Scott, the story was presented as an abduction – or kidnapping. There was no mention of a sexual relationship between the man and the boy. Roman was also charged with the murder of Grace Silverton and the attempted poisoning of Miss Angela Winston.

Before the story appeared, I had already departed, but not before the toxicology report revealed that the Horlicks had been laced with liquid strychnine. I suppose I am lucky that I am still alive to relate this story at all.

Much to the dismay of Miss Angela, the body of the loyal sheepdog, Sandy, was never discovered. It was almost as if the dog never really existed.

Mr George Maxwell's short trip to America had proven a fortuitous one. He had met with the American conservator of Miss Angela's enormous estate. Her mother's cousin had contacted the attorney, feeling that since she was Angela's nearest relative, perhaps she should raise the child as her own. Fearing that this was just an attempt to secure her fortune, Mr Maxwell and the American attorney had flown to Wisconsin to visit this relative's farm. To their pleasant surprise, they discovered a most beautiful and prosperous dairy on the outskirts of Appleton. It was a small town with small town values, a suitable place in America to bring up a girl who was American after all.

Another plus was the fact that the American cousins, the Andersons, already had five children of their own, including a daughter Angela's age, with whom she would share a bedroom. A far cry from Tower House! There would be no motive for doing away with young Angela in this setting. After what had transpired in England, and the disappearance of Scott Pemberton, with the consent of a judge, the will was changed so that if Miss Angela died before she reached twenty-one, her fortune would be turned over to her late father's charitable foundation. The Andersons, in fact, would not accept one penny for Angela's room and board at their farm. 'One day, when she is older, and if she wants to go to one of those fancy European schools, she can pay for that out of her own pocket.'

There would be no use or room for a nanny on this Wisconsin dairy farm. Angela and I were in tears when I saw her off at Southampton docks. She was sailing on the Queen Mary that soon, during the Second World War, would no longer ferry passengers but carry troops to fight for their country.

'Will I ever see you again, Nanny?' the

adorable girl asked plaintively as she squeezed my hand tightly because she did not wish to let go. George Maxwell was accompanying her. He was standing patiently nearby.

I didn't want to lie again. I had told too many falsehoods already. My former husband and his mistress were dead because of it. I squeezed her hand as tightly as she squeezed mine. 'You know the story we read by P.L. Travers about Mary Poppins?'

'Yes.'

'Remember how Mary Poppins magically arrives when some little girl is in need, and then when things are better she simply vanishes?'

'Yes.'

'You must think of me like that, Miss Angela. You must think that Nanny Irene Prescott was put on this earth to take care of you, to protect darling Angela Winston, and now that my job is completed, task done, I will disappear and arrive in some other place where I am needed as well.'

'Won't I need you in America?'

'I don't think so, darling. You will have your new family and all your cousins. You will have a new momma and poppa.'

'Couldn't you come visit?'

'I will come if I am needed.'

'I need you now.'

'Miss Angela, Sandy was there when you

304

needed him, too. They say at Tower House that he just appeared one day out of nowhere. Then, after he protected you, after he saved you from Roman, who wanted to hurt you, he had to go away to save somebody else. I am just like Sandy.'

'Do you think that Sandy will come back one day?'

'If he is needed. He was a guardian angel dog. They come when you need them.'

We hugged each other ever so tightly. Soon they would raise the gangplank. Mr Maxwell had to get the child aboard.

Miss Angela stood on the deck and waved and waved until the Queen Mary was out to sea, the great ship growing smaller and smaller, until finally, when I tore myself away, it appeared no bigger than a ferry boat far out in the Atlantic Ocean.

Miss Angela Winston was the closest I ever came to having a daughter. There is still a void in my heart as I write of her today. I never saw her again or corresponded. In my mind she is still the little girl who needed me during a very desperate period in both our lives.

THIRTY-NINE

It was not safe to remain in London. Even in my disguise, I feared that I might come across someone who would recognise me. I must say that I had become somewhat used to my elderly appearance. There is something to be said for not primping for hours in front of a mirror. I needed a new wig and a new outfit and a vast assortment of make-up. Fearing that it would be too dangerous to shop in London, I booked the train to Reading and completed my shopping there. I wasn't completely pleased with my new wig, but it was more flattering then the grey. It wasn't a blatant red but somewhat in keeping with my former hair colour. The skirt and jacket I purchased were Scotch plaid and most attractive. I even bought a matching cap in case my new wig looked too ridiculous. I checked into a small hotel and slept for hours. I was putting Nanny Prescott permanently to sleep. I would awake as Flora Coombe.

The following afternoon I dined in my room and then departed for the train station. In the light of June I felt like a new woman. My make-up removed years from my visage. Glasses were no longer over my nose: my new outfit was most fetching.

When I arrived in Oxford, I felt as if I was meeting myself. It no longer mattered if I was recognised. Flora Coombe was ready to resume her life.

How I had missed my town – my village – my home. The taxi driver looked at me rather curiously when I asked to be driven to Dovecote Cottage; however, I do not think that he recognised me. He mentioned something about 'that house where the mystery lady was killed,' but I thought it was better not to question him further. I simply stared out of the window at the familiar scenery. The hills were green and the trees abundant with leaves.

It was almost dark when the driver turned onto Dovecote Lane and we drove up to the building. This was no Tower House in Cornwall. It was not nearly as magnificent. It was simply my two-storey home, as familiar to me as a pair of my most comfortable shoes.

I could only glimpse the gardens in the early evening light. Surely they had not been neglected. Blossoms appeared everywhere! How much I owed to Robin Thibodeaux for this great array. I had fool-heartedly and selfishly taken his life. Every day my garden would remind me of my terrible deed.

I tipped the driver generously and stood at my own front door. The house looked dark.

Was anyone at home? I no longer had a key. Would I be able to enter? I hesitated, then rang the bell. Finally, I thought I heard footsteps. A light shone through the parlour window. Another was flicked on outside the door. It opened slowly. Bertie stood before me. The light shone down on me in such a way that my Scottish hat shaded my face.

'Yes?'

'Hello, Bertie.'

Her eyes widened considerably. I knew she recognised my voice. 'Yes?'

'It is I, Bertie, Flora Coombe.'

She began to tremble. 'Me mistress is dead. Dead and gone at the bottom of the lake.'

'No, Bertie,' I replied as calmly as possible. 'I am very much alive. I am standing here before you.'

She began to scream. It was a piercing awful scream that tore at my eardrums. 'A ghost! It's her ghost come to haunt me because I didn't save her!'

I reached out and touched her, to reassure Bertie that I was very much alive. She leaped back and screamed again. 'You can't be alive, ma'am! You can't!'

'I am, Bertie. I am very much alive.'

She staggered back and fell into a chair. She reminded me of a bird all over again, one with wounded wings who could no longer fly. 'But ... but ... where have you been, ma'am? All this time?'

'That is a very good question, Bertie.'

'Where?'

'I don't know, Bertie. I found myself this morning at the Oxford train station. I didn't know where I had been or where I was. I was so frightened. Then suddenly it was as if a fog lifted and I knew how to get home once again. I knew who I was and where I belonged. Bertie, what has happened to me? Where have I been? Where did I get these clothes? I even have money in my purse.'

'Oh, ma'am, it is you!' she exclaimed. 'Come back from the dead!'

Lucretia, my precious Persian pussy, chose this moment to come around the corner and rub against my leg, not one time, but several. She wouldn't leave off until I picked her up and caressed her tenderly. Miss Angela had had her sheepdog. Lucretia was my special cat.

'Oh, ma'am, she remembers you! She's been that miserable since you were dead, whining about the house, sleeping by the stove in the kitchen, but running to the door looking for you every time someone rang.'

The cat purred contentedly as I softly scratched her head. 'My sweet little darling,' I cooed. 'I am happy you didn't forget me.'

'Oh, ma'am,' Bertie said, still attempting to digest the fact that I was really standing before her. 'We should call the inspector.'

'Yes, and David Chasebourne as well. But not tonight, Bertie. I am so tried. I just want to go to sleep in my own bed. Oh, Bertie, how long have I been gone? How long have I been missing?'

'Oh, ma'am, it was last December when they murdered you!'

'Murdered? I do remember someone breaking into my room and that I was awfully afraid. I can't seem to remember anything after that. Where is Mr Thibodeaux? Is he here?'

'Oh, ma'am, there is so much that you don't know.'

I set Lucretia down and collapsed into a chair. The cat immediately jumped into my lap. 'I don't want to hear anymore, Bertie, not tonight. I don't think I could take anymore. I just want to curl up with Lucretia in my own bed. Do you think Cook could fix me a sandwich and a cup of nice hot tea?'

'Oh, ma'am, we don't have Cook anymore. She ... well ... there was nobody to cook for but me. She's working in the city now – in Oxford. She's cooking for some of the boys at the school.'

'Dear me. Well, perhaps we can get her back.'

'Mr Chasebourne was even talking about selling the house.'

'Sell Dovecote Cottage? I would rather die first.'

'We thought you had.'

'I was dead for a while, I suppose, but now I'm back.'

'I could fix you a nice lamb sandwich and a hot cup of tea, ma'am.'

'Oh, thank you, Bertie.' I got slowly to my feet. I suppose in a way I was tired. So much had happened. I wanted to put it all behind me and get back into the familiar routine of my life. I wanted to write again. I wanted to be Flora Coombe. I had missed her.

FORTY

How quickly I returned to my old Dovecote Cottage ways: waking early in the morning with Lucretia curled up contentedly beside me, pulling back the curtains to reveal a beautiful summer day, having breakfast and coffee with the newspaper in my own comfortable bed, retiring to my office and commencing work, returning to an Inspector Hecate novel that was almost completed when I 'disappeared'. The only difficulty was concentrating on a fictional mystery when the one I had actually lived seemed much more fascinating. Afternoons were blissfully spent in my garden.

Speaking of the newspapers, word of my 'reappearance' was leaked to them almost immediately. The extent of the publicity was more than I ever would have imagined. Thank God there were so few available photographs of me, and none of them were recent with the exception of that shot of me hidden beneath the brim of a big hat.

AMNESIA VICTIM RETURNS
WHERE HAS FLORA BEEN?
HUSBAND HANGED IN VAIN

These were some of the headlines that blazed across the British newspapers and other journals throughout the world. Reporters began to haunt my doorstep. I was even snapped once or twice working in the garden, but the large straw hat I wore as protection from the sun shaded my face enough to make it hardly recognisable. Now it was necessary to hire guards to keep them away! The price of fame is steep!

For the first few days I managed to put off Inspector Hanlon, but I quickly ran out of excuses. I was at my writing table when Bertie knocked on the door and made her entry.

'Yes? What is it, Bertie?'

'I am sorry to disturb you, ma'am, when you're at your writing, but the inspector is here again. This time he says that he is not leaving until he speaks with you.'

'I suppose I have to see him, don't. I, Bertie?'

'Oh, yes, ma'am, you must. It is your citizenship duty.'

'Tell me, Bertie, why did you feel it necessary to telephone him on the very night of my return? We could have waited a day or two. I could have had a day or two of peace and quiet before the world found out I was back.'

'It was my citizenship duty, ma'am. He was here in the house that often when you disappeared and he made me promise on my mother's grave that I would telephone if I ever heard or saw you.' She looked as if she was back in the witness box. How I wished I could have observed her performance first-hand.

'On your mother's grave, Bertie? Your mother has passed away?'

'Oh, no, ma'am. It's just what the inspector made me swear on.'

'And it's your "civic" duty, not your "citizenship" duty.'

'Very well, ma'am. Should I show him in?'

How I was dreading the interview. Another performance was required. I did not feel quite up to it. 'I suppose you must, Bertie.'

'Oh, and ma' am?'

'Yes, Bertie.'

'Cook called this morning. She'll be back at work for you starting next Tuesday.'

'Glory be to God.'

'She said she'd much rather come back and cook for you then a bunch of unruly boys who don't know the difference between a patty and a pâté.'

Bertie had scarcely opened the door. The inspector stood on my threshold. He looked more stylish than the first time he had introduced himself to me. He was wearing a light well-tailored summer tan suit with a blue tie for colour. His curly locks had been recently trimmed and he had grown a thin moustache to match. My 'disappearance' had provided him with celebrity. He was now dressed for the role. He stood there staring at me for a moment.

'Yes, it is I, Inspector.'

'You look none the worse for wear.'

'If only I knew what and where the wear was.'

'You are back at work?'

'As are you.' I covered up what I was writing. Why did I always do that? If someone walked in on me as I am writing this very day, I would immediately turn over the pages so that no one can see. We writers are paranoid creatures. At least I am.

'Work is the only thing that takes my mind off the terrible events that transpired while I was "missing".'

'Another Inspector Hecate?'

'Yes. It may be my last. I am planning to retire him at least for awhile.'

'That would be a great loss.'

I was taken aback. 'I thought you had no interest in my inspector.'

'I may have changed my mind. After your disappearance I began to read your books. In fact I think I have had time to read them all.'

'What a shame that it required such adverse circumstances to bring you round.' I gestured to the chair opposite me. 'Will you have a seat, Inspector?'

He sat down immediately. He unbuttoned his jacket so that it hung loosely about his trim figure. 'I must admit that you often fooled me on paper. I thought I had matters well in hand and then you would surprise me.'

'That's my stock in trade, Inspector – the surprise.'

His cold deep-set blue eyes began to bore into me in an attempt to make me feel uncomfortable. I refused to give up and look away. 'I imagined that if you could surprise me so well on paper, no doubt you could surprise me in life as well.'

'Dear me, no,' I responded quickly. 'I am much cleverer in my mysteries. Sometimes these plots take months of thinking and planning to execute.'

He continued to stare. I finally gave up and gave a pretence of arranging the papers about my desk.

'Strange, in all your books I read, there was never any use made of amnesia.'

'Such a hackneyed device, don't you think, Inspector?'

'I suspect you could make it seem fresh and original.'

'Dear me, you are full of compliments today, aren't you?'

'I've gone over the statement you had delivered to the station, Miss Coombe. I have gone over it very carefully.'

'I'm sorry it couldn't be more comprehensive.'

'Still no memory of those missing months, Miss Coombe?'

'I am afraid those days are lost to me, Inspector – perhaps forever.'

'Don't you find it curious that in all that time nobody recognised you?'

'I have wondered about that myself.'

'And with your picture all over the newspapers.'

'Therein lies your answer, I suppose. I have never allowed my photograph to be taken since the day I was old enough to refuse, except for my wedding portrait. I have never liked the way I looked in photographs. I suppose most of us don't. There are very few good photographs of me available, Inspector. Most of them are far from recent.'

'Which brings me to the purpose of my visit. I would like to have a recent photograph of you published in all the newspapers. "Has Anybody Seen This Woman?" I am sure we will receive some sort of response.'

'But I have no recent photograph.'

'We shall have one taken.'

'Dear me,' I said, dreading the very thought of it, 'I suppose I must.'

'I could send over a photographer this afternoon.'

I must have actually blanched. 'A police photographer?!' I shook my head violently. 'Certainly not!'

'But...'

I cut him off immediately. 'Cecil Beaton is an acquaintance of mine. He shall take my photograph. Nobody else!'

'How long will that require?'

'I shall contact him immediately.' I knew that he did not know to whom I was referring. 'Have you heard of Mr Beaton?'

'I am afraid I haven't.'

'He is an artist. He has been after me to take my picture for some time. Now I will acquiesce.'

'We will need this photo as soon as possible.'

'Certainly,' I agreed, 'but in all honesty I cannot see the great rush. The poor unfortunate Robin Thibodeaux is already dead and buried. We cannot bring that innocent soul back from the grave.'

'He was guilty of adultery.'

'I wasn't aware that was punishable by death since the days of Henry VIII.'

'Just for story's sake ... since you are a writer ... what if – suppose ... a woman were to fabricate her own murder so that her husband would be charged and executed for the crime?'

'My, what an intriguing notion, Inspector.'

'Would you let her get away with it?'

'Certainly not. In my books the guilty are always apprehended and prosecuted.'

'What would her punishment be?'

'You would know that better than I, Inspector.'

'I would surmise a lifetime in prison.'

He was scaring me. I refused to let on that I was in any way intimidated. 'My, my, that does sound severe.'

He sat a moment in silence, simply regarding me. Feeling very uncomfortable I busied myself again with my papers.

'Did you ever think, Miss Coombe, that you were perhaps in disguise during this long period of your disappearance?'

'I hardly know what kind of disguise I could effect.'

He hesitated. 'This might be upsetting to you, Miss Coombe, but when you disappeared certain items were left behind.'

'Yes, that is upsetting to me, Inspector.'

'A woman walking around without her teeth and her hair might be quite un-recognisable.'

'I would think she would. I hope that is not how you expect me to pose for Mr Beaton!'

'Your maid, Bertie, informed me that upon your return here you were well dressed, and "everything" was in place.'

'It most certainly was. I am pleased to say when I suddenly realised who I was at Oxford railway station, I was not ashamed of my appearance.'

'Your teeth fit?'

I was truly humiliated. 'Please, Inspector!' But then I knew that I had to answer. 'They fit just fine! If I didn't have teeth I doubt if I could have survived all those months, don't you, Inspector? A woman cannot live on soup alone!'

'I plan to circulate your photograph to every dentist in the country.'

'Dear me, I hope they don't put it up on their walls! I'd hate for someone to have to look at me while they're being drilled.'

The inspector did not find this amusing. I doubt if he had any sense of humour at all. Everything was business to him. He would never give up – a British Mountie out to get his man – me!

'I wonder if I could perhaps have the outfit you arrived home in.'

319

'I suppose so,' I agreed reluctantly, 'but I would like to have it back. I find it most attractive. Wherever I was, my taste seems not to have deserted me.'

'And your ... hair ... your ... wig?'

'What about my hair?'

'Is there a ... trademark?'

'Certainly not!'

'If Bertie could perhaps corroborate this for me.'

I was immediately insulted. This was no acting on my part.

'You don't believe me?'

'Does Inspector Hecate believe any of his suspects?' I must admit, he had me there. I rose from my desk, moved to the study door, opened it and called loudly, 'Bertie!'

She was in the room almost immediately. 'Yes, ma'am?'

'Would you accompany me into my dressing room, please.'

She obviously wondered why. 'Yes, ma'am.' But then, before we started out. 'Will Inspector Hanlon be staying for tea, ma'am?'

My response was swift and crisp. 'Certainly not!'

FORTY-ONE

If anybody has ever heard of me or read any of my books published after 1936, they will no doubt have seen the famous photograph of me by the great Cecil Beaton. It became my official photo for the remainder of my life. It graced my autobiography and it will probably be the cover of this posthumous book as well.

What I like so much about the photo is that it looks almost absolutely nothing like me. I have never looked so aristocratic or glamorous. Cecil Beaton is a genius. He chose my clothes, he posed me and supervised my make-up and hair. For one brief afternoon in his studio I knew what it felt like to be a fashion model or a film star.

Cecil Beaton is an elegant witty man. Somehow I managed to relax in his presence and hold the pose he desired. I am sure many of you have seen it. I am standing before an empty portrait, which gives the entire setting a suggestion of mystery, of something to be solved. I look both quizzical and contemplative, a writer with her mind fiendishly at work.

I hope I do not appear vain when I say that

this photograph became one of Cecil's most celebrated works, to rival his portraits of Dame Edith Sitwell and Lady Diana Cooper. Perhaps this has something to do with my notorious 'disappearance' at the time. The photo was published everywhere and caused quite a stir. It appeared on the front page with the Spanish Civil War!

Naturally, Inspector Hanlon was not pleased with the photograph at all. He insisted that I would not be recognisable, but I told him 'to like it or lump it'. There would be no more photographs of me no matter how much he insisted. If he didn't like that, he could take it up with the Prime Minister, who had called me personally to welcome me back among the living and to request an autographed copy of the very same Beaton photograph.

Did anyone recognise Nanny Irene Prescott from the distinguished Beaton photograph? Almost no one, except for one exception – one person with a keener eye than all the others.

I shall not go into that now. There is more story to relate first.

I must reveal that I reluctantly submitted to examinations by both psychiatrist and hypnotist. You certainly cannot hypnotise a woman unless she is willing, although I pretended to be. In my next life, if there is such a thing, I must come back as an actress. I am quite good at it. No one could doubt that I had fallen under the hypnotist's spell, even though he could not dredge up my 'mysterious hidden past' no matter how hard he tried. Even though he has long since passed away, I shall not reveal the man's name because a book he wrote is still considered somewhat a Bible in his field. His conclusion after our last session: 'Miss Coombe's recent past is so painful to her that it cannot be conjured up without doing irreparable damage to her psyche. Perhaps one day, when she has healed, she will be able to recall those difficult days of her life.'

FORTY-TWO

I wonder what I would title this chapter if this were merely one of my stories. Would it be GOOD TRIUMPHS OVER EVIL, or EVIL TRIUMPHS OVER GOOD? Most of my readers know that I lived 'happily ever after', so perhaps the first title is more appropriate.

The death of Robin Thibodeaux had become a constant nightmare. He drifted into my dreams almost every night. I would often wake up begging forgiveness for what I had done to him. Mary Beth Hewitt would haunt my sleep as well. It wasn't that I couldn't sleep; it was that I could no longer sleep without them. One or the other was always there to remind me of their fate: a razor in her hand and a noose around his neck.

With such demons constantly visiting my sleep, you can well imagine that I welcomed a first evening out when Lord Westmoreland asked me to accompany him to a film playing in Oxford. As usual, his wife was 'under the weather'. I was only too pleased to accompany him.

I remember the film we viewed very well, even though so many years have elapsed. It was the brilliant *Night Must Fall,* based on the celebrated play by our own Emlyn Williams, a film which has since become a classic, though I must admit that the entire experience unnerved me more than I could have imagined.

Unseasonal rain (but it is always seasonal in England) had ruined what was left of the summer, although I suppose my beautiful late blooming flowers relished the refreshment. Everyone knows what the great American poet Henry Wadsworth Longfellow said:

'Into each life some rain must fall,
  Some days must be dark and dreary.'

Such was the case on the evening I accompanied Lord Westmoreland to the cinema. The weather was more than just dreary. A great storm greeted us as we emerged from the theatre. There was deafening thunder, blinding lightning and stinging strands of rain, all the accoutrements of a vicious storm.

I am not sure now whether it was the film or the threatening weather that unsettled me; but, unusually for me, I was insistent upon our return to Dovecote Cottage that Lord Westmoreland accompany me inside the house, especially since it appeared that the electricity had gone out and not a light was burning. 'A sherry or some port or a cordial or whatever you choose for the road,' I remember insisting. 'Something to fortify you for your short drive home.'

'Don't mind if I do.'

As I recall, he never minded when a drink was proffered.

We left the headlights of his Rolls Royce trained on the house. I foraged for some candles in my darkened home. Cook was away and Bertie as well. I suddenly felt queasy, as if I was some silly frightened heroine alone in a big dark house with a storm raging outside. I suppose all women see themselves as heroines in the story of their own life.

Soon candles were burning about the den, the most comfortable room in the house in which to escape a storm and pretend that everything will be all right in the morning. Bunny managed to get a fire going and the room no longer looked so foreboding as it began to warm us.

Outside the rain continued to beat relentlessly against the window as if it wanted to break the glass and drown the house in its fury. Bunny and I sat back in our soft chairs, studied the glow of golden sherry in the firelight and discussed the film we had just seen.

'I never did see the play, you know,' I recall saying. 'Of course I have met Emlyn Williams on more than one occasion. I heard that he was quite brilliant in the role of the murderer, but I must say that this American, Robert Montgomery, was quite marvellous.'

'Not to mention our own Dame May Witty,' Bunny added.

I concurred. 'That was a wonderful scene when he drove her insane, wasn't it?'

'Bloody well written. Almost as good as you, Flora.'

'You flatter me, Bunny. I doubt that I would be very good at writing a play. Too constricting. But I like the title. *Night Must Fall*. I wouldn't have minded coming up with that one.'

There was more thunder and a crack of lightning. Bunny glanced out of the window. 'I doubt that we'll be hunting in weather like this tomorrow.'

'What would you be hunting for?'

'I was hoping for a couple of geese.'

'Dear me, Bunny, can't you let them fly by unmolested?'

'I never go beyond my limit.'

'Even so. It amazes me how fond you are of birds, and yet how eager you are to go out and shoot some.'

'Any bird that has chosen to live in my preserve is off limits. It's only those flying over, such as the geese, who risk their necks.'

'I must warn them to take another route. How does Agnes feel about all this hunting?'

'She abhors it. Do you think I would go hunting so often if she wanted to come along?'

I laughed and shivered almost at the same time. 'Dear me, I think that movie unnerved me more than I realised. I'm starting to feel like Dame May left all alone in her house to be murdered.'

'Next thing you'll be seeing the ghost of Flora's Mill Pond.'

'What ghost?'

'Yours, of course. There were many sightings of you wandering about in your nightgown until people found out you were still alive.'

'Really! The imagination of some people.'

'That wasn't you, Flora, come back to visit the site of your disappearance?'

'Certainly not!'

'But if you had amnesia...'

'I suppose you have a point there, Bunny. I certainly hope that I wasn't running around in my knickers.'

'Until you resurfaced, Flora's Mill Pond had become quite a tourist attraction. I was charging admission, you know, to walk around the lake. Attendance has dropped off considerably.'

'Honestly, Bunny, couldn't you change the name to something else? "Flora's Mill Pond",' I tisked, 'as if I was still buried underneath the water. Besides, it is not a pond in the first place, but a lake.'

'Somehow Mill Pond sounded more poetic, like a George Eliot novel.'

'Even so. What was wrong with "Swan's Way"? I liked that much better.'

'Perhaps I'll go back to that next year when things die down and no one is interested any longer.'

'I hope that will be soon.'

The last round of thunder seemed to shake Dovecote Cottage from its foundations. If that wasn't enough, it sounded as if a bolt of lightning had savaged one of the pine trees beyond the house.

'Bunny, you mustn't drive home in this weather,' I cautioned. 'Perhaps you had better spend the night here until the storm has passed. I am alone tonight. Both Cook and my maid are spending the evening with their families.'

He considered the possibility over a second glass of sherry. 'Thursday night is every servant's night out. I'll telephone Agnes and see if she wouldn't be too frightened without me. She's like a little girl in storms like this. Even hides in the wardrobe and whimpers like a baby. I have to pour her a drink to get her to come out.'

Lord Westmoreland went to telephone his wife, but the phone was dead. 'Our lines must be down as well,' he mused, shaking his grey head. 'Agnes will be beside herself if I don't come home and she can't call out. Agnes couldn't survive without the telephone. She seldom sees any friends now, but she loves talking to them over the telephone.'

'You had best get home then, Bunny.'

'It's not that I don't appreciate the offer. In fact it's very romantic.'

'Oh, Bunny, don't be ridiculous!'

'Why don't you come home with me?'

'Thank you, Bunny, but that's not really necessary.'

I hated to see Lord Westmoreland depart. I stood in the front doorway, the wind blowing at my wig as if the hair were real, rain stinging my cheeks. I closed the door against the torrential storm, in hopes that it would not only keep out the rain but everything bad as well.

There was nothing else to do but go to bed and hope that when I awoke in the morning, the sun would be shining, and all fears of the things that go bump in the night would vanish. A candle flickered in my hand as I crept slowly to my bedroom. If only I could have turned on the wireless and had some music to keep me company, a symphony orchestra to drown out all the mysterious noises in the house that sounded like footsteps just outside my door.

'Is anybody there?' I sang it out loud, even though I knew nobody was. How quickly I scurried into a flannel nightgown with a matching nightcap and crawled beneath the covers. I attempted to read – certainly not a mystery, I think it was a novel by James Hilton – but it was too difficult to read by candlelight; although I was afraid to blow it out and lie alone in the dark with the weather raging outside my window. There was a time not far back when a handsome young man lay beside me. I desperately wanted him back that evening.

The sound of the bedroom window breaking shattered what little composure I had remaining. Now the storm was in my bedroom. My candle died in the wind. Everywhere was darkness and torrent!

There was a figure standing outside the broken window. I could barely discern the outlines of someone very tall who now reached through and opened the French window. 'What is it? Who's there? Who are you?' The questions tore like arrows from my throat. The figure just stood there, silhouetted against the storm outside, but breathing so hard I could actually feel his breath.

'Who are you?' I could scarcely utter the words. Fear had strangled my throat. I became powerless to speak. So this was to be my fate, my punishment, I surmised. For what I had done, I was going to be murdered in my own bed.

How did it happen that the figure's face was suddenly illuminated? I could scarcely believe my eyes. It was Robin's face! There was a noose around his neck! I don't believe in ghosts. Nevertheless, a shrill scream erupted from my being. I was paralysed with fear as it approached the bed as it had in my dreams. Somehow I managed to speak, to sob. 'Robin, Robin,' I wept to the strange figure. 'I am so sorry for what happened to you when I went away! I wanted to save you! I truly did! But I couldn't! I didn't want you to die! Please believe me!'

The figure descended upon my bed. How strong our innate sense of self-preservation. Without even knowing it I reached into my bedside drawer and felt for the small pistol among the other belongings. Soon it was within my grasp. I aimed it at the figure. I fired three shots, streaks of powder in the dark! Something fell from the spectre's hand. The light on its face was extinguished. The figure fell to the floor.

Beyond my door I heard Bertie's scream and a man's voice. 'She's killed him; She's bloody killed him!' Inspector Hanlon and Bertie burst into my chamber. They were carrying torches. Their light revealed the figure of Robin Thibodeaux stretched lifeless beside the bed. 'Where did you get that bloody pistol?' the inspector demanded as he fell to his knees over Robin's body.

'I've had it for years,' I managed to reply. 'My first husband gave it to me in India for the cobras. Can you blame me, Inspector, for shooting an intruder? A ghost?'

'Can't you see it's not a bloody ghost?' He was feeling for Robin's pulse and listening for his breath. 'Now we can't even call a bloody ambulance!'

'Robin Thibodeaux was hanged!'

He looked up at me angrily. 'You can see for yourself that he wasn't. Now you've gone and killed him!'

Somehow, like one of my superior literary heroines, I took a deep breath and gathered my wits about me. 'I doubt that, Inspector.' I looked down at the corpse. 'Robin, you can get up now.'

He crawled slowly to his feet. 'If Robin learn one thing in the bayou, if he hears shots, he lie down and play dead like the possum until the shooting stops. Where I come from, sometimes when they hunt the "coon", they don't mean the furry one.'

The inspector was confused. 'But...?'

'These are blanks, Inspector, meant to scare, not to harm. Since there are no cobras in England, I deemed it wiser to rid myself of real bullets for fear of something like this happening.'

The inspector looked up at Robin. 'You're all right?'

Robin looked taller than I remembered because he was much thinner than he had been previously. Prison had not agreed with him. 'I'm all right for a man who's just been shot at three times. I had forgot about Madame's gun.'

The inspector shook his head. He had not even bothered to remove his fedora in my presence. 'This proves there was no amnesia,' he trumpeted. 'You bloody apologised for Robin's death. I heard you through the door. You said you were sorry for what happened to him when you went away, that you didn't want him to die! That you engineered it.'

Bertie joined forces with the inspector. 'Yes, you did say that, ma'am. I heard you.'

'And you, Robin, what did you hear?' I asked my husband.

'The very same, Madame.'

'Really, Inspector,' I said looking at him

disdainfully. 'What I said wouldn't begin to hold up in a court of law. Of course I went away, but not of my own volition. Yes, I went away, but I still don't know how I went or where.'

'You apologised for his death. You said you wanted to save him but you couldn't.'

'Yes, and I would have – if I'd had my wits about me and wasn't suffering from amnesia and not even knowing I had a husband facing the gallows.'

The inspector steamed a moment in stony silence. He knew that, as usual, I had the upper hand, that he was helpless to convict me. He finally pulled off his hat and slammed it against the bedpost. 'The strings Scotland Yard had to pull to get the bloody prison governor to put out that Thibodeaux had been hanged. They had to go to the Prime Minister. I knew that you faked your whole murder and the minute you knew Thibodeaux was hanged you'd come crawling back with some sort of cock-and-bull amnesia story.'

I was somewhat taken aback by the Prime Minister's involvement. 'You mean Neville went along with this pathetic subterfuge?'

'The P.M. is quite a fan of yours, as you no doubt know. He said that if anybody could fake a disappearance and get away with it, it was Flora Coombe.'

'I suppose that is some sort of compliment.' I studied the narrow figure of my husband. How strange, when you are positive someone is dead, to see him towering over you in your own bedroom. 'Robin,' I began slowly. 'I am genuinely pleased to see that you were not hanged. One death – if not by my own hand – was more than enough. I can now sleep again at night knowing that you are still alive.'

'Robin is sorry, too, that he was not faithful to his Madame. The men in my families are never faithful to their Madames.'

'Well, Robin,' I responded, 'this is the second time you have been saved from execution. I wouldn't attempt a third if I were you.'

'Perhaps Robin can come back and work in the garden for Madame once again. Robin misses his flowers.'

'I doubt that you have read *Candide*, Robin, but Monsieur Voltaire says that we should cultivate our own gardens. I suggest that is what you should do as well. I cannot blossom again as do many of our flowers. I am afraid the bloom is off this rose. I shall content myself with literary romances.'

Robin accepted this. 'What if the big magazine come to Robin again and want me to write the story of how I am almost hung?'

'You'll simply have to find yourself another schoolteacher.' Something suddenly occurred to me. 'And by the way, since you are still alive ... I must begin divorce proceedings.'

Bertie chose this moment to enter the conversation. 'When Inspector told me that Frenchy was still alive, it was like you coming back to life, ma'am.'

I eyed her coldly. She had overstepped her bounds. The one thing I demand is loyalty. 'You were in on this, Bertie, this pathetic attempt to trip me up, to make me confess to something of which I am not guilty.'

She realised that she was in trouble. 'Ma'am, I ... it was my civilised duty ... to assist the police.'

'And how close have you come to this particular police?' Cook had confided in me her suspicions that there was more between Bertie and the inspector than met the eye.

Bertie hesitated. She couldn't lie as readily as I, which is nothing to be proud of, I suppose. 'We've been keeping company, ma'am. Todd would come and stay with me when I was afraid.'

I eyed the inspector suspiciously. 'Was this part of your plan to infiltrate my household?'

'It might have been at first, but I have become genuinely fond of Bertie.'

'Good,' I retorted angrily, 'then you can take her with you, for she is no longer in my employ.'

Bertie was shocked. 'But, ma'am!'

'I demand loyalty, Bertie.'

'But, ma'am...'

'I want you out of this house, Bertie. Just tell me where to send your wages.'

She began to sniffle and whimper. It had no effect on me.

'Well, Inspector,' I said finally, 'are you finished here?'

How reluctant he was to admit defeat. 'Perhaps I am.'

'Then I would be most pleased if everybody left my house.'

Robin looked at me a moment, then retrieved the torch he had dropped.

'I am very pleased that you are still alive, Robin, but you belong home with your own people.'

He nodded his head that he understood. 'Goodbye, kind lady.'

'I expect you to pay for this window,' I informed Inspector Hanlon as he moved towards the door. 'Oh, and Inspector?'

'Yes?' He was holding his hat in his hands. He almost looked contrite.

'It's almost a pity those bullets weren't real. First a man is hanged and then shot. It would make a wonderful ending for a story. Can you be prosecuted for killing a ghost?'

FORTY-THREE

The story isn't quite over yet. There are always the loose ends that have to be tied up.

I mentioned earlier that one person did recognise the face of Nanny Irene Prescott in the sophisticated visage of Flora Coombe as photographed by Cecil Beaton.

Not long after Robin Thibodeaux returned to the United States and I received my divorce, a letter arrived unexpectedly in the mail. The handwriting was familiar and it bore a Romanian postmark. I guessed immediately who it was from. I saved the letter and I will reprint it here.

6 September, 1937

Dear Miss Flora Coombe, or should I say Nanny Prescott?

When I was browsing in a Bucharest bookshop today, I saw a photo of Flora Coombe on the jacket of her new Inspector Hecate mystery book. I knew for certain that it was you. There is something in the eyes that cannot be disguised, even if everything else about the photograph is quite different from the elderly woman who briefly helped me with my studies when I was sent down from Harrow.

Perhaps if you had not confessed to me in the schoolroom at Tower House that you had had a mystery book published, I might never have guessed your true identity. I have since read more about you and realise that I must be the only one who knows your whereabouts during this period of your famous 'amnesia'. You need not worry. Your secret is safe with me as I am certain secrets of mine will be safe with you.

As you can surmise from the postmark, I am living with Roman in his native country of Romania. At first we were taken in by his gypsy relatives and we travelled with them about Eastern Europe in a colourful caravan. Naturally we have changed our names. For a while I even dyed my hair black to fit in better with the others.

Now Roman and I are travelling through Romania and neighbouring countries with a small circus. We have become horse trainers and performers. We put the animals through their paces. They trot about the ring and we perform dangerous stunts upon their backs. I suppose I have run away with the circus like a young man in a story I once read. It is a most exciting life. I have learned to speak Romanian and other Eastern European languages and Roman refers to me as his ward. Only you know what I really am to him.

Does it shock you if I tell you that I wake up every morning in his arms? I doubt it since I know now that you observed us making love in the stable. I am not ashamed of what we have together. Roman makes me feel alive in a way I never did until he first made love to me before I was sent off to school.

Can I be brutally honest and tell you that Roman was my father's lover as well? Their affection for each other began when they were growing up together at Tower House. I don't think that my father ever really loved a woman, but there were duties a Pemberton must perform, for instance, providing an heir (yours truly), and later, a fortune, through the mother of darling Angela.

When my father was drowned, Roman was beside himself with grief. His only consolation was in looking at the son, for, as you know from the portrait of my father in the great hall, we bear a striking resemblance. You mustn't blame Roman. I desired him long before he took me into his bed. I sensed the closeness he had with my father. I had seen them embracing once. I felt shut out and was jealous. I did not feel disgusted. I wonder now if my stepmother's death was truly an accident. Did my father intend for her to drown while he himself was saved so that he would have the money to live in comfort with Roman? Did something go wrong and they both go down with the ship?

When I ask Roman about this he will not deny or confirm. I know my father loved him very much and would have done anything for him, as I would today. He is the most alive man I will ever know.

I must apologise for something, something of which I had no knowledge. I did not know about nor did I assist Roman in his attempt to poison my stepsister so that I would receive her fortune. In my own way I loved little Angela very much and I never would have encouraged such a tragic ending for her.

You wonder how I could forgive Roman for attempting such a thing? Because he loves me so much. He attempted it for me. I cannot condemn him for being solicitous for my welfare, no matter how nefarious his attempt to achieve it.

I miss England and my ancestral home and a way of life that is now denied me: but there are great compensations, such as undying love.

Your former pupil,
Scott Pemberton

How I would have relished sharing Master Scott's sad letter with Inspector Bertram Hawkins of Cornwall. How could I, without revealing my own subterfuge? Other than the untimely death of Mary Beth Hewitt, my great regret was that I could not join forces with Inspector Hawkins – on an equal footing – so to speak. When I told Robin that the bloom was off my rose, it was true, but I think I could have produced one new blossom for that sturdy man of equal age and temperament. It is one of the great regrets of my life. How could he accept me as Flora Coombe when everything about our former relationship had been based upon a lie? No, it was impossible. Besides, I would be giving myself away to quite another inspector who wanted nothing better than to see me shut away in prison so that he could bask in the glory of trapping me.

I thought of Scott Pemberton often. I wondered how he was surviving as the monster Hitler gobbled up Europe until only Sweden and Switzerland remained unmolested. Romania fell to the Germans in 1940 as did France, Belgium, the Netherlands, Luxembourg, Denmark and Norway.

We know now that not only were Jews persecuted and thrown into the cauldrons the Nazis called camps, but gypsies and homosexuals as well.

It was after the liberation that Scott Pemberton resurfaced in England at the age of twenty-four. He caused quite a sensation when he claimed his father's title.

If his photographs in the newspapers were accurate, he had suffered greatly during the war where he had been interred at Fuhlsbuttel, a labour camp near Hamburg where he had to wear a pink insignia to signify his sexual orientation; yet he was still startling handsome in a most ethereal way. He had been separated from Roman almost immediately. The former stable boy at Tower House was killed in an attempt to escape. Meanwhile, the handsome young Scott was handed from commandant to commandant. In the one complete interview he gave to a newspaper writer, he intimated that he had been seduced and mesmerised by Roman when he was too young to know better. When he came to his senses and wished to return to England, it was too late. The Nazis had invaded Romania.

With no money forthcoming from the Winston estate, it had been necessary to sell Tower House during his long absence to pay the mounting estate debts. During the war, the estate was appropriated by the admiralty. Officers had been billeted there.

There was little money left in the Pemberton coffer upon which Scott could live. I wasn't completely surprised to read that he had married an older widow who had been left a fortune by her titled husband. Scott appeared to move rather easily within her crowd, the gentry with too much money and time on their hands. Finally, when he was in his thirties, Scott left her for another man, an American actor. After the actor was killed in a private plane crash, Scott took up with a gentleman closer to his age, an 'angry young man' playwright of the British theatre in the late 1950s, who bludgeoned Scott to death one night in a jealous rage. It was one of the most sensational murder cases of the period and culminated in the playwright hanging himself in prison.

The entire sad affair left me wondering what the young man's life might have been under different circumstances, if there hadn't been a Roman to corrupt him. There have been too many deaths in the Pemberton household. It became a British House of Atreus.

As I conclude these pages, I am making one exception to my edict that absolutely no one shall be given access to this manuscript until the year 2000, a new century which will dawn after I am gone.

Upon my death, whenever it shall be, I wish a copy of these pages to be sent to Mrs Angela Winston Witherspoon at Green Grass Horse Farms in Lexington, Kentucky. Yes, it seems dear little Miss Angela got her pony after all.

I would like the following note to be included with this manuscript:

Dear Miss Angela,

After you read this I think you will understand why Mary Poppins had to go away and leave you.

She was there when you needed her and she has never forgotten her dear sweet charge who made her wish that she had been a nanny all her life.

With deepest love and affection,

Flora (Nanny Prescott) Coombe

At long last this manuscript is complete. Somehow it takes longer to write the truth than fiction. Now it is time to return to my real writing, another instalment in the adventurous life of Nanny Mapleton, who by now has solved as many mysteries as Inspector Hecate, and on several occasions has outsold Dame Agatha Christie's Miss Marple!

POSTSCRIPT

Since I began this history with a quote from the great William Shakespeare, I suppose I should end with a quotation of his as well. It is from his delightful comedy, 'All's Well That Ends Well.'

'The web of our life is of a mingled yarn, Good and ill together.'

The publishers hope that this book has given you enjoyable reading. Large Print Books are especially designed to be as easy to see and hold as possible. If you wish a complete list of our books please ask at your local library or write directly to:

Dales Large Print Books
Magna House, Long Preston,
Skipton, North Yorkshire.
BD23 4ND

This Large Print Book, for people
who cannot read normal print,
is published under the auspices of

THE ULVERSCROFT FOUNDATION